THE GRAYWOLF

SHORT FICTION SERIES

1988

THE
GRAYWOLF
ANNUAL
FOUR:
SHORT
STORIES
BY MEN

EDITED BY SCOTT WALKER

GRAYWOLF PRESS : SAINT PAUL

The stories collected in this *Graywolf Annual* appeared previously in publications, as noted below. We gratefully acknowledge the cooperation of editors, agents, and the authors. The editor gratefully acknowledges Sheila Murphy's assistance in assembling this collection.

IN ORDER OF APPEARANCE

William Kittredge's "Phantom Silver" was first published in *The Iowa Review* and later published by The Kutenai Press. Copyright © 1987 by William Kittredge.

Robert Olmstead's "High-Low-Jack" is from *Soft Water* (Vintage, 1988). Copyright © 1987 by Robert Olmstead.

Raymond Carver's "Menudo" was first published in *Granta*. Copyright © 1987 by Raymond Carver.

Richard Ford's "Great Falls" was first published in *Granta*. Copyright © 1987 by Richard Ford.

Stuart Dybek's "Chopin In Winter" was first published in *Chicago* magazine. Copyright © 1984 by Stuart Dybek.

David Long's "Clearance" was published in *The Flood of '64* (Ecco Press, 1987). Copyright © 1987 by David Long.

Charles Baxter's "How I Found My Brother" was first published in the *Indiana Review*. Copyright © 1987 by Charles Baxter.

Tobias Wolff's "The Other Miller" was first published in *The Atlantic Monthly*. Copyright © 1986 by Tobias Wolff.

Frederick Busch's "Dog Song" was first published in *The Georgia Review*. Copyright © 1985 Frederick Busch.

Alan Cheuse's "The Quest for Ambrose Bierce" was first published in *Candace & Other Stories*. Copyright © 1980 by Alan Cheuse.

Christopher Zenowich's "On the Roof" is published here for the first time. It is part of *Economics of the Heart* to be published by Harper & Row. Copyright © 1987 by Christopher Zenowich.

Paul Griner's "Worboys' Transaction" is published here for the first time. Copyright © 1987 by Paul Griner.

Tim O'Brien's "The Things They Carried" was first published in *Esquire*. Copyright © 1986 by Tim O'Brien.

Publication of this volume is made possible in part by a grant from the National Endowment for the Arts, and in part by generous contributions to Graywolf Press from individuals, corporations and foundations. Support was provided by the Minnesota State Arts Board and by United Arts, of which Graywolf is a member agency.

ISBN 1-55597-103-2 / ISSN 0743-7471
First Printing, 1988
9 8 7 6 5 4 3 2
Published by GRAYWOLF PRESS
Post Office Box 75006, Saint Paul, Minnesota 55175.
All rights reserved.

THE GRAYWOLF SHORT FICTION SERIES

CONTENTS

✦

THE GRAYWOLF ANNUAL FOUR:

SHORT STORIES BY MEN

WILLIAM KITTREDGE

✛

Phantom Silver

THE GREAT WHITE HORSE rears above the rolling horizon, which is golden and simple in the sunset, and those sparkling hooves strike out into the green light under dark midsummer thunderclouds. Far away there is rain, and barn swallows drop like thrown stones through clouds of mosquitoes near the creek. A single planet and then stars grow luminous against the night, and the great horse is gone. Moths bat against the screen around the veranda porch, and we are left in that dreamed yesteryear where the masked man rides away. The light is cold in the early morning, and the silver bullet rests on the mantle like a trophy. Only in the morning is it possible to think of that masked man as old and fat and slow and happy.

THAT CREW of clean-shaven Texas Rangers was all brave and unmasked in the beginning, before the Cavendish gang did them in, leaving him for dead and alone, his comrades sprawled around him and killed. They had ridden into a box canyon, and rifle fire crackled from the surrounding rims. They were ambushed; horses reared and screamed; the good men fell, and in only a few beats of a heart it was over. The Cavendish boys walked the stony ground amid the bodies and smiled as if they would live forever.

But he was not dead, only scarred. Revenge became his great obsession, revenge and justice, notions which served him like two sides of a coin, and he changed like a stone into gold. He rode that white stallion named Silver, he disguised himself behind that mask, he traveled with his dark companion, and they began their endless conquest of wrong-doing.

There was ranch after ranch saved from eastern bankers and monied second sons from Baltimore. Always another gold shipment to be rescued. Another sod-buster and his family to be protected. Another evil law-man to be confounded. Another wagon train saved from the clutches of circling savages. How many homesteaders' wives stood in the doorway of plain unpainted cabins with that silver bullet still warm in their hands while they wondered aloud who that masked man could have been, and the great stallion reared?

THE REAL BEGINNING was a mortal family, a strong handed father and a mother who split their wood, and two children, a brother and a sister, all of them having come west to Texas after the Civil War. They had been living as they were supposed to live in a juniper log cabin alongside the Brazos River before that summer morning when Comanche came down like slaughtering, screaming rain.

They thought they were safe. The Comanche had been corralled for seven years on the Oklahoma Territory, eating mainly on dole meat, and the father was a slow-spoken German other white men did not deal with easily, and so left mostly alone. But there on that bright morning was the truth, Comanche out of season.

Down in the bulrushes near the water of the Brazos there was another morning sort of time and the dumb blankness of eyes rolled back to their extreme station, the hardness of lean hipbones under the flesh, handholds as this brother mounts his sister from behind, the younger brother, the older sister, her skirt tossed up where they were down there on the matted

grass, hidden from the house by tulles and nodding downy cat-
tails, the sister on her knees and elbows and the brother behind, going weak and dizzy that morning with her and afraid
the screaming he heard so distantly might be her or even himself, but that was foolish, they were practiced and wouldn't. He
stopped, crouched over her, listening, and she thrust herself
back against him.

"Don't you quit now," she said.

But he did. He had. The screaming he heard was not really
screaming, not fearfulness, that came later, but high-pitched
joyous whooping, and now he could hear the horses, the hooves beating down the hard-packed wagon road. There were lots
of them, and riding hard.

"Don't you stop," she said, but it was too late for that, already
he had fallen back away from her, turning, knowing there was
no way to see anything from where they were, that was why
they were safe there on those hidden mornings down near the
river. Already he was frightened, and later he would sense she
had always been stronger, had always cared more than he did
about what was going on right at the time; later he would understand it was an undivided mind that gave her what proved
in time to be the strength of her indifference.

"Dammit," she said. "Then get yourself together."

What she meant was for him to pull up his pants and tuck in
his shirttail, and to do it quietly. It was her that kept him quiet
and crouching there those next hours as the smoke from the
burning cabin and the barns rose thin and white into the clear
sky, after the first bellowing from their father and their mother's frantic shrieking, after the horses had gone away, as the
smoke dwindled and twilight came and the frogs called to one
another in the quiet. It was her that kept him crouching and
hidden there until the next day; they were saved at least in the
sense that they could walk away, they were not killed and not
captured, not bloody and hairless like the bodies of their father
and mother.

SHE WAS SIXTEEN that summer of 1867, and he was two years younger, and for a few months, after they had walked those miles upstream to the nearest homestead on the Brazos, toward the Palo Pinto, they were pitied and fed. Then October began to settle into fall, and in November the green-headed mallards and the Canada geese and the Sandhill Crane began coming south, circling and calling as they settled toward the river. The clump of pink-blooming roses on the south wall of the cabin froze, the tamarack hung dark red against the gray hillslopes and the big cottonwood flared yellow one morning in the sun, but the real cold came all in one day the week before Thanksgiving, weather a line of shadow on the morning horizon, the air greasy and hushed all that day and at twilight a hard northern wind and driven sleety rain. But they didn't leave until after the Thanksgiving goose and all the fixings. It was her that decided.

"We are going," she said.

By Christmas they had hooked wagon rides south to San Antonio, and she would no longer let him touch her. "If we had been going to stay there we would have stayed forever," she said, and after the beginning of the new year she took to leaving him alone for days while she went around to the taverns on the banks of the San Antonio River, and she came home with money. She had her blankets in the room they shared, but she would not let him come under them with her.

"You have done me what damage you could," she said. It was not that she did not love him, she explained, it was simply that the damage was done. He took to breaking horses for a livery stable. He had always been good with horses. He could not remember his parents, they had gone away into those scalped bodies the Comanche left behind, he could not think about them at all, and the thing he hated most was the notion of horses he loved being driven north toward the territories by those savages.

Three summers later when he was seventeen she left him behind altogether. "You are man enough," she said. "You take care of yourself like I am going to take care of myself." She was loading just a few things into saddle bags, rich-looking carved-leather bags provided by the tubercular-looking white-haired man she was with, a man who wore one quick gun and claimed to be a medical doctor, although no one had ever known him to cure anything.

"We are going to settle north," she said, talking about her reasons for traveling, as though the white-haired man meant nothing. "He is going to do some work," she said, talking about the eastern Wyoming Territory around Laramie. "Things are cleaner in the north," she said, before she rode off alongside her man. "But you stay around here. You can be what you want to be around here."

By the next summer he was riding with the Texas Rangers and thinking about the man she had ridden away with, going north to some trouble centering around the long-horned cattle being driven that way out of Texas in the great herds, thinking about how he was going to learn this law business clean, getting set for another one-day meeting with that white-haired medical doctor. He could not stop thinking about her with that man, in his bed, on her knees and her elbows as she had been when the Comanche struck. He knew she was that way with the white-haired man, and he watched them in the darkness and kept his hands off himself, getting ready.

Then in the spring of 1876 the Cavendish gang left him there shot in the face, thinking him dead on the rocky dry riverbed, and there came along the single man without a tribe on his paint horse, the good dark man who found him and nursed him, and he recalled that long-ago morning the Comanche struck and knew this was a different life. As he recovered, he knew childishness was left behind, that somewhere in the kindness of this new companion there was a force he would hold always steady against what, until now, he had thought he loved: her white flesh in the sunlight that morning while she crouched with her skirt thrown forward.

For a long while things were so easily clear, there was this

8 THE GRAYWOLF ANNUALTHE GRAYWOLF ANNUAL

new friend and there was the great white horse, and both sides of what was right, like the Indian and buffalo on the United States nickel. The mask and silver bullets were emblems of the need to be distant if you were to be great and correct. Emblems were only ways of getting the work done, he understood that, even though the mask covered that dark purple scar, the twisted hole that had been his nostrils before the Cavendish gang shot him down and rode away, thinking he was dead, seeing as he looked drowned in blood.

What luck that he could shoot so perfectly without any sense of aiming, the silver bullets were after all part of the way he thought, the shooting more a business of balance and intent than anything he understood, the bullets just going where he saw they would, as though he could see a pistol in the hand of some craven man and shoot it away with only a thought.

Those were the legendary wandering years when he did not think about his sister. There was plenty of time; time was a trapeze that only swung you back and forth. Those were the years our union advanced in its skip-step way toward the Pacific and the meeting of fresh water with salt tides in the Golden Gate, the years our passenger pigeons were clubbed out of trees and Indian children were clubbed out of bushes as the nation made ready for the clubbing of Cuba and the Philippines and China. The Pony Express riders mounted their quickly saddled horses at a run while savages burned the way stations behind them; all but the impounded remnants of our sixty-odd million buffalo were slaughtered for their tongues and humps and hides and bones; the long-horned cows wore their way north to the grassy plains of Montana and Wyoming, surviving stampede while the lightning flashed, surviving quicksand on the Platte, only to perish in the snowy blizzard of 1885. The horse-drawn stages scattered dust between towns like Helena and Butte, Goldfield and Tonapah, carrying treasure in their strongboxes and enticing weak black-hatted men into banditry; the railroads came, building their graded roadbeds inexorably up through the passes, over Donner Summit and through the Ma-

rias in the northern Rockies; the nester fought the cattle bar-
ons; the cattle men fought the sheep and the rich fought the
poor; the barbed wire fought the wind; the sod-grass was
plowed under; the streets of Carson City were paved with brick
that had served as ballast on sailing ships from China; Joseph
and Looking Glass fought off tourists in Yellowstone, which
was already a National Park, before losing everything they had
suffered for in the Bear Paw Mountains. Somewhere far away
the last visionary chiefs were dying. Crazy Horse was dead, and
what there was to defend was somehow over as the first popping of the internal combustion engine began to be heard.
There was nothing right left to do most of the time, nothing at
all to do, and our man who began down on the Brazos was not
yet fifty years of age, still quick-handed as he had ever been,
and bored.

In 1912 Tonto found a woman and stayed in Grants Pass
amid blossoming spring apple and cherry trees and what the
masked man called wine-berries. The woman had come west as
a child from the plains after her toes were frozen off in the af-
termath of the great Ghost Dance massacre on the Pine Ridge
Reservation of South Dakota in December of 1891. "We were
like animals," the woman said, "so they let us run."

The earth shook San Francisco where he knew she was,
where she had to be, that most sin-filled and elegant city, with
water all around. The trench warfare began in Europe, and he
was too old. Over there they fought each other from craft in
the air, he would have liked that, it seemed right, and he was
too old. Then the war was over and he started toward the coast,
rode the white horse through the mountains of northern New
Mexico, along the old trails that had been graded into road-
ways, wintered alongside a lake in the Sierras, and in spring
drifted down to the valley towns of California, wondering what
next, trying to stay furtive, hiding out, taking his time on his
way San Francisco, perfecting disguises.

He was old and alone with the white horse, thinking of her
hair, the dark marks of age on her hands, which would be like

his. The man she left San Antonio with was no doubt dead, but she would have another in San Francisco. In some elegant house on one of those hills she would be pouring tea from a silver service, pouring steadily, her hands not shaking at all. He would lift the delicate cup made of fragile English porcelain, and she would smile.

The summer day was cool that close to the ocean as he came up the old El Camino into the Mission District. Off west the Twin Peaks were green with forest and above them the gray fog stood like an arrested wave. The Pacific was over there and he had never seen an ocean, real waves coming from Asia. The solid ground felt precarious, like it might tip and slip away without the strength of the continent spread around. He smiled at himself, knowing he should have come here when he would have liked this walking on eggs, this vast uneasiness was so much more important to confront than some fool with a model 1873 Colt revolver. So he stabled the white horse in a barn on the swampy ground of the upper Mission, and he rode an electrified trolley car out toward the ocean, to see what it was.

It was like he was invisible, disguised as an old man with a shot-off nose that was impossibly ugly to look at. The black man at the livery stable had treated him like a customer, and the people crowding around him on the trolley car talked and laughed like this was what they did all the time—as though his wound were only a matter of accident. Four seats down there was an old woman with an enormous goiter on the side of her neck, and no one looked at her either. Except for him, he watched her, and once she looked up and caught him and smiled.

They passed beyond the Twin Peaks, beneath the fog and out onto the grassy dune-land that descended toward the sea. The trolley line ended, and a boardwalk went on. He felt he was coming toward the edge of what he had always been. But it wasn't. The air was heavy with dampness, the fog thick around him, the waves gray and white the little way out he could see, but it wasn't like the edge of anything. He took off his boots and left them in the sand, walked down until the cold water lapped on his blue-white feet, and rolled himself a cigarette. He fired one shot out into the very center of that gray circle of oncoming water and fog and smiled at himself because there was nothing there to disarm.

Of course she wasn't up there on those hills in some rich man's house. He knew that. She would not have gone that way. Down on Market Street, the next day after he slept in the stable beside the white horse, that was where she would be. She would be in the right place, down with the injured where arrogance was equal to foolishness. Over the years she would have figured it out. She would have left the white-haired man before he died, she would have gone right and poor.

But she was not there. This day he went without his guns again, without his mask and the gun-belt stocked with silver bullets. The white horse munched oats calmly as if this were not a new world, and he walked the barrooms, expecting to see her laughing and quarreling, maybe selling flowers on a street corner. That night he stayed in a room which smelled of urine and ammonia and the old nervous sweat, not really sleeping, just resting there and dreaming she was nearby. But she was not. He walked the muddy streets toward the outskirts of the city as a common man, and she was not there.

At least he had not recognized her.

So it was her turn.

He went back to the only things there were: his mask, his silence, those guns, the great white horse. No matter what the comforts of nearby water, he would not be a common man.

Trussed out in his black leather gun-belt so she would see, he would be what he had always been, so prepared for whatever happened he had always been able to see the moment of his own death: the lurking coward, the high-power rifle and the shot from behind, the loud after-crack echoing where the Staked Plains fall off the Cap Rock in west Texas, swallows flushing and turning through the afternoon, deer in thickets by the Brazos lifting their heads after the impact, as the darkness closed and the far away silence began. These last gunless days of searching in this city where even the sound of the last rifle shot would be lost amid the cobbled streets, as he went aimlessly where she might be, that moment of dying seemed closer.

But he would not die dumb and amiable. So he made inquiries. Who was the most evil and wretched man in this town? She would see, he thought, as the great horse cantered on the bricks. He would not be a common man.

There was no worst man, but there was the man rumored to own the worst men. From far above we see the city on the hills in the sunlight of that morning, the water gleaming around the ferry boats, the sidewalk crowds along Market Street and the trolley cars clanging, the square black automobiles and the masked man on his white horse cantering proudly between the stone buildings, up from the Mission and then down Market toward the building where the ferry boats were docking.

The white horse prances and his mane blows in the sea breeze. The masked man stops before a tavern. In through the gleaming clean windows he can see old men and old women lost in the great interior depths. In his steady voice he calls out the worst man in San Francisco, an old Chinese gentleman with a white thin beard and so the story went, hords of killer functionaries, both white and oriental, some brutal, some cunning. The masked man sits his horse with his hands poised at his guns. At least his old magic will bring down one or two before he goes, even though the deer along the Brazos will never hear of it. But the aged Chinese gentleman comes out alone, wearing a long brocade gown decorated with silver and gold thread, and he holds his hands together before him, as though praying.

"You come in," he says in his quavering voice, gesturing at the masked man.

"You come in with us," he says.

"You shake your hands at your sides," he says, "and you feel the sun on your back, and the great knot will untie itself."

"Feel the warmth," he says, "move your fingers."

"Twist your head on your neck, and feel the cracking as things come loose. Feel the movement of each finger, the warmth of the sun and the coolness of the sea." The Chinese gentleman begins moving his hands up and down at his sides in motions like those of newborn birds, the deep sleeves on his embroidered gown flapping as if he might at any moment fly.

As if his body might at last be doing what it wants with him, the masked man finds his fingers flexing and unlocking and his head slowly turning from one side to the other, lifting and falling as the old small bones began to crack apart from one another. "Feel the aching in your joints," the Chinese gentleman says.

Like a child out on that street astride his great white horse the masked man knows something has begun. It is important in this old age to risk foolishness. The heavy revolvers at his sides will never again be part of what he is; he feels encumbered by these trappings of greatness, the guns and heavy silver bullets in the stiff leather belt.

"Step down," the Chinese gentleman says, "and accept this present from an old man." From the folds in his gown the Chinese gentleman produces an orange, which he holds as a gift toward the masked man.

"They are the sweetest in all the world," the Chinese gentleman says. "In the south of China they are like fire amid the emerald leaves."

Thus the masked man comes to stand in the cool and cavernous darkness of the tavern with his fingers feeling like feathers, a China Orange before him on the hardwood surface of the bar. The people around him are old and talking as old people will, sometimes gesturing angrily, but talking. A fat old woman with bright red lipstick and a pink flowered dress, who could never have been his sister, rubs at his neck, digging her thumbs between the blades of his shoulders, and there as the masked man listens to the cracking of bones loosening themselves from one another he knows the knot is coming undone, unstringing him from what he has always been, and the guns at his side are a heavy and foolish weight.

"You stay here with us," the Chinese gentleman says.

The masked man lifts his guns from their holsters and places them carefully on the worn mahogany surface of the bar. Alongside them he places a silver bullet, and he orders a drink, a round for the house, for what he calls his friends, and an Irish bartender in a stiff collar sets him up a bottle of whiskey and accepts the silver bullet at payment. The masked man peels off his mask and stands barefaced beside the aged Chinese gentleman and does not feel mutilated as he sips his drink and listens to this society he has joined, the old Finns and the French and Britishers around him talking, the crackling of old men, old women telling of childbirth after raising the drinks he has bought to toast him silently.

"There was a morning . . . " The masked man begins to speak, but no one is paying any special attention, so he peels the soft glowing China Orange, stripping the peel away in a long spool and then separating the sections and aligning them before him on the bar before eating the first one. For him it is over. He will be ancient when the great fires blossom over Dresden and Japan, after the millions die, and he will not know he should care. Salmon die in turbines and he does not know at all.

But there was a moment when great silence descended. Beyond the Staked Plains and the Cap Rock of west Texas the swallows flushed and turned through the afternoon. Deer in thickets by the Brazos lifted their heads. In our silence amid bulrushes by the river, a girl crouches on her knees with her skirt thrown forward, her flesh so perfectly white under the fresh morning sun. "Don't you stop," she says, and that great white horse rears above the rolling horizon, which is golden and simple in the sunset, sparkling hooves striking out into the green light under dark midsummer thunderclouds, and far away there is rain as the stars grow luminous.

ROBERT OLMSTEAD

✛

High-Low-Jack

Big George Gilbus and his sidekick Cutler were on the lam. As the story goes, they fell asleep one night, drunk, and the kettle of water Cutler kept on the burner to humidify the air cooked out dry. It started to melt, liquefied by the heat that rose up from the 1932 Hotpoint deluxe electric stove the boys had re-wired that morning.

The fire that ensued burned down four hundred acres of prime Adirondack State Park. For Big George's wife, it was the last of the last times. For Cutler it was the end of his stay in paradise. He'd already tangled with the park authorities on a number of occasions. In the past, they'd taken umbrage over such things as the location of his trailer, his septic system, and his ignorance of fish and game laws, most specifically the taking of fish by use of high explosives and army ordnance he acquired from a buddy in the National Guard.

Cutler would have snuck out from under this one too if not for the fact that he put in for a pay voucher to cover the hours he and Big·George spent helping to combat the flames that engulfed the ranger station and tourist center. Both men were convinced that Rockefeller himself had the troopers hot on their trail, pounding over the New York State Thruway and up and down the Northway, setting out roadblocks, checkpoints and bulletins.

Their first stop was at Big George's house. It was empty except for a note from his wife tacked to the wall with a ten-penny nail. It said, "I read it in the papers. Hasta luego!" She'd even swept the floor and washed the windows.

Big George and Cutler loaded every tool they could into the Dodge Power Wagon and high-tailed it for the woods of Maine where Big George had a cousin, Beecher.

After hiding out in Jackman, they moved on to Skowhegan where they started a cash and barter construction company. They moved into an abandoned Esso station and set up housekeeping. There was room for them, their equipment, the pickup and a small wood shop. They kept the windows covered up and the truck inside the first bay.

Cutler built a frame and platform on the high lift. It held his box spring and mattress. He raised it two feet off the concrete and left it there for a bed. He liked it until one night Big George raised him up to the ceiling and yelled, fire. Cutler rolled out over the side and dropped right through the air to the floor below. Half way down he righted himself like a cat would, and landed on both feet.

"You son of a whore," he said, doubling his fists and dancing on the balls of his feet that must have stung like hell. "You son of a whore. I'm going to take you down a peg or two."

Big George sat up in bed and looked at his friend, slowly shaking his head.

"Jesus, Cutler. That was remarkable how you did that. I never saw a man do what you just did. I've seen roofers come out of the sky like that and get all busted up, but not you. You're a regular free-fall artist. I have decided that whatever you do to me will be a small price to pay for what I have just witnessed."

"Now that you mention it, it was really something wasn't it," Cutler said, letting his hands fall to his sides.

"I wouldn't shit you, old buddy. Never saw a man do what you just did."

"Good for you, George. I'm happy for you."

The next morning Cutler padlocked the hand valve on the

compressor. He then hid the hacksaw blades and the key to the acetylene and oxygen so Big George wouldn't have any way to cut the lock. Later in the day, Big George asked him where they were hid in case he needed them when Cutler wasn't around, but Cutler still wouldn't tell.

Every night as they'd pull up, it was Cutler's habit to jump out of the moving vehicle and run up the overhead door so Big George could pull in. Big George'd shut down the rig and Cutler'd run down the overhead door clattering it along its tracks. Then Big George'd step out onto the oil-stained concrete floor, slam shut the door of the Dodge and pull open the door of the Frigidaire which was always stocked with beer.

Soon word got around as to how the two men had come to be in Maine. Big George's cousin swore on a stack of Bibles that he didn't tell a soul. George knew *he* didn't tell anyone and Cutler swore he didn't breathe a word of it to a soul either, living *or* dead. He said he was certain and for Cutler to say he was certain was enough for any man to believe him. It didn't matter though because people didn't care how they'd come to be in Maine. If the truth were to be known, most people probably admired them for coming into the state under the circumstances they did, being as how they'd left a bit of New York state charred.

As far as women went, both men were beyond the age of need. They neither had the energy nor the ambition to go out and track them after a full day's work. They tended to talk about their mothers and how they should have loved them more when they had the chance. They made plans about jumping in the truck one day and taking the risk of driving west so they could put flowers on the dead women's graves. They'd drive through Quebec to Montreal, maybe catch an Expos game. They'd buy flowers from a girl on a street corner and then descend on New York State by cover of darkness like bandits in the night. Cutler was certain he knew a back way into Charubusco. After so much talk, they finally decided to go.

Friday afternoon they shut down the job. They planned on

leaving that night for their trip back home. As they approached the station, there was an unfamiliar car parked by the
pumps. Big George drove by two or three times before he recognized it as his cousin Beecher's black Impala.

Cutler jumped out and ran up the door while Big George
rolled in. Asel and Beecher slipped in behind the truck nearly
taking the closing door across the tops of their heads. Big
George opened the Frigidaire and handed out beer to everyone.

"I have business with you, George," Beecher said. "I want
you to train this man in your craft. I'll pay half his wage. In return, you have to teach him, work him and keep him under
wraps."

"Now hold on just a minute. I don't know a damn thing
you're saying. You don't even say hello to me. I'll tell you what.
You go to the store and buy some grub for the weekend and
hole up with us. That will give you time to explain everything.
Me and Cutler can't just walk into this thing blind. We got a
business to run and we don't take charity cases. Besides, we
were getting ready to leave on a little vacation."

"That's right, Beecher. Me and George, we're hung out to
dry here a little bit, if you know what I mean. Stay the weekend
like your cousin says. We'll stay too."

"I'll stay, but why the hell do I have to buy all the food?"
Beecher said, feeling as though there would be no easy way to
get around the problem.

"Don't be that way," Big George said. "We have been taking
our dinners down the road where we did a little work in ex-
change for suppers. It's the kind of place where you eat from
the same kettle, the same loaf. We can't go waltzing in there
with you and your friend here. There would be questions to
answer and you know that neither me nor Cutler are too clear
minded. He ain't a damn hippie, is he?"

"Nor a beatnik," Cutler broke in "I won't live with no beatnik
nor a hippie. Neither of them are clean."

"Tell Cutler he isn't a beatnik or a hippie, Beecher. Tell him he isn't."

"Jesus Christ," Beecher said, "His name is Asel and he's in a little trouble that is no cause of his own. He ain't a beatnik and he ain't a hippie. He's a guide, an authentic Maine guide. Now shut your god damn mouth you little pip squeak."

Asel drank the beer Big George'd given him. It was cold in his hand and he liked the way it felt in his throat. He rocked forward on his feet, thinking there might be trouble.

Beecher raised up his shoulder and puffed out his chest, trying to make himself look big. It scared off most people, but not Cutler, because Cutler always took them out at the knees. He didn't care how big they were. To him, Beecher was just some big god damn cuckoo flower even if he was George's cousin.

Cutler hunched down and began to skirt Beecher. He didn't like Beecher moving in on them the way he did. He wanted to knock him down and gouge his eye. The thought took hold and began to have an importance all its own. Beecher could feel it coming.

Cutler rose up on the balls of his feet, only to feel two arms come around him and clamp his own flush against his sides. Something hard jabbed him under his left shoulder blade and he stayed there, not being able to move.

"Let him go, Ace," Big George said. "We're all friends here. You and me will talk while good cousin Beecher goes for groceries and while good friend Cutler washes his face so he can go too."

Asel let go of Cutler and stepped back. The four men stood looking from one to the other.

"Go wash your face," Big George said and Cutler went over to the hose. When he came back Big George put an arm around him and pulled him close.

"That's better, isn't it."

"I don't like getting manhandled," Cutler said looking at Asel.

"You go. You show Beecher where the grocery store is."

"Come on, Beech."

Beecher and Cutler raised up the overhead door just enough to slip out underneath it. They got in Beecher's Impala and drove off to the grocery store. Beecher would use the pay phone to call home. Cutler and Big George didn't have a phone. They had a bulletin board where people could leave messages if they needed work done.

"So what have you got in there kid?"

Asel pulled back his coat. He unholstered his revolver and handed it to Big George.

"Nice," Big George said, ".44 Blackhawk. Good gun. Now I'll tell you, if you're smart, you're going to give Cutler a little something to soothe his ruffled feathers. He doesn't like to be manhandled."

Asel looked up at Big George and nodded his head. He knew it was the right thing to do. "Fair enough," he said. "I don't need enemies."

"Cutler would probably prefer a little piece of your ear, but if not that, something out of your kit would be fine. The trick is, you're going to have to make him think that it isn't a present. You're going to have to give him something without giving it to him."

Asel nodded, more as a way of moving the conversation along, than out of agreement.

"Now tell me what's going on here," Big George went on. "I don't have to know a lot. Beecher is usually right on the mark when it comes to others. If he wants me to take care of you, that's okay."

Asel told Big George about how he'd been in the woods these past years and how he hiked out and Averell was gone. He told him how Beecher had moved in and took care of him the second time around and about Beecher thinking he owed him something but how it wasn't true.

"Beecher's like that. He takes in strays. He always has. It doesn't seem as though Beecher owes you anything, but if he says so then he must be sure in his head that he does. Beecher's word is good enough for me. Consider yourself part of the crew. Just remember, we stay fairly tight-lipped around here. A lot of people do it by nature, but me and Cutler are more or less forced into it. We don't mind."

Big George gave Asel a tour of the station while they waited for Beecher and Cutler to return. He showed him the bays and the grease pit. He took him to the upstairs storage room and into the office. He showed him the men's room and finally the one bay they'd sheeted in with plywood and used for a combination kitchen and bedroom. Big George took Asel outside to show him the bulletin board. They had constructed a roof over it and hung a tiny door with a window to protect it from the elements.

"People are able to open the door and leave messages," Big George said. "It's why we don't need a phone."

Big George was satisfied that Asel would be good to have around. He considered him to be someone who'd keep his business tight to his vest. He liked the way Asel moved and he liked the way Asel's eyes were wide awake while the rest of him seemed a little tired.

"We got a big job coming up. We'll need an extra hand. It's the parsonage, the church and the house next door. A new Reverend is coming in. A real spark plug. The people of the congregation picked up the house to turn over into a day care center. They've got a government person who's coming in to run the show."

Asel didn't like to hear that it was a government person. It reminded him of Borst and the idiot boys. Big George could tell it made him uneasy and he liked that.

"Don't worry about it. We're told she's from an outfit called VISTA. College students, mostly. It's something for the ones who can't be soldiers or hippies. More likely it'll be some refugee off a commune who won't admit it, but would rather get back inside daddy's checkbook. Probably sick of raising bean sprouts by day and sneaking cup cakes by night."

Big George started to laugh. If Cutler had been there he would have too. They would have carried on into the night until it hurt to laugh anymore.

The bell in the office rang. Big George looked out to see Beecher's Impala pulling in by the pumps. He and Asel went out to help carry stuff in.

"Now Beech," Big George said, "We're all set here. You hit the road. There'll be no need to send money. We'll make out fine."

Beecher started to talk but Big George held up his hand to stop him. He then smiled and lowered his hand to take Beecher's.

"Don't be such a stranger from now on."

Beecher was grateful. He got back in the car and pulled onto the highway. It dawned on him that Big George had sprung him for the weekend. He turned the car around. He figured he'd go down to Old Orchard for a few days and maybe have some fun.

The next morning, Asel's education began. The trip Big George and Cutler had planned to take to their mothers' graves was forgotten. Cutler pulled chairs up to the desk in the office. He put on his baseball cap and rolled up his sleeves. Big George set out the coffee pot and a box of cinnamon doughnuts. Cutler broke open a deck of cards and began riffling them in his hands.

"Now we see what you're made of, Ace. We're going to play a little high-low-jack. Also known as Old Sledge, pitch and all-fours. You might have heard of it. It's a card game for three. Sometimes it can be played in partners but given how there's only three of us we'd have to resort to floating partners which is a concept I don't think you're ready for. Now the object is to win of course. To do that you have special scoring points. The highest trump, the lowest trump, the jack, the ace and the ten. Now these can change during the course of a game and during the course of hand. There are special hand signals and I *know* you're not ready for them. Highest and lowest scores share the pot. Alright, let us begin."

As the morning went on, Asel was obliged to go into his kit and put up his belongings one at a time. Cutler's mouth hung open and Big George's forehead went deep with lines as they watched him come up with knives, compasses, guns, ammo, loaders, tackle, rods, first aid supplies, candle lanterns, cook sets, binoculars, hatchets, a meat saw and a machete.

By noon, he was cleaned out except for the Ruger and already into his future earnings. Big George and Cutler held a conference in the grease pit. They decided that the game would be chalked up as a learning experience. They told Asel, he could have his gear back, but after that it would be dog eat dog, destructive and ruthless competition without self-restraint. Asel agreed to this and felt bound to play a few more hands so they could win things legitimately, maybe a clutch knife, or the machete. Asel thought that would make them feel better about the kindnesses they'd directed his way.

Asel began to win. At two o'clock, he and Cutler owned it all, the business and everything. At four o'clock, things changed such that he and Big George owned it all and by seven o'clock that night, he was the sole proprietor. Big George and Cutler were tapped out. They didn't have any more to bet. They sat back and looked across the table at Asel, for some sign.

"It ain't right," Cutler said. "It just ain't right."

"Well, it happened," Big George told him. "You and your god damn card games. Sometimes you think you're so smart, Mister Cutler. Well, you got your tit caught in the wringer this time."

Asel remembered the old man saying just such a thing about someone else. He looked at the men. He said, "That sure was dog eat dog, wasn't it. I won everything. Everything for keeps."

Asel smiled and then he began to laugh. He lit a match and began burning markers. The other two men began to laugh with him. Cutler took out his zippo and helped burn up the slips of paper. They jumped up and clapped each other on the back. They sent cans skittering across the floor, spilling out stale beer and Cutler's cigarette butts.

"We'll do good together," Big George said. "We'll do a bang up job. Now Ace, tomorrow around eleven, a few of the local boys get up a game in bay two. There will be the selectmen and the constable, but don't you fret, it's just a way that Cutler and me have of keeping tabs on those boys. They're the town's finest and it's strictly penny-ante stuff."

RAYMOND CARVER

✛

Menudo

I CAN'T SLEEP, but when I'm sure my wife Vicky is asleep, I get up and look through our bedroom window, across the street, at Oliver and Amanda's house. Oliver has been gone for three days, but his wife Amanda is awake. She can't sleep either. It's four in the morning, and there's not a sound outside — no wind, no cars, no moon even — just Oliver and Amanda's place with the lights on, leaves heaped up under the front windows.

A couple of days ago, when I couldn't sit still, I raked our yard — Vicky's and mine. I gathered all the leaves into bags, tied off the tops, and put the bags alongside the curb. I had an urge then to cross the street and rake over there, but I didn't follow through. It's my fault things are the way they are across the street.

I've only slept a few hours since Oliver left. Vicky saw me moping around the house, looking anxious, and decided to put two and two together. She's on her side of the bed now, scrunched onto about ten inches of mattress. She got into bed and tried to position herself so she wouldn't accidentally roll into me while she slept. She hasn't moved since she lay down, sobbed, and then dropped into sleep. She's exhausted. I'm exhausted too.

I've taken nearly all of Vicky's pills, but I still can't sleep. I'm keyed up. But maybe if I keep looking I'll catch a glimpse of Amanda moving around inside her house, or else find her peering from behind a curtain, trying to see what she can see over here.

What if I do see her? So what? What then?

Vicky says I'm crazy. She said worse things too last night. But who could blame her? I told her — I had to — but I didn't tell her it was Amanda. When Amanda's name came up, I insisted it wasn't her. Vicky suspects, but I wouldn't name names. I wouldn't say who, even though she kept pressing and then hit me a few times in the head.

"What's it matter *who* ?" I said. "You've never met the woman," I lied. "You don't know her." That's when she started hitting me.

I feel *wired*. That's what my painter friend Alfredo used to call it when he talked about friends of his coming down off something. *Wired*. I'm wired.

This thing is nuts. I know it is, but I can't stop thinking about Amanda. Things are so bad just now I even find myself thinking about my first wife, Molly. I loved Molly, I thought, more than my own life.

I keep picturing Amanda in her pink night-gown, the one I like on her so much, along with her pink slippers. And I feel certain she's in the big leather chair right now, under the brass reading lamp. She's smoking cigarettes, one after the other. There are two ashtrays close at hand, and they're both full. To the left of her chair, next to the lamp, there's an end table stacked with magazines — the usual magazines that nice people read. We're nice people, all of us, to a point. Right this minute, Amanda is, I imagine, paging through a magazine, stopping every so often to look at an illustration or a cartoon.

Two days ago, in the afternoon, Amanda said to me, "I can't read books any more. Who has the time?" It was the day after Oliver had left, and we were in this little café in the industrial part of the city. "Who can concentrate any more?" she said stirring her coffee. "Who reads? Do you read?" (I shook my head.)

"Somebody must read, I guess. You see all these books around in store windows, and there are those clubs. Somebody's reading," she said. "Who? I don't know anybody who reads."

That's what she said, apropos of nothing — that is, we weren't talking about books, we were talking about our *lives*. Books had nothing to do with it.

"What did Oliver say when you told him?"

Then it struck me that what we were saying — the tense, watchful expressions we wore — belonged to the people on afternoon TV programs that I'd never done more than switch on and then off.

Amanda looked down and shook her head, as if she couldn't bear to remember.

"You didn't admit who it was you were involved with, did you?"

She shook her head again.

"You're sure of that?" I waited until she looked up from her coffee.

"I didn't mention any names, if that's what you mean."

"Did he say where he was going, or how long he'd be away?" I said, wishing I didn't have to hear myself. This was my neighbor I was talking about. Oliver Porter. A man I'd helped drive out of his home.

"He didn't say where. A hotel. He said I should make my arrangements and be gone — *be gone,* he said. It was like biblical the way he said it — out of his house, out of his *life,* in a week's time. I guess he's coming back then. So we have to decide something real important, real soon, honey. You and I have to make up our minds pretty damn quick."

It was her turn to look at me now, and I know she was looking for a sign of life-long commitment. "A week," I said. I looked at my coffee, which had gotten cold. A lot had happened in a little while, and we were trying to take it in. I don't know what long-term things, if any, we'd thought about those months as we moved from flirtation to love, and then afternoon assignations. In any case, we were in a serious fix now.

Very serious. We'd never expected — not in a hundred years — to be hiding out in a café, in the middle of the afternoon, trying to decide matters like this.

I raised my eyes, and Amanda began stirring her coffee. She kept stirring it. I touched her hand, and the spoon dropped out of her fingers. She picked it up and began stirring again. We could have been anybody drinking coffee at a table under fluorescent lights in a run-down café. Anybody, just about. I took Amanda's hand and held it, and it seemed to make a difference.

V ICKY'S STILL SLEEPING on her side when I go downstairs. I plan to heat some milk and drink that. I used to drink whisky when I couldn't sleep, but I gave it up. Now it's strictly hot milk. In the whisky days I'd wake up with this tremendous thirst in the middle of the night. But, back then, I was always looking ahead : I kept a bottle of water in the fridge, for instance. I'd be dehydrated, sweating from head to toe when I woke, but I'd wander out to the kitchen and could count on finding that bottle of cold water in the fridge. I'd drink it, all of it, down the hatch, an entire quart of water. Once in a while I'd use a glass, but not often. Suddenly I'd be drunk all over again and weaving around the kitchen. I can't begin to account for it — sober one minute, drunk the next.

The drinking was part of my destiny — according to Molly, anyway. She put a lot of stock in destiny.

I feel wild from lack of sleep. I'd give anything, just about, to be able to go to sleep, and sleep the sleep of an honest man.

Why do we have to sleep anyway? And why do we tend to sleep less during some crises and more during others? For instance, that time my dad had his stroke. He woke up after a coma — seven days and nights in a hospital bed — and calmly said "Hello" to the people in his room. Then his eyes picked me out. "Hello, son," he said. Five minutes later, he died. Just like that — he died. But, during that whole crisis, I never took my clothes off and didn't go to bed. I may have catnapped in a waiting-room chair from time to time, but I never went to bed and slept.

And then a year or so ago I found out Vicky was seeing somebody else. Instead of confronting *her*, I went to bed when I heard about it, and stayed there. I didn't get up for days, a week maybe — I don't know. I mean, I got up to go to the bathroom, or else to the kitchen to make a sandwich. I even went out to the living room in my pajamas, in the afternoon, and tried to read the papers. But I'd fall asleep sitting up. Then I'd stir, open my eyes and go back to bed and sleep some more. I couldn't get enough sleep.

It passed. We weathered it. Vicky quit her boyfriend, or he quit her, I never found out. I just know she went away from me for a while, and then she came back. But I have the feeling we're not going to weather this business. This thing is different. Oliver has given Amanda that ultimatum.

Still, isn't it possible that Oliver himself is awake at this moment and writing a letter to Amanda, urging reconciliation? Even now he might be scribbling away, trying to persuade her that what she's doing to him and their daughter Beth is foolish, disastrous, and finally a tragic thing for the three of them.

No, that's insane. I know Oliver. He's relentless, unforgiving. He could slam a croquet ball into the next block — and has. He isn't going to write any such letter. He gave her an ultimatum, right? — a *diktat* — and that's that. A week. Four days now. Or is it three? Oliver may be awake, but if he is, he's sitting in a chair in his hotel room with a glass of iced vodka in his hand, his feet on the bed, TV turned on low. He's dressed, except for his shoes. He's not wearing shoes — that's the only concession he makes. That and the fact he's loosened his tie.

Oliver is relentless.

I HEAT THE MILK, spoon the membrane from the surface and pour it up. Then I turn off the kitchen light and take the cup into the living room and sit on the sofa, where I can look across the street at the lighted windows. But I can hardly sit still. I keep fidgeting, crossing one leg and then the other. I feel like I could throw off sparks, or break a window — maybe rearrange all the furniture.

The things that go through your mind when you can't sleep! Earlier, thinking about Molly, for a moment I couldn't even remember what she *looked* like, for Christ's sake, yet we were together for years, more or less continuously, since we were kids. Molly, who said she'd love me forever. The only thing left was the memory of her sitting and weeping at the kitchen table, her shoulders bent forward, and her hands covering her face. *Forever,* she said. But it hadn't worked out that way. Finally, she said, it didn't matter, it was of no real concern to her, if she and I lived together the rest of our lives or not. Our love existed on a "higher plane." That's what she said to Vicky over the phone that time, after Vicky and I had set up housekeeping together. Molly called, got hold of Vicky, and said, "You have your relationship with him, but I'll always have mine. His destiny and mine are linked."

My first wife, Molly, she talked like that. "Our destinies are linked". She didn't talk like that in the beginning. It was only later, after so much had happened, that she started using words like "cosmic" and "empowerment" and so forth. But our destinies are *not* linked — not now, anyway, if they ever were. I don't even know where she is now, not for certain.

I think I could put my finger on the exact time, the real turning point, when it came undone for Molly. It was after I started seeing Vicky, and Molly found out. They called me up one day from the high school where Molly taught and said, "Please. Your wife is doing handsprings in front of the school. You'd better get down here." It was after I took her home that I began hearing about "higher power" and "going with the flow" — stuff of that sort. Our destiny had been "revised". And if I'd been hesitating before, well, I left her then as fast as I could — this woman I'd known all my life, the one who'd been my best friend for years, my intimate, my confidante. I bailed out on her. For one thing, I was scared. *Scared*.

This girl I'd started out with in life, this sweet thing, this gentle soul, she wound up going to fortune tellers, palm readers, *crystal ball gazers,* looking for answers, trying to figure out what she should do with her life. She quit her job, drew out her teacher's retirement money, and thereafter never made a decision without consulting the *I Ching.* She began wearing strange clothes — clothes with permanent wrinkles and a lot of burgundy and orange. She even got involved with a group that sat around, I'm not kidding, trying to levitate.

When Molly and I were growing up together, she was a part of me and, sure, I was a part of her, too. We loved each other. It *was* our destiny. I believed in it then myself. But now I don't know what to believe in. I'm not complaining, simply stating a fact. I'm down to nothing. And I have to go on like this. No destiny. Just the next thing meaning whatever you think it does. Compulsion and error, just like everybody else.

Amanda? I'd like to believe in her, bless her heart. But she was looking for somebody when she met me. That's the way with people when they get restless: they start up something, knowing that's going to change things for good.

I'd like to go out in the front yard and shout something. "None of this is worth it!" That's what I'd like people to hear.

"Destiny," Molly said. For all I know she's still talking about it.

ALL THE LIGHTS are off over there now, except for that light in the kitchen. I could try calling Amanda on the phone. I could do that and see how far it gets me! What if Vicky heard me dialing or talking on the phone and came downstairs? What if she lifted the receiver upstairs and listened? Besides, there's always the chance Beth might pick up the phone. I don't want to talk to any kids this morning. I don't want to talk to anybody. Actually, I'd talk to Molly, if I could, but I can't any longer —

she's somebody else now. She isn't *Molly* any more. But — what can I say? — I'm somebody else, too.

I wish I could be like everybody else in this neighborhood — your basic, normal, unaccomplished person — and go up to my bedroom, and lie down, and sleep. It's going to be a big day today, and I'd like to be ready for it. I wish I could sleep and wake up and find everything in my life different. Not necessarily just the big things, like this thing with Amanda or the past with Molly. But things clearly within my power.

Take the situation with my mother: I used to send money every month. But then I started sending her the same amount in twice-yearly sums. I gave her money on her birthday, and I gave her money at Christmas. I thought: I won't have to worry about forgetting her birthday, and I won't have to worry about sending her a Christmas present. I won't have to worry, period. It went like clockwork for a long time.

Then last year she asked me — it was in between money-times, it was in March, or maybe April — for a radio. A radio, she said, would make a difference to her.

What she wanted was a little clock radio. She could put it in her kitchen and have it out there to listen to while she was fixing something to eat in the evening. And she'd have the clock to look too, so she'd know when something was supposed to come out of the oven, or how long it was until one of her programs started.

A little clock radio.

She hinted around at first. She said, "I'd sure like to have a radio. But I can't afford one. I guess I'll have to wait for my birthday. That little radio I had, it fell and broke. I miss a radio." *I miss a radio.* That's what she said when we talked on the phone, or else she'd bring it up when she'd write.

Finally — what'd I say? I said to her over the phone that I couldn't afford any radios. I said it in a letter too, so she'd be sure and understand. *I can't afford any radios,* is what I wrote. I can't do any more, I said, than I'm doing. Those were my very words.

But it wasn't true! I could have done more. I just said I couldn't. I could have afforded to buy a radio for her. What would it have cost me? Thirty-five dollars? Forty dollars or less including tax. I could have sent her a radio through the mail. I could have had somebody in the store do it, if I didn't want to go to the trouble myself. Or else I could have sent her a forty-dollar check along with a note saying, *This money is for your radio, mother.*

I could have handled it in any case. Forty dollars — are you kidding? But I didn't. I wouldn't part with it. It seemed there was a *principle* involved. That's what I told myself anyway — there's a principle involved here.

Ha.

Then what happened? She died. She *died.* She was walking home from the grocery store, back to her apartment, carrying her sack of groceries, and she fell into somebody's bushes and died.

I took a flight out there to make the arrangements. She was still at the coroner's, and they had her purse and her groceries behind the desk in the office. I didn't bother to look in the purse they handed me. But what she had from the grocery store was a jar of Metamucil, two grapefruits, a carton of cottage cheese, a quart of buttermilk, some potatoes and onions and a package of ground meat that was beginning to change color.

Boy! I cried when I saw those things. I couldn't stop. I didn't think I'd ever quit crying. The woman who worked at the desk was embarrassed and brought me a glass of water. They gave me a bag for my mother's groceries and another bag for her personal effects — her purse and her dentures. Later, I put the dentures in my coat pocket and drove them down in a rental car and gave them to somebody at the funeral home.

THE LIGHT in Amanda's kitchen is still on. It's a bright light that spills out on to all those leaves. Maybe she's like I am, and she's scared. Maybe she left that light burning as a night-light. Or maybe she's still awake and is at the kitchen table, under the light, writing me a letter. Amanda is writing me a letter, and somehow she'll get it into my hands later on when the real day starts.

Come to think of it, I've never had a letter from her since we've known each other. All the time we've been involved — six months, eight months — and I've never once seen a scrap of her handwriting. I don't even know if she's *literate* that way.

I think she is. Sure, she is. She talks about books, doesn't she? It doesn't matter of course. Well, a little, I suppose. I love her in any case, right?

But I've never written anything to her, either. We always talked on the phone or else face-to-face.

Molly, she was the letter writer. She used to write me even after we weren't living together. Vicky would bring her letters in from the box and leave them on the kitchen table without a word. Finally the letters dwindled away, became more and more infrequent and bizarre. When she did write, the letters gave me a chill. They were full of talk about "auras" and "signs." Occasionally she reported a voice that was telling her something she ought to do or some place she should go. And once she told me that no matter what happened, we were still "on the same frequency." She always knew exactly what I felt, she said. She "beamed in on me," she said, from time to time. Reading those letters of hers, the hair on the back of my neck would tingle. She also had a new word for destiny: *Karma*. "I'm following out my karma," she wrote. "Your karma has taken a bad turn."

I'D LIKE to go to sleep, but what's the point? People will be getting up soon. Vicky's alarm will go off before much longer. I wish I could go upstairs and get back in bed with my wife, tell her I'm sorry, there's been a mistake, let's forget all this — then go to sleep and wake up with her in my arms. But I've forfeited

that right. I'm outside all that now, and I can't get back inside!
But say I did that. Say I went upstairs and slid into bed with
Vicky as I'd like to do. She might wake up and say, *You bastard.
Don't you dare touch me, son of a bitch.*

What's she talking about, anyway? I wouldn't touch her. Not
in that way, I wouldn't.

After I left Molly, after I'd pulled out on her, about two
months after, then Molly really did it. She had her real collapse
then, the one that'd been coming on. Her sister saw to it that
she got the care she needed. What am I saying? *They put her
away.* They had to, they said. They put my wife away. By then I
was living with Vicky, and trying not to drink whisky. I couldn't
do anything for Molly. I mean, she was there, I was here, and I
couldn't have gotten her out of that place if I'd wanted to. But
the fact is, I didn't want to. She was in there, they said, because
she *needed* to be in there. Nobody said anything about destiny.
Things had gone beyond that.

And I didn't even go visit her — not once! At the time, I
didn't think I could stand seeing her in there. But, Christ, what
was I? A fair-weather friend? We'd been through plenty. But
what on earth would I have said to her? *I'm sorry about all this,
honey.* I could have said that, I guess. I intended to write, but I
didn't. Not a word. Anyway, when you get right down to it,
what could I have said in a letter? *How are they treating you, baby?
I'm sorry you're where you are, but don't give up. Remember all the
good times? Remember when we were happy together? Hey, I'm sorry
they've done this to you. I'm sorry it turned out this way. I'm sorry
everything is just garbage now.* I'm sorry, Molly.

I didn't write. I think I was trying to forget about her, to pretend she didn't exist. Molly who?

I left my wife and took somebody else's: Vicky. Now I think
maybe I've lost Vicky, too. But Vicky won't be going away to
any summer camp for the mentally disabled. She's a hard case.
She left her former husband, Joe Kraft, and didn't bat an eye; I
don't think she ever lost a night's sleep over it.

Vicky Kraft-Hughes. Amanda Porter. This is where my destiny has brought me? To this street in this neighborhood, messing up the lives of these women?

Amanda's kitchen light went off when I wasn't looking. The room that was there is gone now, like the others. Only the porch light is still burning. Amanda must have forgotten it, I guess. Hey, Amanda.

ONCE WHEN MOLLY was away in that place and I wasn't in my right mind — let's face it, I was crazy too — one night I was at my friend Alfredo's house, a bunch of us drinking and listening to records. I didn't care any longer what happened to me. Everything, I thought, that could happen had happened. I felt unbalanced. I felt lost. Anyway there I was at Alfredo's. His paintings of tropical birds and animals hung on every wall in his house, and there were paintings standing around in the rooms, leaning against things — table legs, say, or his brick-and-board bookcase, as well as being stacked on his back porch. The kitchen served as his studio, and I was sitting at the kitchen table with a drink in front of me. An easel stood off to one side in front of the window that overlooked the alley, and there were crumpled tubes of paint, a palette and some brushes lying at one end of the table. Alfredo was making himself a drink at the counter a few feet away. I loved the shabby economy of that little room. The stereo music that came from the living room was turned up, filling the house with so much sound the kitchen windows rattled in their frames. Suddenly I began to shake. First my hands began to shake, and then my arms and shoulders, too. My teeth started to chatter. I couldn't hold the glass.

"What's going on, man?" Alfredo said, when he turned and saw the state I was in. "Hey, man, what is it? What's going on with you?"

I couldn't tell him. What could I say? I thought I was having some kind of an attack. I managed to raise my shoulders and let them drop.

Then Alfredo came over, took a chair and sat down beside

me at the kitchen table. He put his big painter's hand on my shoulder. I went on shaking. He could feel me shaking.

"What's wrong with you, man? I'm real sorry about everything, man. I know it's real hard right now." Then he said he was going to fix *menudo* for me. He said it would be good for what ailed me. "Help your nerves, man," he said. "Calm you right down." He had all the ingredients for *menudo*, he said, and he'd been wanting to make some anyway.

"You listen to me. Listen to what I say, man. I'm your family now, man," Alfredo said.

It was two in the morning, we were drunk, there were these other drunk people in the house and the stereo was going full blast. But Alfredo went to his fridge and opened it and took some stuff out. He closed the fridge door and looked in his freezer compartment. He found something in a package. Then he looked around in his cupboards. He took a big pan from the cabinet under the sink, and he was ready.

Tripe. He started with tripe and about a gallon of water. Then he chopped onions and added them to the water, which had started to boil. He put *chorizo* sausage in the pot. After that, he dropped peppercorns into the boiling water and sprinkled in some chili powder. Then came the olive oil. He opened a big can of tomato sauce and poured that in. He added cloves of garlic, some slices of white bread, salt and lemon juice. He opened another can — it was hominy — and poured that in the pot, too. He put it all in, and then he turned the heat down and put a lid on the pot.

I watched him. I sat there shaking while Alfredo stood at the stove making *menudo*, talking — I didn't have any idea what he was saying — and, from time to time, he'd shake his head, or else start whistling to himself. Now and then people drifted into the kitchen for beer. But all the while Alfredo went on very seriously looking after his *menudo*. He could have been home, in Morelia, making *menudo* for his family on New Year's day.

People hung around in the kitchen for a while, joking, but

Alfredo didn't joke back when they kidded him about cooking *menudo* in the middle of the night. Pretty soon they left us alone. Finally, while the *menudo* was cooking and Alfredo stood at the stove with a spoon in his hand, watching me, I got up slowly from the table. I walked out of the kitchen into the bathroom, and then opened another door off the bathroom to the spare room — where I lay down on the bed and fell asleep. When I woke it was mid-afternoon. The *menudo* was gone. The pot was in the sink, soaking. Those other people must have eaten it! They must have eaten it and grown calm. Everyone was gone, and the house was quiet.

I never saw Alfredo more than once or twice afterwards. After that night, our lives took us in separate directions. And those other people who were there — who knows where they went? I'll probably die without ever tasting *menudo*. But who can say?

Is this what it all comes down to then? A middle-aged man involved with his neighbor's wife, linked to an angry ultimatum? What kind of destiny is that? A week, Oliver said. Three or four days now.

A CAR PASSES outside with its lights on. The sky is turning grey, and I hear some birds starting up. I decide I can't wait any longer. I can't just sit here, doing nothing — that's all there is to it. I can't keep waiting. I've waited and waited and where's it gotten me? Vicky's alarm will go off soon, Beth will get up and dress for school, Amanda will wake up, too. The entire neighborhood.

On the back porch I find some old jeans and a sweat-shirt, and I change out of my pajamas. Then I put on my white canvas shoes — "wino" shoes Alfredo would have called them. Alfredo, where are you?

I go outside to the garage, and find the rake and some lawn bags. By the time I get around to the front of the house with the rake, ready to begin, I feel I don't have a choice in the matter any longer. It's light out — light enough at any rate for what I have to do. And then, without thinking about it any more, I start to rake. I rake our yard, every inch of it. It's important it be done right, too. I set the rake right down into the turf and pull hard. It must feel to the grass like it does to us whenever someone gives our hair a hard jerk. Now and then a car passes in the street and slows, but I don't look up from my work. I know what the people in the cars must be thinking, but they're dead wrong — they don't know the half of it. How could they? I'm happy, raking.

I finish our yard and put the bag out next to the curb. Then I begin next door on the Baxters" yard. In a few minutes Mrs. Baxter comes out on her porch, wearing her bathrobe. I don't acknowledge her. I'm not embarrassed, and I don't want to appear unfriendly. I just want to keep on with what I'm doing.

She doesn't say anything for a while, and then she says, "Good morning, Mr. Hughes. How are you this morning?"

I stop what I'm doing and run my arm across my forehead. "I'll be through in a little while," I say. "I hope you don't mind."

"We don't mind," Mrs. Baxter says. "Go right ahead, I guess." I see Mr. Baxter standing in the doorway behind her. He's already dressed for work in his slacks and sports coat and tie. But he doesn't venture on to the porch. Then Mrs. Baxter turns and looks at Mr. Baxter, who shrugs.

It's OK, I've finished here anyway. There are other yards, more important yards for that matter. I kneel, and, taking a grip low down on the rake handle, I pull the last of the leaves into my bag and tie off the top. Then, I can't help it, I just stay there, kneeling on the grass with the rake in my hand. When I look up, I see the Baxters come down the porch steps together and move slowly toward me through the wet, sweet-smelling grass. They stop a few feet away and look at me closely.

"There now," I hear Mrs. Baxter say. She's still in her robe and slippers. It's nippy out; she holds her robe at the throat. "You did a real fine job for us, yes, you did."

I don't say anything. I don't even say, "You're welcome."

They stand in front of me a while longer, and none of us says anything more. It's as if we've come to an agreement on something. In a minute, they turn around and go back to their house. High over my head, in the branches of the old maple — the place where these leaves come from — birds call out to each other. At least I think they're calling to each other.

Suddenly a car door slams. Mr. Baxter is in his car in the drive with the window rolled down. Mrs. Baxter says something to him from the front porch which causes Mr. Baxter to nod slowly and turn his head in my direction. He sees me kneeling there with the rake, and a look crosses his face. He frowns. In his better moments, Mr. Baxter is a decent, ordinary guy — a guy you wouldn't mistake for anyone special. But he *is* special. In my book, he is. For one thing he has a full night's sleep behind him, and he's just embraced his wife before leaving for work. But even before he goes, he's already expected home a set number of hours later. True, in the grander scheme of things, his return will be an event of small moment — but an event nonetheless.

Baxter starts his car and races the engine for a minute. Then he backs effortlessly out of the drive, brakes and changes gears. As he passes on the street, he slows and looks briefly in my direction. He lifts his hand off the steering wheel. It could be a salute or a sign of dismissal. It's a sign, in any case. And then he looks away toward the city. I get up and raise my hand, too — not a wave, exactly, but close to it. Some other cars drive past. One of the drivers must think he knows me because he gives his horn a friendly little tap. I look both ways and then cross the street.

RICHARD FORD

✛

Great Falls

THIS IS NOT a happy story. I warn you.

My father was a man named Jack Russell, and when I was a young boy in my early teens, we lived with my mother in a house to the east of Great Falls, Montana, near the small town of Highwood and the Highwood Mountains and the Missouri River. It is a flat, treeless benchland there, all of it used for wheat farming, though my father was never a farmer, but was brought up near Tacoma, Washington, in a family that worked for Boeing.

He — my father — had been an Air Force sergeant and had taken his discharge in Great Falls. And instead of going home to Tacoma, where my mother wanted to go, he had taken a civilian's job with the Air Force, working on planes, which was what he liked to do. And he had rented the house out of town from a farmer who did not want it left standing empty.

The house itself is gone now — I have been to the spot. But the double row of Russian olive trees and two of the outbuildings are still standing in the milkweeds. It was a plain, two-story house with a porch on the front and no place for the cars. At the time, I rode the school bus to Great Falls every morning and my father drove in while my mother stayed home.

My mother was a tall pretty woman, thin, with black hair and slightly sharp features that made her seem to smile when she wasn't smiling. She had grown up in Wallace, Idaho, and gone to college a year in Spokane, then moved out to the coast, which is where she met Jack Russell. She was two years older than he was, and married him, she said to me, because he was young and wonderful looking, and because she thought they could leave the sticks and see the world together — which I suppose they did for a while. That was the life she wanted, even before she knew much about wanting anything else or about the future.

When my father wasn't working on airplanes, he was going hunting or fishing, two things he could do as well as anyone. He had learned to fish, he said, in Iceland, and to hunt ducks up on the DEW line — stations he had visited in the Air Force. And during the time of this — it was 1960 — he began to take me with him on what he called his "expeditions." I thought even then, with as little as I knew, that these were opportunities other boys would dream of having but probably never would. And I don't think that I was wrong in that.

It is a true thing that my father did not know limits. In the spring, when we would go east to the Judith River Basin and camp up on the banks, he would catch a hundred fish in a weekend, and sometimes more than that. It was all he did from morning until night, and it was never hard for him. He used yellow corn kernels stacked onto a #4 snelled hook, and he would rattle this rig-up along the bottom of a deep pool below a split-shot sinker, and catch fish. And most of the time, because he knew the Judith River and knew how to feel his bait down deep, he could catch fish of good size.

It was the same with ducks, the other thing he liked. When the northern birds were down, usually by mid-October, he would take me and we would build a cattail and wheat-straw blind on one of the tule ponds or sloughs he knew about down the Missouri, where the water was shallow enough to wade. We would set out his decoys to the leeward side of our blind, and he would sprinkle corn on a hunger-line from the decoys to where we were. In the evenings when he came home from the base, we would go and sit out in the blind until the roosting flights came and put down among the decoys — there was never calling involved. And after a while, sometimes it would be an hour and full dark, the ducks would find the corn, and the whole raft of them — sixty, sometimes — would swim in to us. At the moment he judged they were close enough, my father would say to me, "Shine, Jackie," and I would stand and shine a seal-beam car light out onto the pond, and he would stand up beside me and shoot all the ducks that were there, on the water if he could, but flying and getting up as well. He owned a Model 11 Remington with a long-tube magazine that would hold ten shells, and with that many, and shooting straight over the surface rather than down onto it, he could kill or wound thirty ducks in twenty seconds' time. I remember distinctly the report of that gun and the flash of it over the water into the dark air, one shot after another, not even so fast, but measured in a way to hit as many as he could.

What my father did with the ducks he killed, and the fish, too, was sell them. It was against the law then to sell wild game, and it is against the law now. And though he kept some for us, most he would take — his fish laid on ice, or his ducks still wet and bagged in the burlap corn sacks — down to the Great Northern Hotel, which was still open then on Second Street in Great Falls, and sell them to the Negro caterer who bought them for his wealthy customers and for the dining car passengers who came through. We would drive in my father's Plymouth to the back of the hotel — always this was after dark — to a concrete loading ramp and lighted door that were close enough to the yards that I could sometimes see passenger trains waiting at the station, their car lights yellow and warm inside, the passengers dressed in suits, all bound for someplace far away from Montana — Milwaukee or Chicago or New York City, unimaginable places to me, a boy fourteen years old, with my father in the cold dark selling illegal game.

The caterer was a tall, stooped-back man in a white jacket, who my father called "Professor Ducks" or "Professor Fish,"

and the Professor referred to my father as "Sarge." He paid a
quarter per pound for trout, a dime for whitefish, a dollar for a
mallard duck, two for a speckle or a blue goose, and four dollars for a Canada. I have been with my father when he took
away a hundred dollars for fish he'd caught and, in the fall,
more than that for ducks and geese. When he had sold game in
that way, we would drive out 10th Avenue and stop at a bar
called The Mermaid which was by the air base, and he would
drink with some friends he knew there, and they would laugh
about hunting and fishing while I played pinball and wasted
money in the jukebox.

It was on such a night as this that the unhappy things came
about. It was in late October. I remember the time because
Halloween had not been yet, and in the windows of the houses
that I passed every day on the bus to Great Falls, people had
put pumpkin lanterns, and set scarecrows in their yards in
chairs.

My father and I had been shooting ducks in a slough on the
Smith River, upstream from where it enters on the Missouri.
He had killed thirty ducks, and we'd driven them down to the
Great Northern and sold them there, though my father had
kept two back in his corn sack. And when we had driven away,
he suddenly said, "Jackie, let's us go back home tonight. Who
cares about those hard-dicks at The Mermaid. I'll cook these
ducks on the grill. We'll do something different tonight." He
smiled at me in an odd way. This was not a thing he usually
said, or the way he usually talked. He liked The Mermaid, and
my mother — as far as I knew — didn't mind it if he went there.

"That sounds good," I said.

"We'll surprise your mother," he said. "We'll make her
happy."

We drove out past the air base on Highway 87, past where
there were planes taking off into the night. The darkness was
dotted by the green and red beacons, and the tower light swept
the sky and trapped planes as they disappeared over the flat
landscape toward Canada or Alaska and the Pacific.

"Boy-oh-boy," my father said — just out of the dark. I looked
at him and his eyes were narrow, and he seemed to be thinking
about something. "You know, Jackie," he said, "your mother
said something to me once I've never forgotten. She said,
'Nobody dies of a broken heart.' This was somewhat before
you were born. We were living down in Texas and we'd had
some big blow-up, and that was the idea she had. I don't know
why." He shook his head.

He ran his hand under the seat, found a half-pint bottle of
whiskey, and held it up to the lights of the car behind us to see
what there was left of it. He unscrewed the cap and took a
drink, then held the bottle out to me. "Have a drink, son," he
said. "Something oughta be good in life." And I felt that something was wrong. Not because of the whiskey, which I had
drunk before and he had reason to know about, but because of
some sound in his voice, something I didn't recognize and did
not know the importance of, though I was certain it was important.

I took a drink and gave the bottle back to him, holding the
whiskey in my mouth until it stopped burning and I could swallow it a little at a time. When we turned out the road to Highwood, the lights of Great Falls sank below the horizon, and I
could see the small white lights of farms, burning at wide distances in the dark.

"What do you worry about, Jackie," my father said. "Do you
worry about girls? Do you worry about your future sex life? Is
that some of it?" He glanced at me, then back at the road.

"I don't worry about that," I said.

"Well, what then?" my father said. "What else is there?"

"I worry if you're going to die before I do," I said, though I
hated saying that, "or if Mother is. That worries me."

"It'd be a miracle if we didn't," my father said, with the half-
pint held in the same hand he held the steering wheel. I had
seen him drive that way before. "Things pass too fast in your
life, Jackie. Don't worry about that. If I were you, I'd worry we
might not." He smiled at me, and it was not the worried, ner-

vous smile from before, but a smile that meant he was pleased. And I don't remember him ever smiling at me that way again.

We drove on out behind the town of Highwood and onto the flat field roads toward our house. I could see, out on the prairie, a moving light where the farmer who rented our house to us was disking his field for winter wheat. "He's waited too late with that business," my father said and took a drink, then threw the bottle right out the window. "He'll lose that," he said, "the cold'll kill it." I did not answer him, but what I thought was that my father knew nothing about farming, and if he was right it would be an accident. He knew about planes and hunting game, and that seemed all to me.

"I want to respect your privacy," he said then, for no reason at all that I understood. I am not even certain he said it, only that it is in my memory that way. I don't know what he was thinking of. Just words. But I said to him, I remember well, "It's all right. Thank you."

We did not go straight out the Geraldine Road to our house. Instead my father went down another mile and turned, went a mile and turned back again so that we came home from the other direction. "I want to stop and listen now," he said. "The geese should be in the stubble." We stopped and he cut the lights and engine, and we opened the car windows and listened. It was eight o'clock at night and it was getting colder, though it was dry. But I could hear nothing, just the sound of air moving lightly through the cut field, and not a goose sound. Though I could smell the whiskey on my father's breath and on mine, could hear the motor ticking, could hear him breathe, hear the sound we made sitting side by side on the car seat, our clothes, our feet, almost our hearts beating. And I could see out in the night the yellow lights of our house, shining through the olive trees south of us like a ship on the sea. "I hear them, by God," my father said, his head stuck out the window. "But they're high up. They won't stop here now, Jackie. They're high flyers, those boys. Long gone geese."

There was a car parked off the road, down the line of wind-break trees, beside a steel thresher the farmer had left there to rust. You could see moonlight off the taillight chrome. It was a Pontiac, a two-door hard-top. My father said nothing about it and I didn't either, though I think now for different reasons.

The floodlight was on over the side door of our house and lights were on inside, upstairs and down. My mother had a pumpkin on the front porch, and the wind chime she had hung by the door was tinkling. My dog, Major, came out of the quonset shed and stood in the car lights when we drove up.

"Let's see what's happening here," my father said, opening the door and stepping out quickly. He looked at me inside the car, and his eyes were wide and his mouth drawn tight.

We walked in the side door and up the basement steps into the kitchen, and a man was standing there — a man I had never seen before, a young man with blond hair, who might've been twenty or twenty-five. He was tall and was wearing a short-sleeved shirt and beige slacks with pleats. He was on the other side of the breakfast table, his fingertips just touching the wooden tabletop. His blue eyes were on my father, who was dressed in hunting clothes.

"Hello," my father said.

"Hello," the young man said, and nothing else. And for some reason I looked at his arms, which were long and pale. They looked like a young man's arms, like my arms. His short sleeves had each been neatly rolled up, and I could see the bottom of a small green tattoo edging out from underneath. There was a glass of whiskey on the table, but no bottle.

"What's your name?" my father said, standing in the kitchen under the bright ceiling light. He sounded like he might be going to laugh.

"Woody," the young man said and cleared his throat. He looked at me, then he touched the glass of whiskey, just the rim of the glass. He wasn't nervous, I could tell that. He did not seem to be afraid of anything.

"Woody," my father said and looked at the glass of whiskey. He looked at me, then sighed and shook his head. "Where's Mrs. Russell, Woody? I guess you aren't robbing my house, are you?"

Woody smiled. "No," he said. "Upstairs. I think she went upstairs."

"Good," my father said, "that's a good place." And he walked straight out of the room, but came back and stood in the doorway. "Jackie, you and Woody step outside and wait on me. Just stay there and I'll come out." He looked at Woody then in a way I would not have liked him to look at me, a look that meant he was studying Woody. "I guess that's your car," he said.

"That Pontiac." Woody nodded.

"Okay. Right," my father said. Then he went out again and up the stairs. At that moment the phone started to ring in the living room, and I heard my mother say, "Who's that?" And my father say, "It's me. It's Jack." And I decided I wouldn't go answer the phone. Woody looked at me, and I understood he wasn't sure what to do. Run, maybe. But he didn't have run in him. Though I thought he would probably do what I said if I would say it.

"Let's just go outside," I said.

And he said, "All right."

Woody and I walked outside and stood in the light of the floodlamp above the side door. I had on my wool jacket, but Woody was cold and stood with his hands in his pockets, and his arms bare, moving from foot to foot. Inside, the phone was ringing again. Once I looked up and saw my mother come to the window and look down at Woody and me. Woody didn't look up or see her, but I did. I waved at her, and she waved back at me and smiled. She was wearing a powder-blue dress. In another minute the phone stopped ringing.

Woody took a cigarette out of his shirt pocket and lit it. Smoke shot through his nose into the cold air, and he sniffed, looked around the ground and threw his match on the gravel. His blond hair was combed backwards and neat on the sides, and I could smell his aftershave on him, a sweet, lemon smell. And for the first time I noticed his shoes. They were two-tones, black with white tops and black laces. They stuck out below his baggy pants and were long and polished and shiny, as if he had been planning on a big occasion. They looked like shoes some country singer would wear, or a salesman. He was handsome, but only like someone you would see beside you in a dime store and not notice again.

"I like it out here," Woody said, his head down, looking at his shoes. "Nothing to bother you. I bet you'd see Chicago if the world was flat. The Great Plains commence here."

"I don't know," I said.

Woody looked up at me, cupping his smoke with one hand. "Do you play football?"

"No," I said. I thought about asking him something about my mother. But I had no idea what it would be.

"I *have* been drinking," Woody said, "but I'm not drunk now."

The wind rose then, and from behind the house I could hear Major bark once from far away, and I could smell the irrigation ditch, hear it hiss in the field. It ran down from Highwood Creek to the Missouri, twenty miles away. It was nothing Woody knew about, nothing he could hear or smell. He knew nothing about anything that was here. I heard my father say the words, "That's a real joke," from inside the house, then the sound of a drawer being opened and shut, and a door closing. Then nothing else.

Woody turned and looked into the dark toward where the glow of Great Falls rose on the horizon, and we both could see the flashing lights of a plane lowering to land there. "I once passed my brother in the Los Angeles airport and didn't even recognize him," Woody said, staring into the night. "He recognized *me*, though. He said, 'Hey, bro, are you mad at me, or what?' I wasn't mad at him. We both had to laugh."

Woody turned and looked at the house. His hands were still in his pockets, his cigarette clenched between his teeth, his arms taut. They were, I saw, bigger, stronger arms than I had thought. A vein went down the front of each of them. I wondered what Woody knew that I didn't. Not about my mother — I didn't know anything about that and didn't want to — but about a lot of things, about the life out in the dark, about coming out here, about airports, even about me. He and I were not so far apart in age, I knew that. But Woody was one thing, and I was another. And I wondered how I would ever get to be like him, since it didn't necessarily seem so bad a thing to be.

"Did you know your mother was married before?" Woody said.

"Yes," I said. "I knew that."

"It happens to all of them, now," he said. "They can't wait to get divorced."

"I guess so," I said.

Woody dropped his cigarette into the gravel and toed it out with his black-and-white shoe. He looked up at me and smiled the way he had inside the house, a smile that said he knew something he wouldn't tell, a smile to make you feel bad because you weren't Woody and never could be.

It was then that my father came out of the house. He still had on his plaid hunting coat and his wool cap, but his face was as white as snow, as white as I have ever seen a human being's face to be. It was odd. I had the feeling that he might've fallen inside, because he looked roughed up, as though he had hurt himself somehow.

My mother came out the door behind him and stood in the floodlight at the top of the steps. She was wearing the powder-blue dress I'd seen through the window, a dress I had never seen her wear before, though she was also wearing a car coat and carrying a suitcase. She looked at me and shook her head in a way that only I was supposed to notice, as if it was not a good idea to talk now.

My father had his hands in his pockets, and he walked right up to Woody. He did not even look at me. "What do you do for a living?" he said, and he was very close to Woody. His coat was close enough to touch Woody's shirt.

"I'm in the Air Force," Woody said. He looked at me and then at my father. He could tell my father was excited.

"Is this your day off, then?" my father said. He moved even closer to Woody, his hands still in his pockets. He pushed Woody with his chest, and Woody seemed willing to let my father push him.

"No," he said, shaking his head.

I looked at my mother. She was just standing, watching. It was as if someone had given her an order, and she was obeying it. She did not smile at me, though I thought she was thinking about me, which made me feel strange.

"What's the matter with you?" my father said into Woody's face, right into his face — his voice tight, as if it had gotten hard for him to talk. "Whatever in the world is the matter with you? Don't you understand something?" My father took a revolver pistol out of his coat and put it up under Woody's chin, into the soft pocket behind the bone, so that Woody's whole face rose, but his arms stayed at his sides, his hands open. "I don't know what to do with you," my father said. "I don't have any idea what to do with you. I just don't." Though I thought that what he wanted to do was hold Woody there just like that until something important took place, or until he could simply forget about all this.

My father pulled the hammer back on the pistol and raised it tighter under Woody's chin, breathing into Woody's face — my mother in the light with her suitcase, watching them, and me watching them. A half a minute must've gone by.

And then my mother said, "Jack, let's stop now. Let's just stop."

My father stared into Woody's face as if he wanted Woody to consider doing something — moving or turning around or anything on his own to stop this — that my father would then put a stop to. My father's eyes grew narrowed, and his teeth were gritted together, his lips snarling up to resemble a smile. "You're crazy, aren't you?" he said. "You're a god-damned crazy man. Are you in love with her, too? Are you, crazy man? Are you? Do you say you love her? Say you love her! Say you love her so I can blow your fucking brains in the sky."

"All right," Woody said. "No. It's all right."

"He doesn't love me, Jack. For God's sake," my mother said. She seemed so calm. She shook her head at me again. I do not think she thought my father would shoot Woody. And I don't think Woody thought so. Nobody did, I think, except my father himself. But I think he did, and was trying to find out how to.

My father turned suddenly and glared at my mother, his eyes shiny and moving, but with the gun still on Woody's skin. I think he was afraid, afraid he was doing this wrong and could mess all of it up and make matters worse without accomplishing anything.

"You're leaving," he yelled at her. "That's why you're packed. Get out. Go on."

"Jackie has to be at school in the morning," my mother said in just her normal voice. And without another word to any one of us, she walked out of the floodlamp light carrying her bag, turned the corner at the front porch steps and disappeared toward the olive trees that ran in rows back into the wheat.

My father looked back at me where I was standing in the gravel, as if he expected to see me go with my mother toward Woody's car. But I hadn't thought about that — though later I would. Later I would think I should have gone with her, and that things between them might've been different. But that isn't how it happened.

"You're sure you're going to get away now, aren't you, mister?" my father said into Woody's face. He was crazy himself, then. Anyone would've been. Everything must have seemed out of hand to him.

"I'd like to," Woody said. "I'd like to get away from here."

"And I'd like to think of some way to hurt you," my father

said and blinked his eyes. "I feel helpless about it." We all heard the door to Woody's car close in the dark. "Do you think that I'm a fool?" my father said.

"No," Woody said. "I don't think that.

"Do you think you're important?"

"No," Woody said. "I'm not."

My father blinked again. He seemed to be becoming someone else at that moment, someone I didn't know. "Where are you from?"

And Woody closed his eyes. He breathed in, then out, a long sigh. It was as if this was somehow the hardest part, something he hadn't expected to be asked to say.

"Chicago," Woody said. "A suburb of there."

"Are your parents alive?" my father said, all the time with his blue magnum pistol pushed under Woody's chin.

"Yes," Woody said. "Yessir."

"That's too bad," my father said. "Too bad they have to know what you are. I'm sure you stopped meaning anything to them a long time ago. I'm sure they both wish you were dead. You didn't know that. But I know it. I can't help them out, though. Somebody else'll have to kill you. I don't want to have to think about you anymore. I guess that's it."

My father brought the gun down to his side and stood looking at Woody. He did not back away, just stood, waiting for what I don't know to happen. Woody stood a moment, then he cut his eyes at me uncomfortably. And I know that I looked down. That's all I could do. Though I remember wondering if Woody's heart was broken and what any of this meant to him. Not to me, or my mother, or my father. But to him, since he seemed to be the one left out somehow, the one who would be lonely soon, the one who had done something he would someday wish he hadn't and would have no one to tell him that it was all right, that they forgave him, that these things happen in the world.

Woody took a step back, looked at my father and at me again as if he intended to speak, then stepped aside and walked away toward the front of our house, where the wind chime made a noise in the new cold air.

My father looked at me, his big pistol in his hand. "Does this seem stupid to you?" he said. "All this? Yelling and threatening and going nuts? I wouldn't blame you if it did. You shouldn't even see this. I'm sorry. I don't know what to do now."

"It'll be all right," I said. And I walked out to the road. Woody's car started up behind the olive trees. I stood and watched it back out, its red taillights clouded by exhaust. I could see their two heads inside, with the headlights shining behind them. When they got into the road, Woody touched his brakes, and for a moment I could see that they were talking, their heads turned toward each other, nodding. Woody's head and my mother's. They sat that way for a few seconds, then drove slowly off. And I wondered what they had to say to each other, something important enough that they had to stop right at that moment and say it. Did she say, *I love you?* Did she say, *This is not what I expected to happen?* Did she say, *This is what I've wanted all along?* And did he say, *I'm sorry for all this,* or *I'm glad,* or *None of this matters to me?* These are not the kinds of things you can know if you were not there. And I was not there and did not want to be. It did not seem like I should be there. I heard the door slam when my father went inside, and I turned back from the road where I could still see their taillights disappearing, and went back into the house where I was to be alone with my father.

THINGS SELDOM END in one event. In the morning I went to school on the bus as usual, and my father drove in to the air base in his car. We had not said very much about all that had happened. Harsh words, in a sense, are all alike. You can make them up yourself and be right. I think we both believed that we were in a fog we couldn't see through yet, though in a while, maybe not even a long while, we would see lights and know something.

In my third-period class that day a messenger brought a note for me that said I was excused from school at noon, and I should meet my mother at a motel down 10th Avenue South — a place not so far from my school — and we would eat lunch together.

It was a gray day in Great Falls that day. The leaves were off the trees and the mountains to the east of town were obscured by a low sky. The night before had been cold and clear, but today it seemed as if it would rain. It was the beginning of winter in earnest. In a few days there would be snow everywhere.

The motel where my mother was staying was called the Tropicana, and was beside the city golf course. There was a neon parrot on the sign out front, and the cabins made a U shape behind a little white office building. Only a couple of cars were parked in front of cabins, and no car was in front of my mother's cabin. I wondered if Woody would be here, or if he was at the air base. I wondered if my father would see him there, and what they would say.

I walked back to cabin 9. The door was open, though a DO NOT DISTURB sign was hung on the knob outside. I looked through the screen and saw my mother sitting on the bed alone. The television was on, but she was looking at me. She was wearing the powder-blue dress she had had on the night before. She was smiling at me, and I liked the way she looked at that moment, through the screen, in shadows. Her features did not seem as sharp as they had before. She looked comfortable where she was, and I felt like we were going to get along, no matter what had happened, and that I wasn't mad at her — that I had never been mad at her.

She sat forward and turned the television off. "Come in, Jackie," she said, and I opened the screen door and came inside. "It's the height of grandeur in here, isn't it?" My mother looked around the room. Her suitcase was open on the floor by the bathroom door, which I could see through and out the window onto the golf course, where three men were playing under the milky sky. "Privacy can be a burden, sometimes," she said, and reached down and put on her high-heeled shoes. "I didn't sleep very well last night, did you?"

"No," I said, though I had slept all right. I wanted to ask her where Woody was, but it occurred to me at that moment that he was gone now and wouldn't be back, that she wasn't thinking in terms of him and didn't care where he was or ever would be.

"I'd like a nice compliment from you," she said. "Do you have one of those to spend?"

"Yes," I said. "I'm glad to see you.

"That's a nice one," she said and nodded. She had both her shoes on now. "Would you like to go have lunch? We can walk across the street to the cafeteria. You can get hot food."

"No," I said. "I'm not really hungry now."

"That's okay," she said and smiled at me again. And, as I said before, I liked the way she looked. She looked pretty in a way I didn't remember seeing her, as if something that had had a hold on her had let her go, and she could be different about things. Even about me.

"Sometimes, you know," she said, "I'll think about something I did. Just anything. Years ago in Idaho, or last week, even. And it's as if I'd read it. Like a story. Isn't that strange?"

"Yes," I said. And it did seem strange to me because I was certain then what the difference was between what had happened and what hadn't, and knew I always would be.

"Sometimes," she said, and she folded her hands in her lap and stared out the little side window of her cabin at the parking lot and the curving row of other cabins. "Sometimes I even have a moment when I completely forget what life's like. Just altogether." She smiled. "That's not so bad, finally. Maybe it's a disease I have. Do you think I'm just sick and I'll get well?"

"No. I don't know," I said. "Maybe. I hope so." I looked out the bathroom window and saw the three men walking down the golf course fairway carrying golf clubs.

"I'm not very good at sharing things right now," my mother

said. "I'm sorry." She cleared her throat, and then she didn't say anything for almost a minute while I stood there. "I *will* answer anything you'd like me to answer, though. Just ask me anything, and I'll answer it the truth, whether I want to or not. Okay? I will. You don't even have to trust me. That's not a big issue with us. We're both grown-ups now."

And I said, "Were you ever married before?"

My mother looked at me strangely. Her eyes got small, and for a moment she looked the way I was used to seeing her — sharp-faced, her mouth set and taut. "No," she said. "Who told you that? That isn't true. I never was. Did Jack say that to you? Did your father say that? That's an awful thing to say. I haven't been that bad."

"He didn't say that," I said.

"Oh, of course he did," my mother said. "He doesn't know just to let things go when they're bad enough."

"I wanted to know that," I said. "I just thought about it. It doesn't matter.

"No, it doesn't," my mother said. "I could've been married eight times. I'm just sorry he said that to you. He's not generous sometimes."

"He didn't say that," I said. But I'd said it enough, and I didn't care if she believed me or didn't. It was true that trust was not a big issue between us then. And in any event, I know now that the whole truth of anything is an idea that stops existing finally.

"Is that all you want to know, then?" my mother said. She seemed mad, but not at me, I didn't think. Just at things in general. And I sympathized with her. "Your life's your own business, Jackie," she said. "Sometimes it scares you to death it's so much your own business. You just want to run."

"I guess so," I said.

"I'd like a less domestic life, is all." She looked at me, but I didn't say anything. I didn't see what she meant by that, though I knew there was nothing I could say to change the way her life would be from then on. And I kept quiet.

In a while we walked across 10th Avenue and ate lunch in the cafeteria. When she paid for the meal I saw that she had my father's silver-dollar money clip in her purse and that there was money in it. And I understood that he had been to see her already that day, and no one cared if I knew it. We were all of us on our own in this.

When we walked out onto the street, it was colder and the wind was blowing. Car exhausts were visible and some drivers had their lights on, though it was only two o'clock in the afternoon. My mother had called a taxi, and we stood and waited for it. I didn't know where she was going, but I wasn't going with her.

"Your father won't let me come back," she said, standing on the curb. It was just a fact to her, not that she hoped I would talk to him or stand up for her or take her part. But I did wish then that I had never let her go the night before. Things can be fixed by staying; but to go out into the night and not come back hazards life, and everything can get out of hand.

My mother's taxi came. She kissed me and hugged me very hard, then got inside the cab in her powder-blue dress and high heels and her car coat. I smelled her perfume on my cheeks as I stood watching her. "I used to be afraid of more things than I am now," she said, looking up at me, and smiled. "I've got a knot in my stomach, of all things." And she closed the cab door, waved at me, and rode away.

I WALKED BACK toward my school. I thought I could take the bus home if I got there by three. I walked a long way down 10th Avenue to Second Street, beside the Missouri River, then over to town. I walked by the Great Northern Hotel, where my father had sold ducks and geese and fish of all kinds. There were no passenger trains in the yard and the loading dock looked small. Garbage cans were lined along the edge of it, and the door was closed and locked.

As I walked toward school I thought to myself that my life

had turned suddenly, and that I might not know exactly how or which way for possibly a long time. Maybe, in fact, I might never know. It was a thing that happened to you — I knew that — and it had happened to me in this way now. And as I walked on up the cold street that afternoon in Great Falls, the questions I asked myself were these : why wouldn't my father let my mother come back ? Why would Woody stand in the cold with me outside my house and risk being killed ? Why would he say my mother had been married before, if she hadn't been ? And my mother herself — why would she do what she did ? In five years my father had gone off to Ely, Nevada, to ride out the oil strike there, and been killed by accident. And in the years since then I have seen my mother from time to time — in one place or another, with one man or other — and I can say, at least, that we know each other. But I have never known the answer to these questions, have never asked anyone their answers. Though possibly it — the answer — is simple : it is just low-life, some coldness in us all, some helplessness that causes us to misunderstand life when it is pure and plain, makes our existence seem like a border between two nothings, and makes us no more or less than animals who meet on the road — watchful, unforgiving, without patience or desire.

STUART DYBEK

✣

Chopin in Winter

THE WINTER *Dzia-Dzia* came to live with us in Mrs. Kubiac's building on 18th Street was the winter that Mrs. Kubiac's daughter, Marcy, came home pregnant from college in New York. Marcy had gone there on a music scholarship, the first person in Mrs. Kubiac's family to go to high school, let alone college.

Since she had come home I had seen her only once. I was playing on the landing before our door and as she came up the stairs we both nodded hi. She didn't look pregnant. She was thin, dressed in a black coat, its silvery fur collar pulled up around her face, her long blond hair tucked into the collar. I could see the snowflakes on the fur turning to beads of water under the hall light bulb. Her face was pale and her eyes the same startled blue as Mrs. Kubiac's.

She passed me almost without noticing and continued up the next flight of stairs, then paused and, leaning over the banister, asked, "Are you the same little boy I used to hear crying at night?"

Her voice was gentle, yet kidding.

"I don't know," I said.

"If your name is Michael and if your bedroom window is on the fourth floor right below mine, then you are," she said. "When you were little sometimes I'd hear you crying your

heart out at night. I guess I heard what your mother couldn't.
The sound traveled up."

"I really woke you up?"

"Don't worry about that. I'm a very light sleeper. Snow falling wakes me up. I used to wish I could help you as long as we
were both up together in the middle of the night with everyone
else snoring."

"I don't remember crying," I said.

"Most people don't once they're happy again. It looks like
you're happy enough now. Stay that way, kiddo," she smiled. It
was a lovely smile. Her eyes seemed surprised by it. "Too-da-
loo," she waved her fingers.

"Too-da-loo," I waved after her. A minute after she was
gone I began to miss her.

OUR LANDLADY, Mrs. Kubiac, would come downstairs for
tea in the afternoons and cry while telling my mother about
Marcy. Marcy, Mrs. Kubiac said, wouldn't tell her who the
child's father was. She wouldn't tell the priest. She wouldn't go
to church. She wouldn't go anywhere. Even the doctor had to
come to the house, and the only doctor that Marcy would allow
was Dr. Shtulek, her childhood doctor.

"I tell her, 'Marcy, darling, you have to do something,' " Mrs.
Kubiac said. " 'What about all the sacrifices, the practice, the
lessons, teachers, awards? Look at rich people — they don't let
anything interfere with what they want.' "

Mrs. Kubiac told my mother these things in strictest confi-
dence, her voice at first a secretive whisper, but growing increasingly louder as she recited her litany of troubles. The
louder she talked the more broken her English became, as if
her worry and suffering were straining the language past its
limits. Finally, her feelings overpowered her; she began to
weep and lapsed into Bohemian, which I couldn't understand.

I would sit out of sight beneath the dining-room table, my

plastic cowboys galloping through a forest of chair legs, while I listened to Mrs. Kubiac talk about Marcy. I wanted to hear everything about her, and the more I heard the more precious the smile she had given me on the stairs became. It was like a secret bond between us. Once I became convinced of that, listening to Mrs. Kubiac seemed like spying. I was Marcy's friend and conspirator. She had spoken to me as if I was someone apart from the world she was shunning. Whatever her reasons for the way she was acting, whatever her secrets, I was on her side. In daydreams I proved my loyalty over and over.

At night we could hear her playing the piano — a muffled rumbling of scales that sounded vaguely familiar. Perhaps I actually remembered hearing Marcy practicing years earlier, before she had gone on to New York. The notes resonated through the kitchen ceiling while I wiped the supper dishes and *Dzia-Dzia* sat soaking his feet. *Dzia-Dzia* soaked his feet every night in a bucket of steaming water into which he dropped a tablet that fizzed, immediately turning the water bright pink. Between the steaming water and pink dye, his feet and legs, up to the knees where his trousers were rolled, looked permanently scalded.

Dzia-Dzia's feet seemed to be turning into hooves. His heels and soles were swollen nearly shapeless and cased in scaly calluses. Nails, yellow as a horse's teeth, grew gnarled from knobbed toes. *Dzia-Dzia*'s feet had been frozen when as a young man he walked most of the way from Crakow to Gdansk in the dead of winter escaping service in the Prussian army. And later he had frozen them again mining for gold in Alaska. Most of what I knew of *Dzia-Dzia*'s past had mainly to do with the history of his feet.

Sometimes my uncles would say something about him. It sounded as if he had spent his whole life on the move — selling dogs to the Igorot in the Philippines after the Spanish-American War; mining coal in Johnson, Pennsylvania; working barges on the Great Lakes; riding the rails out west. No one in the family wanted much to do with him. He had deserted them so often, my uncle Roman said, that it was worse than growing up without a father.

My grandma had referred to him as *Pan Djabel,* "Mr. Devil," though the way she said it sounded as if he amused her. He called her a *górel,* a hillbilly, and claimed that he came from a wealthy, educated family that had been stripped of their land by the Prussians.

"Landowners, all right!" Uncle Roman once said to my mother. "Besides acting like a bastard, according to Ma he actually *was* one in the literal sense."

"Romey, shhh, what good's bitter?" my mother said.

"Who's bitter, Ev? It's just that he couldn't even show up to bury her. I'll never forgive that."

Dzia-Dzia hadn't been at Grandma's funeral. He had disappeared again and no one had known where to find him. For years *Dzia-Dzia* would simply vanish without telling anyone, then suddenly show up out of nowhere to hang around for a while, ragged and smelling of liquor, wearing his two suits one over the other, only to disappear yet again.

"Want to find him? Go ask the bums on Skid Row," Uncle Roman would say.

My uncles said he lived in boxcars, basements, and abandoned buildings. And when, from the window of a bus, I'd see old men standing around trash fires behind billboards, I'd wonder if he was among them.

Now that he was very old and failing he sat in our kitchen, his feet aching and numb as if he had been out walking down 18th Street barefoot in the snow.

IT WAS MY AUNTS and uncles who talked about *Dzia-Dzia* "failing." The word always made me nervous. I was failing, too — failing spelling, English, history, geography, almost everything except arithmetic, and that only because it used numbers instead of letters. Mainly, I was failing penmanship. The nuns complained that my writing was totally illegible, that I spelled like a DP, and threatened that if I didn't improve they might have to hold me back.

Mother kept my failures confidential. It was *Dzia-Dzia*'s they discussed during Sunday visits in voices pitched just below the level of an old man's hearing. *Dzia-Dzia* stared fiercely, but didn't deny what they were saying about him. He hadn't spoken since he had reappeared and no one knew whether his muteness was caused by senility or stubbornness, or if he'd gone deaf. His ears had been frozen as well as his feet. Wiry white tufts of hair that matched his horned eyebrows sprouted from his ears. I wondered if he would hear better if they were trimmed.

Though *Dzia-Dzia* and I spent the evenings alone together in the kitchen he didn't talk any more than he did on Sundays. Mother stayed in the parlor, immersed in her correspondence courses in bookkeeping. The piano rumbled above us through the ceiling. I could feel it more than hear it, especially the bass notes. Sometimes a chord would be struck that made the silverware clash in the drawer and the glasses hum.

Marcy had looked very thin climbing the stairs, delicate, incapable of such force. But her piano was massive and powerful-looking. I remembered going upstairs once with my mother to visit Mrs. Kubiac. Marcy was away at school then. The piano stood unused — top lowered, lid down over the keys — dominating the apartment. In the afternoon light it gleamed deeply, as if its dark wood were a kind of glass. Its pedals were polished bronze and looked to me more like pedals I imagined motormen stamping to operate streetcars.

"Isn't it beautiful, Michael?" my mother asked.

I nodded hard, hoping that Mrs. Kubiac would offer to let me play it, but she didn't.

"How did it get up here?" I asked. It seemed impossible that it could fit through a doorway.

"Wasn't easy," Mrs. Kubiac said, surprised. "Gave Mr. Kubiac a rupture. It come all the way on the boat from Europe. Some old German, a great musician, brang it over to give concerts, then got sick and left it. Went back to Germany. God knows what happened to him — I think he was a Jew. They auctioned it off to pay his hotel bill. That's life, huh? Otherwise who could afford it? We're not rich people."

"It must have been very expensive anyway," mother said.

"Only cost me a marriage," Mrs. Kubiac said, then laughed but it was forced. "That's life too, huh?" she asked. "Maybe a woman's better off without a husband?" And then, for just an instant, I saw her glance at my mother then look away. It was a glance I had come to recognize from people when they caught themselves saying something that might remind my mother or me that my father had been killed in the war.

THE SILVERWARE would clash and the glasses hum. I could feel it in my teeth and bones as the deep notes rumbled through the ceiling and walls like distant thunder. It wasn't like listening to music, yet more and more often I would notice *Dzia-Dzia* close his eyes, a look of concentration pinching his face as his body swayed slightly. I wondered what he was hearing. Mother had said once that he'd played the fiddle when she was a little girl, but the only music I'd even seen him show any interest in before was the *Frankie Yankovitch Polka Hour,* which he turned up loud and listened to with his ear almost pressed to the radio. Whatever Marcy was playing, it didn't sound like Frankie Yankovitch.

Then one evening, after weeks of silence between us, punctuated only by grunts, *Dzia-Dzia* said, "That's boogie-woogie music."

"What, *Dzia-Dzia?*" I asked, startled.

"Music the boogies play."

"You mean from upstairs? That's Marcy."

"She's in love with a colored man."

"What are you telling him, Pa?" Mother demanded. She had just happened to enter the kitchen while *Dzia-Dzia* was speaking.

"About boogie-woogie." *Dzia-Dzia*'s legs jiggled in the bucket so that the pink water sloshed over onto the linoleum.

"We don't need that kind of talk in the house."

"What talk, Evusha?"

"He doesn't have to hear that prejudice in the house," Mom said. "He'll pick up enough on the street."

"I just told him boogie-woogie."

"I think you better soak your feet in the parlor by the heater," Mom said. "We can spread newspaper."

Dzia-Dzia sat, squinting as if he didn't hear.

"You heard me, Pa. I said soak your feet in the parlor," Mom repeated, on the verge of shouting.

"What, Evusha?"

"I'll yell as loud as I have to, Pa."

"Boogie-woogie, boogie-woogie, boogie-woogie," the old man muttered as he left the kitchen, slopping barefoot across the linoleum.

"Go soak your head while you're at it," Mom muttered behind him, too quietly for him to hear.

MOM HAD ALWAYS insisted on polite language in the house. Someone who failed to say "please" or "thank you" was as offensive to her ears as someone who cursed.

"The word is 'yes,' not 'yeah,' " she would correct. Or "If you want 'hey,' go to a stable." She considered "ain't" a form of laziness, like not picking up your dirty socks.

Even when they got a little drunk at the family parties that took place at our flat on Sundays, my uncles tried not to swear, and they had all been in the army and marines. Nor were they allowed to refer to the Germans as Krauts, or the Japanese as

Nips. As far as Mom was concerned, of all the misuses of language, racial slurs were the most ignorant, and so the most foul.

My uncles didn't discuss the war much anyway, though whenever they got together there was a certain feeling in the room as if beneath the loud talk and joking they shared a deeper, sadder mood. Mom had replaced the photo of my father in his uniform with an earlier photo of him sitting on the running board of the car they'd owned before the war. He was grinning and petting a neighbor's Scottie. That one and their wedding picture were the only photos that Mom kept out. She knew I didn't remember my father, and she seldom talked about him. But there were a few times when she had read me sections from his letters. There was one section in particular that she read at least once a year. It had been written while he was under bombardment, shortly before he was killed.

> When it continues like this without letup you learn what it is to really hate. You begin to hate them as a people and want to punish them all — civilians, women, children, old people — it makes no difference, they are all the same, none of them innocent, and for a while your hate and anger keep you from going crazy with fear. But if you let yourself hate and believe in hate, then no matter what else happens, you've lost. Eve, I love our life together and want to come home to you and Michael, as much as I can, the same man who left.

I wanted to hear more, but didn't ask. Perhaps because everyone seemed to be trying to forget. Perhaps because I was afraid. When the tears would start in Mom's eyes I caught myself wanting to glance away as Mrs. Kubiac had.

THERE WAS SOMETHING MORE besides Mom's usual standards for the kind of language allowed in the house, that caused her to lose her temper and kick *Dzia-Dzia* out of his spot in the kitchen. She had become even more sensitive, especially where *Dzia-Dzia* was concerned, because of what had happened with Shirley Popel's mother.

Shirley's mother had died recently. Mom and Shirley had been best friends since grade school, and after the funeral, Shirley came back to our house and poured out the story.

Her mother had broken a hip falling off a curb while sweeping the sidewalk in front of her house. She was a constantly smiling woman without any teeth who, everyone said, looked like a peasant. After 40 years in America she could barely speak English, and even in the hospital refused to remove her babushka.

Everyone called her Babushka, Babush for short, which means "granny," even the nuns at the hospital. On top of her broken hip, Babush caught pneumonia, and one night Shirley got a call from the doctor saying Babush had taken a sudden turn for the worse. Shirley rushed right over, taking her 13-year-old son, Rudy. Rudy was Babushka's favorite, and Shirley hoped that seeing him would instill the will to live in her mother. It was Saturday night and Rudy was dressed to play at his first dance. He wanted to be a musician and was wearing clothes he had bought with money saved from his paper route. He'd bought them at Smoky Joe's on Maxwell Street — blue suede loafers, electric-blue socks, a lemon-yellow one-button roll-lapel suit with padded shoulders and pegged trousers, and a parrot-green satin shirt. Shirley thought he looked cute.

When they got to the hospital they found Babush connected to tubes and breathing oxygen.

"Ma," Shirley said, "Rudy's here."

Babush raised her head, took one look at Rudy, and smacked her gray tongue.

"Rudish," Babush said, "you dress like nigger." Then suddenly her eyes rolled; she fell back, gasped, and died.

"And those were her last words to any of us, Ev," Shirley wept, "words we'll carry the rest of our lives, but especially poor little Rudy — *you dress like nigger*."

For weeks after Shirley's visit, no matter who called, Mom would tell them Shirley's story over the phone.

"Those aren't the kind of famous last words we're going to hear in this family if I can help it," she promised more than once, as if it were a real possibility. "Of course," she'd sometimes add, "Shirley always has let Rudy get away with too much. I don't see anything cute about a boy going to visit his grandmother at the hospital dressed like a hood."

ANY LAST WORDS *Dzia-Dzia* had he kept to himself. His silence, however, had already been broken. Perhaps in his own mind that was a defeat that carried him from failing to totally failed. He returned to the kitchen like a ghost haunting his old chair, one that appeared when I sat alone working on penmanship.

No one else seemed to notice a change, but it was clear from the way he no longer soaked his feet. He still kept up the pretense of sitting there with them in the bucket. The bucket went with him the way ghosts drag chains. But he no longer went through the ritual of boiling water: boiling it until the kettle screeched for mercy, pouring so the linoleum puddled and steam clouded around him, and finally dropping in the tablet that fizzed furiously pink, releasing a faintly metallic smell like a broken thermometer.

Without his bucket steaming, the fogged windows cleared. Mrs. Kubiac's building towered a story higher than any other on the block. From our fourth-story window I could look out even with the roofs and see the snow gathering on them before it reached the street.

I sat at one end of the kitchen table copying down the words that would be on the spelling test the next day. *Dzia-Dzia* sat at the other mumbling incessantly, as if finally free to talk about the jumble of the past he'd never mentioned — wars, revolutions, strikes, journeys to strange places, all run together, and music, especially Chopin.

"Chopin," he'd whisper hoarsely, pointing to the ceiling with the reverence of nuns pointing to heaven. Then he'd close his eyes and his nostrils would widen as if he were inhaling the fragrance of sound.

It sounded no different to me, the same muffled thumping and rumbling we'd been hearing ever since Marcy had returned home. I could hear the intensity in the crescendos that made the silverware clash, but it never occurred to me to care what she was playing. What mattered was that I could hear her play each night, could feel her playing just a floor above, almost as if she were in our apartment. She seemed that close.

"Each night Chopin — it's all she thinks about, isn't it?"

I shrugged.

"You don't know?" *Dzia-Dzia* whispered, as if I were lying and he was humoring me.

"How should I know?"

"And I suppose how should you know the *Grande Valse brillante* when you hear it either? How should you know Chopin was twenty-one when he composed it? — about the same age as the girl upstairs. He composed it in Vienna, before he went to Paris. Don't they teach you that in school? What are you studying?"

"Spelling."

"Can you spell *dunkoff*?"

The waves of the keyboard would pulse through the warm kitchen and I would become immersed in my spelling words, and after that in penmanship. I was in remedial penmanship. Nightly penmanship was like undergoing physical therapy. While I concentrated on the proper slant of my letters my left hand smeared graphite across the loose-leaf paper.

Dzia-Dzia, now that he was talking, no longer seemed content to sit and listen in silence. He would continually interrupt.

"Hey, Lefty, stop writing with your nose. Listen how she plays."

"Don't shake the table, *Dzia-Dzia*."

"You know this one? No? *Valse brillante*."

"I thought that was the other one."

"What other one? The E-flat? That's *Grande Valse brillante*. This one's A-flat. Then there's another A-flat — Opus 42 — called *Grande Valse*. Understand?"

He rambled on like that about A- and E-flats and sharps and opuses and I went back to compressing my capital *M*'s. My homework was to write 500 of them. I was failing penmanship yet again, my left hand, as usual, taking the blame it didn't deserve. The problem with *M* wasn't my hand. It was that I had never been convinced that the letters could all be the same widths. When I wrote, *M* automatically came out twice as broad as *N*, *H* double the width of *I*.

"This was Paderewski's favorite waltz. She plays it like an angel."

I nodded, staring in despair at my homework. I had made the mistake of interconnecting the *M*'s into long strands. They hummed in my head, droning out the music, and I wondered if I had been humming aloud. "Who's Paderewski?" I asked, thinking it might be one of *Dzia-Dzia*'s old friends, maybe from Alaska.

"Do you know who's George Washington, who's Joe DiMaggio, who's Walt Disney?"

"Sure."

"I thought so. Paderewski was like them, except he played Chopin. Understand? See, deep down inside, Lefty, you know more than you think."

INSTEAD OF GOING into the parlor to read comics or play with my cowboys while Mom pored over her correspondence courses, I began spending more time at the kitchen table, lingering over my homework as an excuse. My spelling began to improve, then took a turn toward perfection; the slant of my handwriting reversed toward the right; I began to hear melodies in what had sounded like muffled scales.

Each night *Dzia-Dzia* would tell me more about Chopin, describing the preludes or ballades or mazurkas, so that even if I
hadn't heard them I could imagine them, especially *Dzia-Dzia*'s
favorites, the nocturnes, shimmering like black pools.

"She's playing her way through the waltzes," *Dzia-Dzia* told
me, speaking as usual in his low, raspy voice as if we were having a confidential discussion. "She's young, but already knows
Chopin's secret — a waltz can tell more about the soul than a
hymn."

By my bedtime the kitchen table would be shaking so much
that it was impossible to practice penmanship any longer. Across from me, *Dzia-Dzia,* his hair, eyebrows, and ear tufts wild
and white, swayed in his chair, his eyes squeezed closed, with a
look of rapture on his face as his fingers pummeled the tabletop. He played the entire width of the table, his body leaning
and twisting as his fingers swept the keyboard, left hand
pounding at those chords that jangled silverware, while his
right raced through runs across tacky oilcloth. His feet pump-
ed the empty bucket. If I watched him, then closed my eyes, it
sounded as if two pianos were playing.

One night *Dzia-Dzia* and Marcy played so that I expected at
any moment the table would break and the ceiling would collapse. The bulbs began to flicker in the overhead fixture, then
went out. The entire flat went dark.

"Are the lights out in there too?" Mom yelled from the parlor. "Don't worry, it must be a fuse."

The kitchen windows glowed with the light of snow. I looked
out. All the buildings down 18th Street were dark and the
streetlights were out. A snow-removal machine spraying wings
of snow, its yellow lights revolving, disappeared down 18th like
the last blinks of electricity. There wasn't any traffic. The block
looked deserted, as if the entire city was deserted. Snow was
filling the emptiness, big flakes floating steadily and softly between the darkened buildings, coating the fire escapes, while
on the roofs a blizzard blew sideways, swirling into clouds.

Marcy and *Dzia-Dzia* never stopped playing.

"Michael, come in here by the heater, or if you're going to stay in there put the burners on," Mom called.

I lit the burners on the stove. They hovered in the dark like blue crowns of flame, flickering *Dzia-Dzia*'s shadow across the walls. His head pitched, his arms flew up as he struck the notes. The walls and window-panes shook with gusts of wind and music. I imagined plaster dust wafting down, coating the kitchen, a fine network of cracks spreading through the dishes.

"Michael?" Mother called.

"I'm sharpening my pencil." I stood by the sharpener grinding it as hard as I could, then sat back down and went on writing. The table rocked under my point, but the letters formed perfectly. I spelled new words, words I'd never heard before, yet as soon as I wrote them their meanings were clear, as if they were in another language, one in which words were understood by their sounds, like music. After the lights came back on I couldn't remember what they meant and threw them away.

Dzia-Dzia slumped back in his chair. He was flushed and mopped his forehead with a paper napkin.

"So, you liked that one," he said. "Which one was it?" he asked. He always asked me that, and little by little I had begun recognizing their melodies.

"The Polonaise," I guessed. "In A-flat Major."

"Ahhh," he shook his head in disappointment. "You think everything with a little spirit is the Polonaise."

"The *Revolutionary* Etude!"

"It was a waltz," *Dzia-Dzia* said.

"How could that be a waltz?"

"A posthumous waltz. You know what 'posthumous' means?"

"What?"

"It means music from after a person's dead. The kind of waltz that has to carry back from the other side. Chopin wrote it to a young woman he loved. He kept his feelings for her secret, but never forgot her. Sooner or later feelings come bursting out. The dead are as sentimental as anyone else. You know what happened when Chopin died?"

"No."

"They rang the bells all over Europe. It was winter. The Prussians heard them. They jumped on their horses. They had cavalry then, no tanks, just horses. They rode until they came to the house where Chopin lay on a bed next to a grand piano. His arms were crossed over his chest and there was plaster drying on his hands and face. The Prussians rode right up the stairs and barged into the room, slashing with their sabers, their horses stamping and kicking up their front hooves. They hacked the piano and stabbed the music, then wadded up the music into the piano, spilled on kerosene from the lamps, and set it on fire. Then they rolled Chopin's piano to the window — it was those French windows, the kind that open out and there's a tiny balcony. The piano wouldn't fit, so they rammed it through, taking out part of the wall. It crashed three stories into the street and when it hit made a sound that shook the city. The piano lay there smoking and the Prussians rode over it and left. Later, some of Chopin's friends snuck back and removed his heart and sent it in a little jeweled box to be buried in Warsaw."

Dzia-Dzia stopped and listened. Marcy had begun to play again very faintly. If he had asked me to guess what she was playing I would have said a prelude, the one called the *Raindrop*.

I HEARD THE PRELUDES on Saturday nights, sunk up to my ears in bath water. The music traveled from upstairs through the plumbing, and resonated as clearly underwater as if I had been wearing earphones.

There were other places I discovered where Marcy's playing carried. Polonaises sometimes reverberated down an old trash chute that had been papered over in the dining room. Even in the parlor, provided no one else was listening to the radio or flipping pages of a newspaper, it was possible to hear the faintest hint of mazurkas around the sealed wall where the stovepipe from the space heater disappeared into what had once been a fireplace. And when I went out to play on the landing, bundled up as if I was going out to climb on the drifts piled along 18th Street, I could hear the piano echoing down the hallways. I began to creep higher up the stairs to the top floor, until finally I was listening at Mrs. Kubiac's door, ready to jump away if it should suddenly open, hoping I would be able to think of some excuse for being there, and at the same time almost wishing they would catch me.

I didn't mention climbing the stairs in the hallway, nor any of the other places I'd discovered, to *Dzia-Dzia*. He never seemed interested in any place other than the kitchen table. It was as if he were attached to the chair, rooted in his bucket.

"Going so early? Where you rushing off to?" he'd ask at the end of each evening, no matter how late, when I'd put my pencil down and begun buckling my books into my satchel.

I'd leave him sitting there, feet in his empty bucket his fingers, tufted with the same white hair as his ears, still tracing arpeggios across the tabletop, though Marcy had already stopped playing. I didn't tell him how from my room, a few times lately after everyone was asleep, I could hear her playing as clearly as if I were sitting at her feet.

M ARCY PLAYED less and less, especially in the evenings after supper, which had been her regular time.

Dzia-Dzia continued to shake the table nightly, eyes closed, hair flying, fingers thumping, but the thump of his fingers against the oilcloth was the only sound other than his breathing — rhythmic and labored as if he were having a dream or climbing a flight of stairs.

I didn't notice at first, but *Dzia-Dzia*'s solos were the start of his return to silence.

"What's she playing, Lefty?" he demanded more insistently than ever, as if still testing whether I knew.

Usually now, I did. But after a while I realized he was no longer testing. He was asking because the sounds were becoming increasingly muddled to him. He seemed able to feel the pulse of the music, but could no longer distinguish the melodies. By asking me, he hoped perhaps that if he knew what Marcy was playing he would hear it clearly himself.

Then he began to ask what she was playing when she wasn't playing at all.

I would make up answers. "The Polonaise . . . in A-flat Major."

"The Polonaise! You always say that. Listen harder. Are you sure it's not a waltz?"

"You're right, *Dzia-Dzia*. It's the *Grande Waltz.*"

"The *Grande Waltz* . . . which one is that?"

"A-flat, Opus 42. Paderewski's favorite, remember? Chopin wrote it when he was twenty-one, in Vienna."

"In Vienna?" *Dzia-Dzia* asked, then pounded the table with his fist. "Don't tell me numbers and letters! A-flat, Z-sharp, Opus Zero, Opus a thousand! Who cares? You make it sound like a bingo game instead of Chopin."

I was never sure if he couldn't hear because he couldn't remember, or couldn't remember because he couldn't hear. His hearing itself still seemed sharp enough.

"Stop scratching with that pencil all the time, Lefty, and I wouldn't have to ask you what she's playing," he'd complain.

"You'd hear better, *Dzia-Dzia*, if you'd take the kettle off the stove."

He was slipping back into his ritual of boiling water. The kettle screeched like a siren. The windows fogged. Roofs and weather vanished behind a slick of steam. Vapor ringed the overhead light bulbs. The vaguely metallic smell of the fizzing pink tablets hung at the end of every breath.

Marcy played hardly at all by then. What little she played was

muffled, far off as if filtering through the same fog. Sometimes, staring at the windows, I imagined 18th Street looked
that way, with rings of vapor around the streetlights and headlights, clouds billowing from exhaust pipes and manhole covers, breaths hanging, snow swirling like white smoke.

Each night water hissed from the kettle's spout as from a
blown valve, rumbling as it filled the bucket, filling until it
slopped over pink onto the warped linoleum. *Dzia-Dzia* sat,
bony calves half submerged, trousers rolled to his knees. He
was wearing two suits again, one over the other, always a sure
sign he was getting ready to travel, to disappear without saying
good-bye. The fingers of his left hand still drummed uncon-
sciously along the tabletop as his feet soaked. Steam curled up
the arteries of his scalded legs, hovered over his lap, smoldered
up the buttons of his two vests, traced his mustache and white
tufts of hair until it enveloped him. He sat in a cloud, eyes
glazed, fading.

I BEGAN TO GO to bed early. I would leave my homework un-
finished, kiss Mother goodnight, and go to my room.

My room was small, hardly space for more than the bed and
bureau. Not so small, though, that *Dzia-Dzia* couldn't have fit.
Perhaps, had I told him that Marcy played almost every night
now after everyone was sleeping, he wouldn't have gone back
to filling the kitchen with steam. I felt guilty, but it was too late,
and I shut the door quickly before steam could enter and fog
my window.

It was a single window. I could touch it from the foot of the
bed. It opened onto a recessed, three-sided air shaft and faced
the roof of the building next door. Years ago a kid my age
named Freddy had lived next door and we still called it Freddy's roof.

Marcy's window was above mine. The music traveled down
as clearly as Marcy said my crying had traveled up. When I
closed my eyes I could imagine sitting on the Oriental carpet

beside her huge piano. The air shaft actually amplified the music just as it had once amplified the arguments between Mr. and Mrs. Kubiac, especially the shouting on those nights after Mr. Kubiac had moved out, when he would return drunk and try to move back in. They'd argued mostly in Bohemian, but when Mr. Kubiac started beating her, Mrs. Kubiac would yell out in English, "Help me, police, somebody, he's killing me!" After a while the police would usually come and haul Mr. Kubiac away. I think sometimes Mom called them. One night Mr. Kubiac tried to fight off the police and they gave him a terrible beating. "You're killing him in front of my eyes!" Mrs. Kubiac began to scream. Mr. Kubiac broke away and, with the police chasing him, ran down the hallways pounding on doors, pleading for people to open up. He pounded on our door. Nobody in the building let him in. That was their last argument.

The room was always cold and I'd slip, still wearing my clothes, under the goose-feather-stuffed *piersyna* to change into my pajamas. It would have been warmer with the door open even a crack, but I kept it closed because of the steam. A steamed bedroom window reminded me too much of the winter I'd had pneumonia. It was one of the earliest things I could remember: the gurgling hiss of the vaporizer and smell of benzoin while I lay sunk in my pillows watching steam condense to frost on the pane until daylight blurred. I could remember trying to scratch through the frost with the key to a wind-up mouse so that I could see how much snow had fallen, and Mother catching me. She was furious that I had climbed out from under the warmth of my covers and asked me if I wanted to get well or to get sicker and die. Later, when I asked Dr. Shtulek if I was dying, he put his stethoscope to my nose and listened. "Not yet," he smiled. Dr. Shtulek visited often to check my breathing. His stethoscope was cold like all the instruments in his bag, but I liked him, especially for unplugging the vaporizer. "We don't need this any more," he confided. Night seemed very still without its steady exhaling. The jingle of snow chains and the scraping of shovels carried from 18th

Street. Maybe that was when I first heard Marcy practicing scales. By then I had grown used to napping during the day and lying awake at night. I began to tunnel under my *piersyna* to the window and scrape at the layered frost. I scraped for nights, always afraid I would get sick again for disobeying. Finally, I was able to see the snow on Freddy's roof. Something had changed while I'd been sick — they had put a wind hood on the tall chimney that sometimes blew smoke into our flat. In the dark it looked as if someone was standing on the roof in an old-fashioned helmet. I imagined it was a German soldier. I'd heard Freddy's landlord was German. The soldier stood at attention, but his head slowly turned back and forth and hooted with each gust of wind. Snow drove sideways across the roof and he stood banked by drifts, smoking a cigar. Sparks flew from its tip. When he turned completely around to stare in my direction with his faceless face, I'd duck and tunnel back under my *piersyna* to my pillows, and pretend to sleep. I believed a person asleep would be shown more mercy than a person awake. I'd lie still, afraid he was marching across the roof to peer in at me through the holes I'd scraped. It was a night like that when I heard Mother crying. She was walking from room to room crying like I'd never heard anyone cry before. I must have called out because she came into my room and tucked the covers around me. "Everything will be all right," she whispered; "go back to sleep." She sat on my bed, toward the foot where she could look out the window, crying softly until her shoulders began to shake. I lay pretending to sleep. She cried like that for nights after my father was killed. It was my mother, not I, whom Marcy had heard.

It was only after Marcy began playing late at night that I remembered my mother crying. In my room, with the door shut against steam, it seemed she was playing for me alone. I would wake already listening and gradually realize that the music had been going on while I slept, that I had been shaping my dreams to it. She played only nocturnes those last weeks of winter. Sometimes they seemed to carry over the roofs, but mostly she played so softly that only the air shaft made it possible to hear. I would sit huddled in my covers beside the window listening, looking out at the white dunes on Freddy's roof. The soldier was long gone, his helmet rusted off. Smoke blew unhooded; black flakes with sparking edges wafted out like burning snow. Soot and music and white gusts off the crests buffeted the pane. Even when the icicles began to leak and the streets to turn to brown rivers of slush, the blizzard in the air shaft continued.

Marcy disappeared during the first break in the weather. She left a note that read: "Ma, Don't worry."

"That's all," Mrs. Kubiac said, unfolding it for my mother to see. "Not even 'love,' not even her name signed. The whole time I kept telling her do something, she sits playing the piano, and now she does something, when it's too late, unless she goes to some butcher. Ev, what should I do?"

My mother helped Mrs. Kubiac call the hospitals. Each day they called the morgue. After a week, Mrs. Kubiac called the police and when they couldn't find Marcy, any more than they had been able to find *Dzia-Dzia,* Mrs. Kubiac began to call people in New York — teachers, old roommates, landlords. She used our phone. "Take it off the rent," she said. Finally, Mrs. Kubiac went to New York herself to search.

When she came back from New York she seemed changed, as if she'd grown too tired to be frantic. Her hair was a different shade of gray so that now you'd never know it had once been blond. There was a stoop to her shoulders as she descended the stairs on the way to novenas. She no longer came downstairs for tea and long talks. She spent much of her time in church, indistinguishable among the other women from the old country, regulars at the morning requiem mass, wearing babushkas and dressed in black like a sodality of widows, droning endless, mournful litanies before the side altar of the Black Virgin of Częstochowa.

By the time a letter from Marcy finally came, explaining that the entire time she had been living on the South Side in a Negro neighborhood near the university, and that she had a son whom she'd named Tatum Kubiac — "Tatum" after a famous jazz pianist — it seemed to make little difference. Mrs. Kubiac visited once, but didn't go back. People had already learned to glance away from her when certain subjects were mentioned — daughters, grandchildren, music. She had learned to glance away from herself. After she visited Marcy she tried to sell the piano, but the movers couldn't figure out how to get it downstairs, nor how anyone had ever managed to move it in.

IT TOOK TIME for the music to fade. I kept catching wisps of it in the air shaft, behind walls and ceilings, under bath water. Echoes traveled the pipes and wallpapered chutes, the bricked-up flues and dark hallways. Mrs. Kubiac's building seemed riddled with its secret passageways. And, when the music finally disappeared, its channels remained, conveying silence. Not an ordinary silence of absence and emptiness, but a pure silence beyond daydream and memory, as intense as the music it replaced, which, like music, had the power to change whoever listened. It hushed the close-quartered racket of the old building. It had always been there behind the creaks and drafts and slamming doors, behind the staticky radios, and the flushings and footsteps and crackling fat, behind the wails of vacuums and kettles and babies, and the voices with their scraps of conversation and arguments and laughter floating out of flats where people locked themselves in with all that was private. Even after I no longer missed her, I could still hear the silence left behind.

DAVID LONG

✛

Clearance

I'D GOTTEN MYSELF nerved up in the night.

Fay would've said, if she'd known, I had no business going up in the mountains alone, a man with young kids, a man not equipped with above-average bravery. But I let the crackle of the fire and the tin of Dinty Moore's and the stack of dry wood by the tent distract me. Sometime late I zipped myself into the bag and watched the coals glow blue through a thickness of rip-stop nylon, not thinking of anything special, baseball at first, the status of the VISA bill, then how jittery Matty, my older boy, looked before launching into his back dives. Outside the stars pummeled down. I was comfortable and reasonably tired, but before long my thoughts got away from me, bounding past the recent trouble with Fay and gravitating toward worst things, zeroing in, ultimately, on the noise a sow grizzly would make plundering down out of last season's huckleberries toward the tent. I'd lost some ground these last couple of years since my father died. Already this spring Mr. Allred, the man who brought us eggs, had been pinned under his tractor, and the aide in Fay's classroom had been told she had a melanoma on her ankle. *Why not me,* I'd learned to think. But all I heard all night was wind coming southeast over the saddle, scouring through the scrub pine.

When I woke it was afternoon. The fire was cold. That last

hour before sunup the light overhead had appeared promis-
ing, but now the sky was thick with coils of heavy, dark-
bottomed clouds. I knelt, rubbed water on my face. The ridge
was pocked with alpine lakes. Clayborn, Lynx, Aspen, the two
Pearls. Some were too marginal for names, shallow glacier-
made gouges that froze solid. Most, though, ran deep enough
for a crop of cutthroat or grayling.

A remnant of ice floated near the deep end, mottled and
flecked with reddish algae. Yesterday, when I'd stopped above
the last grade, the lake had shone up gaudy as a god's eye. Under this afternoon's clouds that fluky ultramarine had gone to
black. The wind tore across it, not slapping up whitecaps but
flashing off into trails of fine erratic shivers. A patch of
meadow lay beyond the outlet; it was too early for color,
though. The slope to the left was all scree, emptying into the
lake. Above the scree, couloirs of broken shale shot another
few hundred feet to the summit.

In the eight years since Fay and I'd moved back to Sperry, I'd
made this trip late every June, in the company of my two oldest
friends, Pat McSherry and John Rittenour. One year there'd
been a drive on at the aluminum plant and McSherry hadn't
been able to take time off until into July and by then the lake
was completely clear of ice. Even so, the three of us were the
only ones there, and the fish struck like they were starved. It
was just over seven miles from where the Forest Service road
quit, slow going early in the season. The shadowed stretches
were still bermed with corn snow, turning to a heavy slush by
afternoon. Even last year, when Rittenour finally married
again, and drove out with Holly and her daughter to visit family in St. Paul, he got back in time and we came as always.

The second morning we scrambled up the mountain. Rittenour led, climbing with light, quick hand holds. McSherry
came next, stubborn as a pitbull. I followed, not in a hurry,
watching their heads bob against the sky. The snow was off the
south face by now and the rock was mostly dry — there were a

few bad spots, up along the cliffs, but we'd worked out a route and stuck with it. The peak was small, sheared flat as a poker table except for a cairn climbers had built over the years. We'd collapse around it, draw up our knees, try to catch our wind.

McSherry's face would be flushed and sweaty. He'd complain about his knees. He'd say he was an old man and wasn't going to climb anymore. We all joked about being old men, but we didn't feel that old yet — I didn't anyway. I was just forty. There was nothing wrong with my knees. I had a good head of hair left, my weight was OK. Fortune, or whatever, had been kind to me, Fay had to remind me sometimes, though in the everyday course of things, Fay wasn't a big believer in Fortune. *It's not in the lap of the gods, Averill,* she'd more likely say. Whichever, it was true I'd missed the war, never broken a bone, never been stitched.

Beyond this summit lay a slice of backcountry valley, then other peaks, silt-colored, chopping north into British Columbia, each band thicker in haze. Even the mildest days had a cool wind, smelling of lichen or, I thought, the rock itself.

"I'm spending the rest of my life right here," I announced once, so close to happy I didn't know anything sensible to say. Rittenour nodded, fluffing out his beard. "We'll tell Fay what you decided on," he said softly.

McSherry snorted, took a long pull off the water bottle.

In a way, I meant that about staying on top, but pretty soon — I don't know — I'd get to kicking the loose stones around, skimming them out into the air.

"Let's head down," I'd say.

"Christ Almighty, we just got here," McSherry would say. "You don't know what you want."

That was other years.

In that first friendly light today I'd traced the whole route in my mind, consoling myself over the lousy night. But now, with the clouds boiling low overhead, it seemed remote and dark, no place to be alone. A fine mist had begun to coat my glasses. I pulled a space blanket from the pack and covered the wood-pile, and after that I told myself I'd better fish.

FAY'D ALREADY TAKEN the boys down to her mother's out-side of Hamilton, standard procedure once school got out. I had to admit I didn't mind having the house to myself — it was only for a few weeks, after all. Some weekends I'd drive down after work on Friday, in time to help Fay get the boys to bed, then the three of us would play cards, or just sit outside and talk until it was too dark. Fay's mother had been widowed years ago, the fall Fay started junior high. Her husband had gone off for weekend duty in the National Guard and — one of those accidents that seem excruciatingly senseless — been crushed between the back of a troop truck and the armory wall. She was a plain, strong-looking woman, in the same style that Fay was, red-cheeked and long-legged, still trim from working with the horses. She must've seen other men now and then, but none were in evidence and there was never talk of another marriage. We got along, Fay's mother and I (better since the boys had been born), though I'd feel her eyes on me sometimes — gray as river stones — and believe she was on the verge of telling me things about myself.

After those weekends I'd get up around five, leave Fay sleeping, and drive straight through to the office. It was a happy-enough arrangement. But this time, this year, Fay'd told me she thought they'd stay all summer. She said it as if she was test-ing me.

"Well, OK," I said.

"I'll call you from the ranch," she said. But she didn't and I didn't call her.

How do these things get started?

For a while I'd been willing to believe it was winter grinding on Fay and me — it's not so fierce here as people imagine, but it's diabolical, it acts like it won't ever end. I found myself tak-ing offense all the time. I didn't like the grudging, snappish thing she did with her voice. I dogged after her, wanting to know how on earth she could talk like that to someone she loved. She sloughed it off — *You're bored, Averill,* that's all she'd say, as if it was a fault in me. Or she'd say, *Please don't buy trouble.* Weeks went by. The boys drifted around the house like a couple of lost satellites.

Fay and I still got together in bed now and then, but we seldom said a word. It was always very late, the bedroom in total darkness. At one point, over the winter, she had her hair cut in a blowzier, more modern style, and switched from her old glasses to a pair of soft contacts. It occurred to me to wonder if she was seeing someone else, and for a while — it sounds funny — I was excited watching her come and go, wondering if she'd take that sort of chance. But it was a poor idea, this suspicion, and when I finally said what I'd been thinking, one night in March, Fay said, *Averill, believe me, it's you or no one.* Her voice wasn't even angry, only, I thought, tired, as if what disappointed her most was that I'd think something so predictable.

Whatever was wrong, I'd begun to believe it was inescapable, a thing in our blood it took sixteen years to grow.

I knew I ought to use this time she was gone to see how I felt, to settle on the next move — I knew she'd be doing that down in Hamilton. But lately things had turned chaotic at the office. Every night I came home dull-headed after a day of trying to sort between the backbiting and the fact. I wasn't up to doing anything constructive. Most of the storm windows were still on, and already the grass had grown wild along the alley. Then it was Thursday night. The ball game on the cable station was over and I was out on the porch steps listening to the neighborhood settle down, watching the last twenty minutes of sunlight bleed through cracks in the back fence. The phone rang. I didn't move at first. I didn't know how we were going to act about this. I was afraid I'd say something meaner than I felt. Still, I couldn't bear to hear it keep bleating in the empty house.

It wasn't her, but Rittenour, canceling.

"I feel funny about this, Averill," he said. "I mean, we can

still reschedule, don't you think?" Holly's daughter Rose Ann
was having tubes put in her ears, he explained. "I thought it
was going to be all cleared up by now, but the medicine just
didn't do that much, so, I don't know, Holly says she wants me
to go on with you and Pat . . . " I could picture him looking off,
blinking, hoping not to offend. "I kind of want to be here, you
know, in case . . . "

I felt this punch of anger.

But I said, "Whatever you think," then added that I was sorry, and that I'd wait up and give McSherry a call when he got
off swing shift. I went back outside with a beer. I could hear the
neighbor's sprinkler slapping against his clapboards and dropping into the hedge. Farther off in the dark I heard the *ack-ack*
of a plastic machine gun and the shrill taunting noises of some
young boys. When the beer was gone I had another. I went inside to call McSherry and give him the news, but as soon as I
heard his voice I knew I was going to lie to him.

FROM WHERE I STOOD on the rocks, I couldn't see two inches
down into the lake. I thought I had a hit once, but then it felt
more like something on the bottom. All I carried was an Eagle
Claw Fay's brother had lent me years ago, with a tired Shake-
speare that clattered as I reeled. The others used flies, damsel
nymphs at ice out. I made do with whatever was left from last
year, Daredevil, Colorado spinner, I didn't care. McSherry
could barely stand to be around me. Sometimes I just used nib-
lets from a can, eating the spares myself. I lobbed a few more
casts, reeled in too fast, and put the pole down on the rocks.

Without the others, I had to admit, it was only killing time.
I'd never loved it anyway, the actual fishing, not like they did. I
tossed most of what I caught back anymore, unless they'd managed to swallow the hook. It was a joke how squeamish I'd gotten. I set off hiking down toward the jam of bleached logs at the
outlet, but it was muddy along the shore, and I found that
walking felt as pointless as the next thing. What time had it got-

ten to be? With the sky so socked-in I could make my best guess and be off by three hours. I considered how fast I could tear down the camp, and where I'd be on the trail when I couldn't see my feet in front of me.

Still, I didn't feel like pulling out, either.

I wondered what Pat or John would do with themselves, alone up here. Fish, drink a little, nap in the tent where it was warm. Fish again later until the light failed. In my rush I hadn't even brought a bottle. I tried picturing Rittenour's airy looping casts, that lovely concentration of McSherry's, his huge hands resting in his lap like driftwood. But when I imagined my friends, I saw them under a bright sun, the leaves on the bushes uncurled and jiggling in the breeze. It was a dumb exercise. They wouldn't have come alone, either of them. It wouldn't have crossed their minds.

And I knew if I'd told them, I wouldn't have come either. McSherry would've gone silent for a second then asked what I thought I'd prove with a stunt like this. He would've said I was a moron not to carry a gun — he never went near the mountains without a .357 Smith & Wesson on his belt. Of course, I hadn't told Fay either. For a moment, I contemplated which was worse. Back at the house I'd gotten fired up, loaded the car that night under the floodlight, making myself believe this was something necessary, even crucial (one of Fay's words), but all that was neutralized by now. It was nothing short of perverse not telling people where you were.

It took most of a matchbook to get the fire going. I boiled a kettle of lake water, sliced off a few rounds of Thuringer, emptied out an envelope of onion soup mix. I crouched on the log, warming my hands around the cup, watching the mountain, the little I could see of it. There was still a wind on top, but it was trapped above the clouds. The bushes near the tent didn't so much as twitch.

There's no way I'm going to sleep, I thought. *I'm going to lie in that tent all night again and tomorrow's going to be just like today.* God, it was bad enough at home without Fay there civilizing the bed. I could fall asleep on the couch with the TV on, but if I stripped down and got under the covers, I'd get so wired I'd feel like I should throw my clothes back on and go to the office. Sometimes I had a glass of brandy, sometimes I broke down and took a pill. Next thing, I'd be awake again, the heartbeat pattering in my ears. I'd swing my legs over the side of the bed and look at the clock. Quarter to three invariably — as if I'd been called for a purpose, then left on my own to guess what it was.

It got dark sooner than I'd figured. Already I couldn't see features in the terrain across the lake, dark shapes was all. The pine had burned into steady coals. I snugged my arms in against my vest and watched my breath.

I couldn't help it, I thought about Fay getting ready for bed, her head cocking to one side as she pulled an earring out. I thought of the nightshirt dropping down, obscuring her limbs. Forty thousand hours I'd spent in bed with her — *unfathomable*. I remembered how her stomach felt under my hand. It had more give after Ned, but still had that flat calm feel from when she was seventeen and we were first lying together by the Bitterroot. I thought about her alone in her old room at her mother's, slantways across the bed, oblivious, and in another few seconds I was picturing my own mother locked up tight and paranoid in her little place down in Arizona.

I wrenched myself up as if standing would scatter my thoughts. The only place to go was down by the lake. So that's where I was, off away from the fire, crunching stones under my boot, when I first heard the plane.

McSherry couldn't bear them. *I swear a man can't lose himself far enough anymore,* he'd say, or just get a foul look and turn his head. He didn't go into it, of course, but I knew it was one of the ways the war still got to him. I didn't have that reflex in me, though. They were only little planes, Pipers or Cherokees, and they weren't so many. From the top of the mountain, if the sun was right, I'd scan the air until I caught sight of the wings glinting across the thermals. If anything, it made me feel farther from home. But in the dark, with the wind gone and the lake flat and the birds at roost, the engine's drone sounded immense.

I waited for the lights to show, the red and green flashing from the wingtips, the strobe on the tail illuminating a portion of cloud. Nothing came but sound, a gruff, untroubled baritone, the pitch creeping up a note or two as it neared the divide. Right away it cheered and diverted me, this sound. I stood looking up like Matty or Ned, mouth open. Then, almost instantly, I felt a crushing envy — here were people who had their lives in hand. I saw them relaxed and flush, buzzing home from the city, deals cut. I stood listening, scolding myself, and then in no time I was back to Fay again, thinking I couldn't have wandered farther off course if I'd tried.

And that's what I was still doing, moments later, when the plane struck the mountain.

I KEPT LISTENING, jerking my head as if there'd be more. I heard the spitting of my fire, nothing else. Even so, I couldn't disbelieve what I'd heard — already the sound, the sequence of it, was scored into my ear. Stub of sheet metal on rock, another longer shearing, wincing noise, an empty beat, then the rattle of dislodged talus kicking downslope. If I lived to be ninety — I knew this instantly — it wasn't going to change the least bit. It would come back like eight or ten other things I heard when my mind blew empty. Fay shaking me, her fingers embedded in my arm, *It's time, Averill! it's time,* in the apartment on Griswold, before Matty came . . . or my mother forlorn as a curlew, also summer, the middle of the night, *Honey, your father's* . . .

But the next part spilled together: throwing on the half-empty pack, running off down the lake, turning back three separate times before I got going right — the first for gloves, the second for my hatchet, and a third time to go back where

I'd been standing when it happened, to stare up again as if I could memorize that spot in the darkness by the angle of my neck.

The flashlight threw out a thick rope of light. I kept it straight on the trail all the way down the side of the lake, dodging deadfall and standing water, trying not to run, but loping anyway, cutting finally up into the scree.

I tacked a few times, stopped for my heart to slow, then kept on, looping my free hand to the side for ballast. Higher up, the rocks had a sheen, and as I swung low, the chill rose around my face. Above the scree, I hit the foot of the wall, roughly where I'd imagined it would be. I followed it south, hoping it would meet the ridgeline. All at once I was in the clouds and my fire no longer showed below.

In another few feet I hit new snow.

Climbing, it was easy not to picture what I was looking for. My mind strayed to a story involving my father, how the family'd sent him into a blizzard to look for his uncle on the road to Cut Bank. This was back in the worst of the '30s — my great-uncle Sumner had torn off to town to vent himself on a government agent. The truck had left the county road and was nosed into the borrow pit, drifted in as high as the tailgate. Uncle Sumner was lying across the seat, his knees up to his chest, his ear frozen to the leather. He always survived in this story (he died many years later at the Lutheran Home, a shock of silvery hair still hiding the disfigured ear). My mother was the one who dredged it up now and then, a preachment on doing what was needed, but my father, though he didn't mind telling it, never acted like it had a point — or if it did, it was that events were sometimes larger than you were. I'd heard it addressed at me a half-dozen times (and at my little brother a few more) without ever deciding which way to see it. What remained was his voice, creeping along, shaded with amazement. I could hear that voice now, mixed up with my own, and all the time I climbed it never occurred to me that I wouldn't find the plane, that I wouldn't jab the light forward through the mist and come straight on it.

Still, I wasn't ready.

Suddenly the shaft of light fell on a section of engine. The rock around it was bare where the snow'd melted. The surface of the metal was still giving off twists of steam. I reached my hand out, then yanked it back and crammed it under my arm and started shooting the light around, but there was nothing else that didn't belong there. I poked uphill a few steps, then a few more, and all at once the light careened off into an expanse of drifting cloud.

THE RIDGELINE was sheer, hardly enough to balance on as I stared down. The plane lay on the other side, where it had to be, just downslope from a brief disturbance in the rock and snow. It was right-side to, a single-engine. Except for the crumpled wings jutting from the roof, it didn't look much bigger than the white Corvette McSherry used to drive. The nose was torn, balled in like scrap, but the tail section was still sleek as a bullet. I could read its numbers without any trouble.

I yelled down, but my voice sounded puny. I called out a second time, sharper, and hung back, waiting.

In a way, I believed I could still scramble down to the passenger's door and swing it free, and find them only stunned — suspended there, waiting for my hand to snake in and release the lap belts. I could see them tumbling out, waking up. It was a potent feeling: their weight bearing down on me, my boots clattering in the loose shale, taking them one at a time (however many there were) down to a sheltered place on the rocks where they could rest while I got blankets . . . but it dispersed almost at once. All it took was another breath and I was crashing down toward the door. It was jammed tight, and I had to beat the safety glass with a rock until it shattered.

THERE WERE TWO of them in the plane, a man maybe ten years my senior, and a woman younger, Fay's age or thereabouts. The clothes were Western, new and expensive. They both wore snap-front jackets too light for the altitude and the weather. The man had been piloting. His arm was strung around the control, his face canted toward the far window, an imposing, important-looking face still slick from shaving. He could've been a rancher, a lawyer . . . I felt an instant, almost fearful deference toward him, toward them both. The woman's head was thrown back, baring an expanse of white neck crowded with strands of Navajo silver. She was blonde and the hair was pulled off her face and hung down over the seat back.

In a moment, I wormed the flashlight into a twist of sheared metal so it shone on a mirror and diffused across the cabin. I busted out the window glass and crawled through the frame, pulled off my glove and put a finger to each of their necks. The skin felt like vinyl, not cold yet and not warm. I let my weight fall back against the leather duffles and department-store packages strewn in back. A bottle had broken in one of them, aftershave or cologne, something sharp and sweet that stung my eyes.

I'd kept my mind clear of the moment of the crash, except to remember how glowery and unstable. the clouds had looked from down at the lake as they shunted and broke against the cliffs. But inside the plane, staring uphill through the remains of the windshield, at the rock skiffed with snow, I had to wonder why it didn't explode and burn.

Or why the whole cabin hadn't been pounded into oblivion.

I kicked at the door until it released, then hauled myself out, urgently, as if the plane might still explode. I backed off, and it was only then, apart from it, that I understood how close they'd come to clearing the ridge. Ten feet maybe. And then I could see the story. He'd had just time enough to jerk back on the control, punching the nose up into the draft, but not enough for the lift to take hold and carry them over the saddle.

So they were just barely dead, I thought.

And this thought was so strange and unanswerable, for a few seconds it held back the others, but then they tumbled ahead anyway. *What would I've done if I'd found a pulse? What if one had been living and the other not? What if they'd been crazy with pain?*

I CRUMPLED the back pages of the Lethbridge paper scavenged from the floor of the cabin and covered them with moss and laid on the deadest, driest wood I could find and drag up the hill. The fire sent up a black smoke; even the paper seemed unwilling to burn hard until I got my face down and blew at the sparks and fed in the twig tips with my fingers. Slowly it came around. In a few minutes, it burned without me. I crashed down through the loose rock toward the treeline where I could hack off some real wood.

Later, using the blade of the hatchet, I jimmied the pilot's door. I unthreaded his left arm and, bracing myself against the wing strut, tugged on his shoulders until they slumped and began to tip out.

A few minutes later I did the same for the woman.

Back in the cabin again, I couldn't find a goddamn thing to cover them with. No blankets or sleeping bags, not even a tarp. Their bags were soft-sided, sparsely packed, just enough for an overnight. I started opening the larger of the two, but as soon as I had the top splayed open I stopped and couldn't bear to keep going. I zipped it back and fitted the straps together and got out.

I'd put the man and woman next to each other, their feet toward the fire, and wedged a seat cushion under each of their heads. After that I walked around for a while, but now that I was through with the work, the chill seeped inside my clothes and I had to sit down by the fire myself.

The damage should've been massive, I knew that — so wretched that a man like me couldn't stand to look. Instead, it scarcely showed. The man's arm had broken, I was fairly certain, also his nose. It was puffy and off-center and a filament of

blood ran slantwise across his cheek and down into his collar.
The woman had a knot at her temple, crossed by a little furl of
cut skin — I'd done worse to my own head being careless in the
cellar.

Their eyes were shut. Whatever kind of clenched expression
they'd had those last four or five seconds, the impact had scattered it. The faces looked incredibly vacant. It was hard to sit so
close and not wonder what their names were, whether they
were married or not — probably, I thought, she was a second
wife, being that much younger. I could see the firelight batting
off her fingers — they were spiny fingers, with glossy, evenly
rounded nails, and they were empty of rings. But that didn't
say much. Even Fay left her ring on the dresser some mornings. I could piece together all kinds of things back in the
plane, but I was tired now and starting to shake a little. I wished
I had some coffee, I wished I could hold it and feel the steam
on my cheeks.

Not long after that, I heard the search planes, first one, coming east from the city airport in Sperry and passing far up the
ridge, then others. The clouds were still locked overhead. For
an hour or so the droning kept up, growing and twisting away
while they tracked a grid above the mountains. The fire was
too little to show through the clouds, I thought, realizing I was
glad of it. All this felt private, of no concern to others.

After the planes had gone home, my fatigue seemed to pass
into a quiet, patient sort of sadness. I wished them better weather: a night with a moon they could follow down out of Canada, flashing on the creeks and the expanse of reservoir, on the
pockets of meltwater lying along the ridge. I sent them a safe
distance above the lake where my tent was, and over me, down
at the edge of the water the way I'd been before, deviling myself. I let them break into the sky above the valley lights, banish-
ing the racket of the engine with bright talk. I felt like I was in
the cockpit with them, my arms looped around their shoulders, my head leaning forward between theirs.

But then, while I was lost in this wishful thinking, a chunk of talus worked loose from the ridge, skipped down and smacked the body of the plane. I shot to my feet and glared back into the dark.

It was quiet again.

Suddenly I couldn't catch my breath. My chest began to heave. Acid splashed up into my throat, gagging me. I yelled out loud, crazy things, to keep from throwing up. But I threw up anyway, the heels of my hands wedged down between the points of the rocks.

I rinsed my lips with snow. I straightened, and slowly my head grew clear. I moved back and forth through the blowing smoke and came to rest finally, staring down at the bodies. At the man's primarily. I looked at the massive chest, the face. My sympathy burned off in an instant. *I don't need to know any more about you than I already know,* I thought. I hated him. I hated him for the killing he'd done, but I hated him with a worse kind of passion, it came to me, for that string of other ridges he'd barely cleared in his life. I didn't need to hear any of what he'd have to say for himself. I knew his laugh by heart, I knew the things he said to the woman as they started out.

There was more of the night left, but I broke up the rest of the larch and threw it on and let it roar.

I pictured daylight starting over the mountains, the pressure rising and the sky coming apart. Then the helicopters dropping into the meadow by the lake's outlet, and the rescuers clattering down from the ridgeline and finding the empty Cessna, then, the couple stretched out here by the fire in their summery clothes, with cushions under their heads. Nobody'd want to speak for a moment, I guessed. One of the men would kick at the ashes for something to do, and find a strip of live coals underneath, and maybe kneel and blow on them and think *What in God's name went on here?*

I put my head down, but didn't sleep.

Sometime after eleven the next morning, I stopped at a cafe up the canyon and ordered eggs and potatoes with gravy, and sat eating and reading *The Missoulian,* running through the box scores, batter by batter. Then, for a long time, I watched the river. It was high in its banks, still fast and discolored with run-off. Despite what you hear, I thought, a man doesn't change overnight, no matter how abrupt his chastening. Still, it could begin that way. I walked out and started the truck. By the time I crossed over the upper valley bridge it was a clear, achingly bright summer's day.

I backed to the shed and unloaded, slipped the tent from its stuff sack and spread it across the picnic table to dry. After that I rolled the mower out and got it running and cut the grass along the alley fence where it came up wild. I stopped to strip off my chamois shirt, then a row later, my T-shirt. I raked the clippings and carried them to the compost, then upended the mower, took the blade off with a crescent wrench, and sat on the back steps in the sun, sharpening it, filing away the gouges. A heavy truck banged across the potholes at the end of our block, downshifted onto Ponderosa, and moved off, leaving the neighborhood suddenly still. There was hardly a shiver of wind in the new leaves. Somewhere, out of sight, a song sparrow called out across the yard and was answered.

I got up and unlocked the house. I left my boots by the door, entered the shade of the kitchen and made my way to the phone.

I let it ring a terrible, implausible number of times, feeling the sweat cool on my shoulders.

It was Fay's mother who finally answered.

"*It's you*," she said. She sounded a little surprised and breathless and, I thought, relieved. "Dear boy," she said, "you nearly missed us."

CHARLES BAXTER

✛

How I Found My Brother

I WAS SEPARATED from my biological mother when I was four months old. Everything from that period goes through the wash of my memory and comes out clean, blank. The existing snapshots of my mother show this very young woman holding me, a baby, at arm's length, like a caught fish, outside in the blaring midday summer sunlight. She's got clothes up on the clothesline in the background, little cotton infant things. In one picture a spotted dog, a mongrel combination of Labrador and Dalmatian, is asleep beside the bassinet. I'd like to know what the dog's name was, but time has swallowed that information. In another picture, a half-empty bottle of Grain Belt Beer stands on the lawn near a wading pool. My mother must have figured that if she could have me, at the age of seventeen, she could also have the beer.

My mother's face in these pictures is having a tough time with daylight. It's a struggle for her to bask in so much glare. She squints and smiles, but the smile is all on one side, the right. The left side stays level, except at the edge, where it slips down. Because of the sunlight and the black-and-white film, my mother's face in other respects is bleached, without details, like a sketch for a face. She's a kid in these pictures and she has a kid's face, with hair pulled back with bobby pins and a slight puffiness in the cheeks, which I think must be bubble gum.

She doesn't look like she's ever been used to the outdoors, the poor kid. Sunlight doesn't become her. It's true she smiled, but then she did give me up. I was too much serious work, too much of a squalling load. Her girlish smile was unsteady and finally didn't include me. She gave me away — this is historical record — to my adoptive parents, Harold and Ethel Harris, who were older and more capable of parental love. She also gave them these photographs, the old kind, with soft sawtooth borders, so I'd be sure to know how she had looked when the unfamiliar sunlight hit her in a certain way. I think her teen-aged boyfriend, my father, took these pictures. Harold and Ethel Harris were my parents in every respect, in love and in their care for me, except for the fact of these pictures. The other children in the family, also adopted, looked at the snapshots of this backyard lady with curiosity but not much else.

My biological father was never a particle of interest to me compared to my adoptive father, Harold Harris, a man who lived a life of miraculous calm. A piano tuner and occasional jazz saxophonist, Harold liked to sit at home, humming and tapping his fingers in the midst of uproar and riot, kids shouting and plaster falling. He could not be riled; he never made a fist. He was the parental hit of any childhood group, and could drive a car competently with children sitting on his shoulders and banging their hands on the side of his head. Genetic inheritance or not, he gave us all a feeling for pitch. Ask me for an F-sharp, I'll give you one. I get the talent from Harold.

I WENT to high school, messed around here and there, did some time in the Navy, and when I was discharged I married my sweetheart of three years, the object of my shipboard love letters, Lynda Claire Norton. We had an apartment. I was clerking at Meijer's Thrifty Acres. I thought we were doing okay. Each night I was sleeping naked next to a sexual angel. At sunrise she would wake me with tender physical comfort,

with hair and fingertips. I was working to get a degree from
night school. Fourteen months after we were married, right on
the day it was due, the baby came. A boy, this was. Jonathan
Harold Harris. Then everything went to hell.

I was crazy. Don't ask me to account for it. I have no background or inclination to explain the human mind. Besides, I'm
not proud of the way I acted. Lynda moved right out, baby and
all, the way any sensible woman would have, and she left me
two empty rooms in the apartment in which I could puzzle myself out.

I had turned into the damndest thing. I was a human monster movie. I'd never seen my daddy shouting the way I had; he
had never carried on or made a spectacle of himself. Where
had I picked up this terrible craziness that made me yell at a
woman who had taken me again and again into her arms? I
wrote long letters to the world while I worked at home on my
model ships, a dull expression on my face. You will say that liquor was the troublemaker here and you would be correct, but
only so far. I had another bad ingredient I was trying to track
down. I broke dishes. My mind, day and night, was muzzy with
bad intentions. I threw a lightbulb against a wall and did not
sweep up the glass for days. Food burned on the stove and then
I ate it. I was committing outrageous offenses against the spirit.
Never, though, did I smash one of the model ships. Give me
credit for that.

I love oceans and the ships that move across them. I believe
in man-made objects that take their chances on the earth's ex-
panses of water. And so it happened that one weekday afternoon I was watching a rerun of *The Caine Mutiny*, with my
workboard set up in front of me with the tiny pieces of my model *Cutty Sark* in separated piles, when the phone rang. For a
moment I believed that my wife had had second thoughts
about my behavior and was going to give me another chance.
To tell the truth, whenever the phone rang, I thought it would
be Lynda, announcing her terms for my parole.

"Hello? Is this Andy Harris?" a man's voice asked.

"This is him," I said. "Who's this?"

"This is your brother." Just like that. Very matter-of-fact. This is your brother. Harold and Ethel Harris had had two other adopted sons, in addition to me, but I knew them. This voice was not them. I gripped the telephone.

Now — and I'm convinced of this — every adopted child fears and fantasizes getting a call like this announcing from out of the blue that someone in the world is a relative and has tracked you down. I know I am not alone in thinking that anyone in the world might be related to me. My biological mother and father were very busy, urgent lovers. Who knows how much procreation they were capable of, together and separately? And maybe they had brothers and sisters, too, as urgent in their own way as my mother and father had been in theirs, filling up the adoption agencies with their offspring. I could never go into a strange city without feeling that I had cousins in it.

Therefore I gripped the telephone, hoping for reason, for the everyday. "This is not my brother," I said.

"Oh yes, it is. Your mother was Alice Barton, right?"

"My mother was Ethel Harris," I said.

"Before that," the voice said, "your mother was Alice Barton. She was my mother, too. This is your brother, Kurt. I'm a couple of years younger than you." He waited. "I know this is a shock," he said.

"You can't find out about me," I said. The room wasn't spinning, but I had an idea that it might. My mouth was open halfway and I was taking short sweaty breaths through it. One shiver took its snaky way down and settled in the lumbar region. "The records are sealed. It's all private, completely secret."

"Not anymore, it isn't," he said. "Haven't you been keeping up? In this country you can find out anything. There are no secrets worth keeping anymore; nobody *wants* privacy, so there isn't any."

He was shoving this pile of ideas at me. *My* thoughts had left

me in a great flight, the whole sad flock of them. "Who are
you?" I asked.

"Your brother Kurt," he said, repeating himself. "Listen, I
won't bore you to explain what I had to do to find you. The fact
is that it's possible. Easy, if you have money. You pay someone
and someone pays someone and eventually you find out what
you want to know. Big surprise, right?" He waited, and when I
didn't agree with him, he started up again, this time with small
talk. "So, I hear that you're married and you have a kid yourself." He laughed. "And I'm an uncle."

"What? No. Now you're only partly right," I said, wanting
very hard to correct this man who said he was my brother. "My
wife left me. I'm living here alone now."

"Oh. I'm sorry about that." He offered his sympathies in a
shallow, masculine way: the compassion offered by princes
and salesmen. "But listen," he said, "you're not alone. It's happened before. Couples separate all the time. You'll get back.
It's not the end of the world. Andy?"

"What?"

"Would you be willing to get together and talk?"

"Talk? Talk about what?"

"Well, about being brothers. Or something else. You can talk
about anything you please." He waited for me to respond, and
I didn't. This was my only weapon — the terrible static of telephone silence. "Look," he said, "this is tough for me. *I'm not a
bad person.* I've been sitting by this phone for an hour. I don't
know if I'm doing the right thing. My wife ... you'll meet
her ... she hasn't been exactly supportive. She thinks this is a
mistake. She says I've gone too far this time. I dialed your number four times before I dialed it to the end. I make hundreds of
business calls but this one I could not do. It may be hard for
you, also: I mean, I take a little getting used to. I can get obsessive about little things. That's how I found you."

"By being obsessive."

"Yeah. Lucille ... that's my wife ... she says it's one of my
faults. Well, I always wanted a brother, you know, blood re-

lated and everything, but I couldn't have one until I found you. But then I thought you might not like me. It's possible. Are you following me?"

"Yes, I am." I was thinking: here I am in my apartment, recently vacated by my wife, talking to a man who says he's my brother. Isn't there a law against this? Someone help me.

"You don't have to like me," he said, his brusque voice starting to stumble over the consonants. That made me feel better. "But that isn't the point, is it?" Another question I didn't have to answer, so I made him wait. "I can imagine what's in your head. But let's meet. Just once. Let's try it. Not at a house. I only live about twenty miles away. I can meet you in Ann Arbor. We can meet in a bar. I *know* where you live. I drove by your building. I believe I've even seen your car."

"Have you seen me?" This brother had been cruising past my house, taking an interest. Do brothers do that? What *do* they do?

"Well, no, but who cares about looks where brothers are concerned? We'll see each other. Listen, there's this place a couple of miles from you, The Wooden Keg. Could we meet there? Tomorrow at three? Are you off tomorrow?"

"That's a real problem for me," I said. "Booze is my special poison."

"Hell, that's all right," he said. "I'll watch out for you. I'm your brother. Oh. There's one other thing. I lied. I look like you. That's how you'll recognize me. I have seen you."

I held on to the telephone a long time after I hung up. I turned my eyes to the television set. José Ferrer was getting drunk and belligerent at a cocktail party. I switched off the set.

I was in that bar one hour before I said I would be, and my feelings were very grim. I wasn't humming. I didn't want him to be stationed there when I came in. I didn't want to be the one who sauntered in through the door and walked the long distance to the bar stool. I didn't want some strange sibling checking out the way I close the distance or blink behind my glasses while my eyes adjust to the light. I don't like people watching me when they think they're going to get a skeleton key to my character. I'm not a door and I won't be opened that easily.

Going into a bar in the midsummer afternoon takes you out of the steel heat and air-hammer sun; it softens you up until you're all smoothed out. This was one of those wood sidewall bars with air that hasn't recirculated for fifty years, with framed pictures of thoroughbreds and cars on the walls next to the chrome decorator hubcaps. A man's bar, smelling of cigarettes and hamburger grease and beer. The brown padded light comes down on you from some recessed source, and the leather cushions on those bar stools are as soft as a woman's hand, and before long the bar is one big bed, a bed on a barge eddying down a sluggish river where you've got nothing but good friends lined up on the banks. This is why I am an alcoholic. It wasn't easy drinking Coca-Cola in that place, that dim halfway house between the job and home, and I was about to slide off my wagon and order my first stiff one when the door cracked open behind me, letting in a trumpet blast of light, and I saw, in doorframe outline, my brother coming toward me. He was taking his own time. He had on a hat. When the door closed and my eyes adjusted, I got a better look at him, and I saw what he said I would see : I saw instantly that this was my brother. The elves had stolen my shadow and given it to him. A version of my face was fixed on a stranger. From the outdoors came this example of me, wearing a coat and tie.

He took a bar stool next to mine and held out his hand. I held out mine and we shook like old friends, which we were a long way from becoming. "Hey," we both said. He had the eyes, the cheek, and the jaw in a combination I had seen only in the mirror. "Andy," he said, refusing to let my hand go. "Good to meet you."

"Kurt," I said. "Likewise." Brother or no brother, I wasn't giving away anything too fast. This is America, after all.

"What're you drinking?" he asked.

"Coke."

"Oh. Right." He nodded. When he nodded, the hat nodded. After he saw me looking at it, he said, "Keeps the sun out of my eyes." He took it off and tried to put it on the bar, but there wasn't enough room for it next to the uncleared beer glasses and the ashtrays, so he stood up and dropped it on a hook over by the popcorn machine. There it was, the only hat. He said, "My eyes are sensitive to light. What about yours?" I nodded. Then he laughed, hit the bar with the broad flat of his hand, and said, "Isn't this great?" I wanted to say, yes, it's great, but the true heart of the secret was that, no, it was not. It was horrifyingly strange without being eventful. You can't just get a brother off the street. But before I could stop him from doing it, he leaned over and put his right arm, not a large arm but an arm all the same, over my shoulders, and he dropped his head so that it came sliding in toward my chest just under the chin. Here was a man dead set on intimacy. When he straightened up, he said, "We're going to have ourselves a day today, that's for sure." His stutter took some of the certainty out of the words. "You don't have to work this afternoon, right?"

"No," I said, "I'm not scheduled."

"Great," he said. "Let me fill you in on myself."

INSTEAD OF GIVING ME his past, he gave me a résumé. He tried to explain his origins. My biological mother, for all the vagueness in her face, had been a demon for good times. She had been passionate and prophylactically carefree. Maybe she had had twenty kids, like old Mother Hubbard. She gave us away like presents to a world that wanted us. This one, this Kurt, she had kept for ten months before he was adopted by some people called Sykes. My brother said that he understood that we — he and I — had two other siblings in Laramie, Wyoming. There might be more he didn't know about. I had a sudden image of Alice Barton as a human stork, flying at tree level and dropping babies into the arms of waiting parents.

Did I relax as my brother's voice took me through his life? Were we related under the skin, and all the way around the block? He talked; I talked. The Sykes family had been bookish types, lawyers, both of them, and Kurt had gone to Michigan State University in East Lansing. He had had certain advantages. No falling plaster or piano tuning. By learning the mysterious dynamics of an orderly life, he had been turned out as a salesman, and now he ran a plastics factory in Southfield, north of Detroit. "A small business," he said in a friendly, smug way. "Just fifteen employees." I heard about his comfortably huge home. I heard about his children, my nephews. From the wallet thick with money and credit cards came the line-up of photos of these beautiful children.

So what was he doing, this successful man, sitting on a bar stool out here, next to his brother, me, the lowly check-out clerk?

"Does anybody have enough friends?" he asked me. "Does anyone have enough *brothers?*" He asked this calmly, but the questions, as questions, were desperate. "Here's what it was," he said. "Two or three times a week I felt like checking in with someone who wasn't a wife and wasn't just a friend. Brothers are a different category, right there in the middle. It's all about *relatedness,* you know what I mean?" I must have scowled. "We can't rush this,' he said. "Let's go have dinner somewhere. My treat. And then let's do something."

"Do what?" I asked.

"I've given that a lot of thought," he said. "What do you do the first time out with your brother? You can't just eat and drink. You can't shop; women do that." Then he looked me square in the eye, smiled, and said, "It's summer. Maybe we could go bowling or play some softball." There was a wild look in his eye. He let out a quick laugh.

WE WENT IN HIS Pontiac Firebird to a German restaurant
and loaded up on sauerbraten. I had a vague sense he was lowering himself to my level but did not say so. He ordered a chest-
sized decorated stein of beer but I stayed on the cola wagon. I
tried to talk about my wife, but it wouldn't come out: all I could
say was that I had a problem with myself as a family man. That
wasn't me. The crying of babies tore me up. Feeding time gave
me inexplicable jitters. I had acted like Godzilla. When I told
him this, he nodded hard, like a yes-man. It was all reasonable
to him.

"Of course," he said. "Of course you were upset and con-
fused." He was understanding me the way I wanted to be understood. I talked some more. Blah blah blah. Outside, it was
getting dark. The bill came, and he paid it: out came the thick
wallet again, and from a major-league collection of credit cards
came the white bank plastic he wanted. I talked more. He
agreed with everything I said. He said, "You're exactly right."
Then I said something else, and he responded, "Yes, you're exactly right."

That was when I knew I was being conned. In real life people
don't say that to you unless they're trying to earn your love in a
hurry. But here he was, Kurt Sykes, visibly my brother, telling
me I was exactly right. It was hard to resist, but I was holding
on, and trying.

"Here's how," he said. He lifted his big stein of beer into the
air, and I lifted my glass of Coke. Click. A big blonde waitress
watched us, her face disciplined into a steel-helmet smile.

AFTER THAT, it was his idea to go outside and play catch. This
activity had all sorts of symbolic meanings for him, but what
was I going to do? Go home and watch television? I myself have
participated in a few softball leagues and the jock way of life is
not alien to me, but I think he believed he could open me up if
we stayed at my level, throwing something back and forth,
grunting and sweating. We drove across town to Buhr Park,

where he unloaded his newly-purchased baseball, his two brand-new gloves, and a shiny new bat. Baseball was on the agenda. We were going to play ball or die. "We don't have to do any hitting," he said. While I fitted the glove to my left hand — a perfect fit, as if he had measured me — he locked the car. I have never had a car worth locking; it was not a goal.

The sun having set, I jogged out across a field of darkening grass. The sky had that blue tablecloth color it gets at dusk just before the stars come out. I had my jeans, sweatshirt, and sneakers on, my usual day-off drag. I had not dressed up for this event. In fact, I was almost feeling comfortable, except for some growing emotional hot-spot I couldn't locate that was making me feel like pushing the baseball into my brother's face. Kurt started to toss the ball toward me and then either noticed his inappropriate dress-for-success formality or felt uncomfortable. He went back to the car and changed into sweat clothes in the half-dark. He could have been seen, but wasn't, except by me. (My brother could change his clothes out in the open, not even bothering to look around to see who would see. What did this mean?)

Now, dressed down, we started to hustle, keeping the rhythms up. He threw grounders, ineptly, his arm stiff and curious. I bent down, made the imaginary play, and pivoted. He picked up the bat and hit a few high flies toward me. Playing baseball with me was his way of claiming friendship. Fine. Stars came out. We moved across the field, closer to a floodlit tennis court, so we had a bit of light. I could see fireflies at the edge of where we were playing. On the court to my right, a high school couple was working their way through their second set. The girl let out little cries of frustration now and then. They were pleasurable to hear. Meanwhile, Kurt and I played catch in the near-dark, following the script that, I could see, he had written through one long sleepless night after another.

As we threw the ball back and forth, he talked. He continued on in his résumé. He was married but had two girl-friends. His wife knew about them both. She did not panic because she expected imperfection in men. Also, he said, he usually voted Republican. He went to parent-teacher-organization meetings.

"I suppose you weren't expecting this," he said.

No, I thought, I was *not* expecting you. I glanced at the tennis court. Clouds of moths and bright bugs swarmed in insect parabolas around the high voltage lights. The boy had a white Huron high school tee shirt on, and white shorts and tennis shoes, and a blue sweatband around his thick damp hair. The girl was dressed in an odd assortment of pink and pastel blue clothes. She was flying the colors and was the better player. He had the force, but she had the accuracy. Between his heat and her coolness, she piled up the points. I let myself watch her; I allowed myself that. I was having a harder and harder time keeping my eyes on my brother.

"You gonna play or look at them?" Kurt asked.

I glanced at him. I thought I'd ignore his question. "You got any hobbies?" I asked.

He seemed surprised. "Hobbies? No. Unless you count women and making money."

"How's your pitch?"

"You mean baseball?"

"No. Music. How's your sense of pitch?"

"Don't have one."

"I do," I said. "F-sharp." And I blew it at him.

He leaned back and grimaced. "How do you know that's F-sharp?"

"My daddy taught me," I said. "He taught me all the notes on the scale. You can live with them. You can become familiar with a note."

"I don't care for music," he said, ending that conversation. We were still both panting a bit from our exertions. The baseball idea was not quite working in the way he had planned. He seemed to be considering the possibility that he might not like me. "What the hell," he said. "Let's go back to that bar."

WHY DID I HIT my brother in that bar? Gentlemen of the bottle, it is you I address now. You will understand when I tell you that when my brother and I entered the bar, cool and smoky and filled with midsummer ballplayers, uniformed men and women, and he thoughtlessly ordered me a Scotch, you will understand that I drank it. Drank it after I saw his wad of money, his credit cards, his wallet-rubbed pictures of the children, my little nephews. He said he would save me from my alcoholism but he did not. Gentlemen, in a state of raw blank irritation I drank down what God and nature have labeled "poison" and fixed with a secret skull-and-crossbones. He bought me this drink, knowing it was bad for me. My mind withdrew in a snap from my brain. The universe is vast, you cannot predict it. From the great resources of anger I pulled my fund, my honest share. But I do not remember how, or exactly why, I said something terrible, and hit my brother.

HE STAGGERED BACK, and he looked at me.

HIS NOSE was bleeding and my knuckles hurt. I was sitting in the passenger side of his car. My soul ached. My soul was lying face down. He was taking me back to my apartment, and I knew that my brother would not care to see me from now on. He would reassert his right to be a stranger. I had lost my wife, and now I had lost him, too.

WE STUMBLED into my living room. I wobbled out to the kitchen, and, booze-sick, filled a dishtowel with ice cubes and brought it to him. My right hand felt swollen. We were going to have ugly bruises, but his were facial and would be worse. Holding the ice to his damaged face, he looked around. Above the ice his eyes flickered on with curiosity. "Ships," he said.

Then he pointed at the worktable against the wall. "What's all that?"

"It's my hobby," I said. The words came slow and wormlike out of my puzzled mouth.

He squinted above the ice. "Bottles? And glue?"

"I build ships in bottles." I sounded like a balloon emptying itself of air. I pointed at the decorator shelf on the west wall, where my three-masted clipper ship, the *Thermopylae,* was on display.

"How long have you done this?" he asked.

"So long I can't remember."

"How do you do it?"

He gave me a chance. Even a bad drunk is sometimes forced to seize his life and to speak. So I went over to the worktable. "You need these." I held up the surgical forceps. I could hardly move my fingers for the pain. Alcoholic darkness sat in a corner with its black bag waiting to cover me entirely. I went on talking. "And these. Surgical scissors." Dried specks of glue were stuck to the tips. "Some people cheat and saw off the bottom of the bottle, then glue it back on once the ship is inside. I don't do it that way. It has to grow inside the bottle. You need a challenge. I build the hull inside. I have used prefab hulls. Then you've got to lay the deck down. I like to do it with deck furnishings already in place: you know, the cabin doors and hatchcovers and cleats and riding bits already in place on the deck. You put the glue on and then you put the deck in, all in one piece, folded up, through the neck, then you fold it out. With all that glue on, you only have one shot. Then you do the rigging inside the bottle. See these masts? The masts are laid down inside the bottle with the bottom of the mast in a hole."

I pointed to the *Cutty Sark,* which I was working on. I did not care if my hands were broken; I would continue this, the only lecture in my head, even if I sounded like a chattering magpie.

"You see, you pull the mast up inside the bottle with a string attached to the mast, and there's a stop in the hole that'll keep the mast from going too far forward. Then you tie the lines that are already on the mast off on the belaying pins and the bits and the cleats." I stopped. "These are the best things I do. I make ships in bottles better than anything else I do in my life."

"Yes." He had been standing over my worktable, but now he was lying on the sofa again.

"I like ships," I said. "When I was growing up, I had pictures on the wall of yachts. I was the only person in the Harris family who was interested in ships."

"Hmm."

"I like sailboats the most." I was talking to myself. "They're in their own class."

"That's interesting," he said. "That's all very interesting, but I wonder if I could lie down here for a while."

"I think you're already doing it."

"I don't need a pillow or a blanket," Kurt said, covered with sweat. "I can lie here just as is."

"I was going to turn on the air conditioner."

"Good. Put it on low."

I went over to the rattletrap machine and turned it on. The compressor started with a mechanical complaint, a sound like *orrr orrr orrr,* and then faster, *orrorrorr.* By the time I got back into the living room, my brother's eyes were closed.

"You're asleep," I said.

"No," he said, "no, I'm not. My eyes are just closed. I'm bruised and taking a rest here. That's all. Why don't you talk to me for a minute while I lie here with this ice. Say anything."

So I TALKED against the demons chittering in the corners of the room. I told my brother about being on a carrier in the Navy. I talked about how I watched the blue lifting swells of the Pacific even when I wasn't supposed to and would get my ass kicked for it. I was hypnotized by sea water, the crazy majesty of horizontal lines. I sleepwalked on that ship, I was so happy. I told him about the rolling progress of oceanic storms, and how the cumulonimbus clouds rose up for what looked like three or four miles into the atmosphere. Straightedged curtains of rain followed us; near the Straits of Gibraltar it once rained for thirty minutes on the forward part of the ship, while the sun burned down on the aft.

I talked about the ship's work, the painting and repairing I did, and I told him about the constant metallic rumble vibrating below-decks. I told him about the smell, which was thick with sterile grease stink that stayed in your nostrils, and the smell of working men. Men away from women, men who aren't getting any, go bad, and they start to smell like metal and fur and meat.

Then I told him about the ships I built, the models, and the originals for them, about the masts and sails, and how, in the water, they had been beautiful things.

"What if they fell?" my brother said.

I didn't understand the question, but thought I would try to answer it anyway. It was vague, but it showed he was still awake, still listening. I wanted to ask, fell from where? But I didn't. I said if a man stood on the mainmast lookout, on a whaler, for example, he could lose his balance. If he tumbled from that height, he might slap the water like he was hitting cement. He might be internally damaged, but if he did come up, they'd throw him a lifebuoy, the white ones made out of cork and braided with a square of rope.

I brought one of the ships toward him. "I've got one here," I said, "tiny, the size of your fingernail."

He looked at it, cleated to the ship above the deck. He studied it and then he gazed at me. "Yes," he said. It was the most painful smile I'd ever seen in an adult human being, and it reminded me of me. I thought of the ocean, which I hadn't viewed for years and might not, ever again. "Yes," my brother said from under the icepack. "Now I get it."

Like strangers sitting randomly together in a midnight peeling-gray downtown bus depot smelling of old leather shoes, we talked until four in the morning, and he left, his face bruised dark, carrying one of my ships, the *Lightning*, under his arm. He came back a week later. We sat in the park this time, not saying much. Then I went to see him, and I met his wife. She's a pleasant woman, a tall blonde who comes fully outfitted with jewels I usually see under glass in display cases. My brother and I know each other better now; we've discovered that we have, in fact, no subjects in common. But it's love, so we have to go on talking, throwing this nonsense into the air, using up the clock. He has apologized for trying to play softball with me; he admits now that it was a mistake.

When I was small, living with Harold and Ethel Harris and the other Harris children, I knew about my other parents, the aching lovers who had brought me into my life, but I did not miss them. They'd done me my favor and gone on to the rest of their lives. No, the only thing I missed was the world: the oceans, their huge distances, their creatures, the tides, the burning water-light I heard you could see at the equator. I kept a globe nearby my boy's bed. Even though I live here, now, no matter where I ever was, I was always homesick for the rest of the world. My brother docs not understand that. He thinks home is where he is now. I show him maps; I tell him about Turkey and the Azores; I have told him about the great variety and beauty of human pigmentation. He listens but won't take me seriously.

When my brother talks now, he fingers his nose, probably to remind me where I hit him. It's a delicate gesture, with a touch of self-pity. With this gesture he establishes a bit of history between us. He wants to look up to me. He's twenty-eight years old, hasn't ever seen Asia, and he says this to me seriously. Have you ever heard the sound of a man's voice from a minaret? I ask him, but he just smiles. He's already called my wife; he has a whole series of happy endings planned, scene by scene. He wants to sit in a chair and see me come into the room, perfected, thanking the past for all it has done for me.

TOBIAS WOLFF

✤

The Other Miller

For two days now Miller has been standing in the rain with the rest of Bravo Company, waiting for some men from another company to blunder down the logging road where Bravo waits in ambush. When this happens, if this happens, Miller will stick his head out of the hole he is hiding in and shoot off all his blank ammunition in the direction of the road. So will everyone else in Bravo Company. Then they will climb out of their holes and get on some trucks and go home, back to the base.

This is the plan.

Miller has no faith in it. He has never yet seen a plan that worked, and this one won't either. He can tell. For one thing, the lieutenant who thought up the plan has been staying away a lot — "doing recon," he claims, but that's a lie. How can you do recon if you don't know where the enemy is? Miller's foxhole has about a foot of water in it. He has to stand on little shelves he's been digging out of the walls, but the soil is sandy and the shelves keep collapsing. That means his boots are wet. Plus his cigarettes are wet. Plus he broke the bridge on his molars the first night out, while chewing up one of the lollipops he'd brought along for energy. It drives him crazy the way the broken bridge lifts and grates when he pushes it with his tongue, but last night he lost his willpower and now he can't keep his tongue away from it.

When he thinks of the other company, the one they're supposed to ambush, Miller sees a column of dry, well-fed men marching farther and farther away from the hole where he stands waiting for them. He sees them moving easily under light packs. He sees them stopping for a smoke break, stretching out on fragrant beds of pine needles under the trees, the murmur of their voices growing more and more faint as one by one they drift into sleep.

It's the truth, by God. Miller knows it like he knows he's going to catch a cold, because that's his luck. If he were in the other company then they'd be the ones standing in holes.

Miller's tongue does something to the bridge, and a surge of pain shoots through him. He snaps up straight, eyes burning, teeth clenched against the yell in his throat. He fights it back and glares around him at the other men. The few he can see look stunned and ashen-faced. Of the rest he can make out only their poncho hoods. The poncho hoods stick out of the ground like bullet-shaped rocks.

At this moment, his mind swept clean by pain, Miller can hear the tapping of raindrops on his own poncho. Then he hears the pitchy whine of an engine. A jeep is splashing along the road, slipping from side to side and throwing up thick gouts of mud behind it. The jeep itself is caked with mud. It skids to a stop in front of Bravo Company's position, and the horn beeps twice.

Miller glances around to see what the others are doing. Nobody has moved. They're all just standing in their holes.

The horn beeps again.

A short figure in a poncho emerges from a clump of trees farther up the road. Miller can tell it's the first sergeant by how little he is, so little that the poncho hangs almost to his ankles. The first sergeant walks slowly toward the jeep, big blobs of mud all around his boots. When he gets to the jeep, he leans his head inside; he pulls it out again a moment later. He looks

down at the road. He kicks at one of the tires in a thoughtful
way. Then he looks up and shouts Miller's name.

Miller keeps watching him. Not until the first sergeant
shouts his name again does Miller begin the hard work of hoist-
ing himself out of the foxhole. The other men turn their ashen
faces up at him as he trudges past their heads.

"Come here, boy," the first sergeant says. He walks a little
distance from the jeep and waves Miller over.

Miller follows him. Something is wrong. Miller can tell, because the first sergeant called him "boy," instead of "shitbird."
Already he feels a burning in his left side, where his ulcer is.

The first sergeant stares down the road. "Here's the thing,"
he begins. He stops and turns to Miller. "Hell's bells, I don't
know. Goddamn it. Listen. We got a priority here from the Red
Cross. Did you know your mother was sick?"

Miller doesn't say anything. He pushes his lips tight together.

"She must have been sick, right?" When Miller remains silent the first sergeant says, "She passed away last night. I'm real
sorry." The first sergeant looks sadly up at Miller, and Miller
watches his right arm beginning to rise under the poncho; then
it falls to his side again. Miller can see that the first sergeant
wants to give his shoulder a man-to-man kind of squeeze, but it
just won't work. You can only do that if you're taller than the
other fellow, or maybe the same size.

"These boys here will drive you back to base," the first sergeant says, nodding toward the jeep. "You give the Red Cross a
call, and they'll take it from there. Get yourself some rest," he
adds. He turns away and walks off toward the trees.

Miller retrieves his gear. One of the men he passes on his way
back to the jeep says, "Hey, Miller, what's the story?"

Miller doesn't answer. He's afraid that if he opens his mouth
he'll start laughing and ruin everything. He keeps his head
down and his lips tight as he climbs into the back seat of the
jeep, and he doesn't look up again until the company is a mile
or so behind. The fat Pfc. sitting beside the driver is watching

him. He says, "I'm sorry about your mother. That's a bummer."

"Maximum bummer," says the driver, another Pfc. He shoots a look over his shoulder. Miller sees his own face reflected for an instant in the driver's sunglasses.

"Had to happen someday," he mumbles, and looks down again.

Miller's hands are shaking. He puts them between his knees and stares through the snapping plastic window at the trees going past. Raindrops rattle on the canvas overhead. He is inside, and everyone else is still outside. Miller can't stop thinking about the others standing around getting rained on, and the thought makes him want to laugh and slap his leg. This is the luckiest he has ever been.

"My grandmother died last year," the driver says. "But that's not the same thing as losing your mother. I feel for you, Miller."

"Don't worry about me," Miller tells him. "I'll get along."

The fat Pfc. beside the driver says, "Look, don't feel like you have to repress just because we're here. If you want to cry or anything just go ahead. Right, Leb?"

The driver nods. "Just let it out."

"No problem," Miller says. He wishes he could set these fellows straight, so they won't feel like they have to act mournful all the way to Fort Ord. But if he tells them what happened they'll turn right around and drive him back to his foxhole.

This is what happened. Another Miller in the battalion has the same initials he's got, W. P., and this Miller is the one whose mother has died. His father passed away during the summer and Miller got that message by mistake too. So he has the lay of the land now; as soon as the first sergeant started asking about his mother, he got the entire picture.

For once, everybody else is on the outside and Miller is on the inside. Inside, on his way to a hot shower, dry clothes, a pizza, and a warm bunk. He didn't even have to do anything wrong to get here; he just did as he was told. It was their own mistake. Tomorrow he'll rest up like the first sergeant ordered him to, go on sick call about his bridge, maybe go downtown to a movie after that. Then he'll call the Red Cross. By the time they get everything straightened out it will be too late to send him back to the field. And the best thing is, the other Miller won't know. The other Miller will have a whole other day of thinking his mother is still alive. You could even say that Miller is keeping her alive for him.

The man beside the driver turns around again and studies Miller. He has little dark eyes in a round, baby-white face covered with beads of sweat. His name tag reads KAISER. Showing little square teeth like a baby's, he says, "You're really coping, Miller. Most guys pretty much lose it when they get the word."

"I would too," the driver says. "Anybody would. Or maybe I should say almost anybody. It's *human,* Kaiser."

"For sure," Kaiser says. "I'm not saying any different. That's going to be my worst day, the day my mom dies." He blinks rapidly, but not before Miller sees his little eyes mist up.

"Everybody has to go sometime," Miller says. "Sooner or later. That's my philosophy."

"Heavy," the driver says. "Really deep."

Kaiser gives him a sharp look and says, "At ease, Lebowitz."

Miller leans forward. Lebowitz is a Jewish name. That means Lebowitz must be a Jew. Miller wants to ask him why he's in the Army, but he's afraid Lebowitz might take it wrong. Instead, he says, conversationally, "You don't see too many Jewish people in the Army nowadays."

Lebowitz looks into the rearview mirror. His thick eyebrows arch over his sunglasses, and then he shakes his head and says something Miller can't make out

"At ease, Leb," Kaiser says again. He turns to Miller and asks him where the funeral is going to be held.

"What funeral?" Miller says.

Lebowitz laughs.

"Back off," Kaiser says. "Haven't you ever heard of shock?"

Lebowitz is quiet for a moment. Then he looks into the rear-view mirror again and says, "Sorry, Miller. I was out of line."

Miller shrugs. His probing tongue pushes the bridge too hard and he stiffens suddenly.

"Where did your mom live?" Kaiser asks.

"Redding," Miller says.

Kaiser nods. "Redding," he repeats. He keeps watching Miller. So does Lebowitz, glancing back and forth between the mirror and the road. Miller understands that they expected a different kind of performance from the one he's given them, more emotional and all. They have seen other personnel whose mothers died and now they have certain standards that he has failed to live up to. He looks out the window. They are driving along a ridgeline. Slices of blue flicker between the trees on the left-hand side of the road; then they hit a space without trees and Miller can see the ocean below them, clear to the horizon under a bright cloudless sky. Except for a few hazy wisps in the treetops they've left the clouds behind, back in the mountains, hanging over the soldiers there.

"Don't get me wrong," Miller says. "I'm sorry she'd dead."

Kaiser says, "That's the way. Talk it out."

"It's just that I didn't know her all that well," Miller says, and after this monstrous lie a feeling of weightlessness comes over him. At first it makes him uncomfortable, but almost immediately he begins to enjoy it. From now on he can say anything.

He makes a sad face and says, "I guess I'd be more broken up and so on if she hadn't taken off on us the way she did. Right in the middle of harvest season. Just leaving us like that."

"I'm hearing a lot of anger," Kaiser tells him. "Ventilate. Own it."

Miller got that stuff from a song, but he can't remember any more. He lowers his head and looks at his boots. "Killed my dad," he says, after a time. "Died of a broken heart. Left me with five kids to raise, not to mention the farm." Miller closes his eyes. He sees a field all plowed up with the sun setting behind it, a bunch of kids coming in from the field with rakes and hoes on their shoulders. As the jeep winds down through the switchbacks he describes his hardships as the oldest child in this family. He is at the end of his story when they reach the coast highway and turn north. All at once the jeep stops rattling and swaying. They pick up speed. The tires hum on the smooth road. The rushing air whistles a single note around the radio antenna. "Anyway," Miller says, "it's been two years since I even had a letter from her."

"You should make a movie," Lebowitz says.

Miller isn't sure how to take this. He waits to hear what else Lebowitz has to say, but Lebowitz is silent. So is Kaiser, who's had his back turned to Miller for several minutes now. Both men stare at the road ahead of them. Miller can see that they have lost interest in him. He is disappointed, because he was having a fine time pulling their leg.

One thing Miller told them was true: he hasn't had a letter from his mother in two years. She wrote him a lot when he first joined the Army, at least once a week, sometimes twice, but Miller sent all her letters back unopened and after a year of this she finally gave up. She tried calling a few times but Miller wouldn't go to the telephone, so she gave that up too. Miller wants her to understand that her son is not a man to turn the other cheek. He is a serious man. Once you've crossed him, you've lost him.

Miller's mother crossed him by marrying a man she shouldn't have married: Phil Dove. Dove was a biology teacher in the high school. Miller was having trouble in the course, and his mother went to talk to Dove about it and ended up getting engaged to him. Miller tried to reason with her, but she wouldn't hear a word. You would think from the way she acted that she had landed herself a real catch instead of someone who talked with a stammer and spent his life taking crayfish apart.

Miller did everything he could to stop the marriage but his mother had blinded herself. She couldn't see what she already had, how good it was with just the two of them. How he was always there when she got home from work, with a pot of coffee already brewed. The two of them drinking their coffee together and talking about different things, or maybe not talking at all — maybe just sitting in the kitchen while the room got dark around them, until the telephone rang or the dog started whining to get out. Walking the dog around the reservoir. Coming back and eating whatever they wanted, sometimes nothing, sometimes the same dish three or four nights in a row, watching the programs they wanted to watch and going to bed when they wanted to and not because some other person wanted them to. Just being together in their own place.

Phil Dove got Miller's mother so mixed up that she forgot how good their life was. She refused to see what she was ruining. "You'll be leaving anyway," she told him. "You'll be moving on, next year or the year after" — which showed how wrong she was about Miller, because he would never have left her, not ever, not for anything. But when he said this she laughed as if she knew better, as if he wasn't serious. He was serious, though. He was serious when he promised he'd stay and he was serious when he promised he'd never speak to her again if she married Phil Dove.

She married him. Miller stayed at a motel that night and two more nights, until he ran out of money. Then he joined the Army. He knew that would get to her, because he was still a month shy of finishing high school, and because his father had been killed while serving in the Army. Not in Vietnam but in Georgia, killed in an accident. He and another man were dipping mess kits in a garbage can full of boiling water and somehow the can fell over on him. Miller was six at the time. Miller's mother hated the Army after that, not because her husband was dead — she knew about the war he was going to, she knew about snipers and booby traps and mines — but because of the way it happened. She said the Army couldn't even get a man killed in a decent fashion.

She was right, too. The Army was just as bad as she thought, and worse. You spent all your time waiting around. You lived a completely stupid existence. Miller hated every minute of it, but he found pleasure in his hatred, because he believed that his mother must know how unhappy he was. That knowledge would be a grief to her. It would not be as bad as the grief she had given him, which was spreading from his heart into his stomach and teeth and everywhere else, but it was the worst grief he had power to cause, and it would serve to keep her in mind of him.

KAISER AND LEBOWITZ are describing hamburgers to each other. Their idea of the perfect hamburger. Miller tries not to listen but their voices go on, and after a while he can't think of anything but beefsteak tomatoes and Gulden's mustard and steaming, onion-stuffed meat crisscrossed with black marks from the grill. He is on the point of asking them to change the subject when Kaiser turns and says, "Think you can handle some chow?"

"I don't know," Miller says. "I guess I could get something down."

"We were talking about a pit stop. But if you want to keep going, just say the word. It's your ball game. I mean, technically we're supposed to take you straight back to base."

"I could eat," Miller says.

"That's the spirit. At a time like this you've got to keep your strength up."

"I could eat," Miller says again.

Lebowitz looks up into the rearview mirror, shakes his head, and looks away again.

They take the next turnoff and drive inland to a crossroads where two gas stations face two restaurants. One of the restaurants is boarded up, so Lebowitz pulls into the parking lot of the Dairy Queen across the road. He turns the engine off and the three men sit motionless in the sudden silence that follows.

It soon begins to fade. Miller hears the distant clang of metal on metal, the caw of a crow, the creak of Kaiser shifting in his seat. A dog barks in front of a rust-streaked trailer next door. A skinny white dog with yellow eyes. As it barks the dog rubs itself, one leg raised and twitching, against a sign that shows an outspread hand below the words KNOW YOUR FUTURE.

They get out of the jeep, and Miller follows Kaiser and Lebowitz across the parking lot. The air is warm and smells of oil. In the gas station across the road a pink-skinned man in a swimming suit is trying to put air in the tires of his bicycle, jerking at the hose and swearing loudly at his inability to make the pump work. Miller pushes his tongue against the broken bridge. He lifts it gently. He wonders if he should try eating a hamburger, and decides that it can't hurt as long as he is careful to chew on the other side of his mouth.

But it does hurt. After the first couple of bites Miller shoves his plate away. He rests his chin on one hand and listens to Lebowitz and Kaiser argue about whether people can actually tell the future. Lebowitz is talking about a girl he used to know who had ESP. "We'd be driving along," he says, "and out of the blue she would tell me exactly what I was thinking about. It was unbelievable."

Kaiser finishes his hamburger and takes a drink of milk. "No big deal," he says. "I could do that." He pulls Miller's hamburger over to his side of the table and takes a bite.

"Go ahead," Lebowitz says. "Try it. I'm not thinking about what you think I'm thinking about," he adds.

"Yes, you are."

"All right, now I am," Lebowitz says, "but I wasn't before."

"I wouldn't let a fortune-teller get near me," Miller says. "The way I see it, the less you know the better off you are."

"More vintage philosophy from the private stock of W. P. Miller," Lebowitz says. He looks at Kaiser, who is eating the last of Miller's hamburger. "Well, how about it? I'm up for it if you are."

Kaiser chews ruminatively. He swallows and licks his lips.

"Sure," he says. "Why not? As long as Miller here doesn't mind."

"Mind what?" Miller asks.

Lebowitz stands and puts his sunglasses back on. "Don't worry about Miller. Miller's cool. Miller keeps his head when men all around him are losing theirs."

Kaiser and Miller get up from the table and follow Lebowitz outside. Lebowitz is bending down in the shade of a dumpster, wiping off his boots with a paper towel. Shiny blue flies buzz around him. "Mind what?" Miller repeats.

"We thought we'd check out the prophet," Kaiser tells him.

Lebowitz straightens up, and the three of them start across the parking lot.

"I'd actually kind of like to get going," Miller says. When they reach the jeep he stops, but Lebowitz and Kaiser walk on. "Now, listen," Miller says, and skips a little to catch up. "I have a lot to do," he says to their backs. "I want to go home."

"We know how broken up you are," Lebowitz tells him. He keeps walking.

"This shouldn't take too long," Kaiser says.

The dog barks once and then, when it sees that they really intend to come within range of its teeth, runs around the trailer. Lebowitz knocks on the door. It swings open, and there stands a round-faced woman with dark, sunken eyes and heavy lips. One of her eyes has a cast; it seems to be watching something beside her while the other looks down at the three soldiers at her door. Her hands are covered with flour. She is a gypsy, an actual gypsy. Miller has never seen a gypsy before, but he recognizes her just as he would recognize a wolf if he saw one. Her presence makes his blood pound in his veins. If he lived in this place he would come back at night with some other men, all of them yelling and waving torches, and drive her out.

"You on duty?" Lebowitz asks.

She nods, wiping her hands on her skirt. They leave chalky streaks on the bright patchwork. "All of you?" she asks.

"You bet," Kaiser says. His voice is unnaturally loud.

She nods again and turns her good eye from Lebowitz to Kaiser, and then to Miller. After she takes Miller in she smiles and rattles off a string of strange sounds, words from another language or maybe a spell, as if she expects him to understand. One of her front teeth is black.

"No," Miller says. "No, ma'am. Not me." He shakes his head.

"Come," she says, and stands aside.

Lebowitz and Kaiser mount the steps and disappear into the trailer. "Come," the woman repeats. She beckons with her white hands.

Miller backs away, still shaking his head. "Leave me alone," he tells her, and before she can answer he turns and walks away. He goes back to the jeep and sits in the driver's seat, leaving both doors open to catch the breeze. Miller feels the heat drawing the dampness out of his fatigues. He can smell the musty wet canvas overhead and the sourness of his own body. Through the windshield, covered with mud except for a pair of grimy half-circles, he watches three boys solemnly urinating against the wall of the gas station across the road.

Miller bends down to loosen his boots. Blood rushes to his face as he fights the wet laces, and his breath comes faster and faster. "Goddamn laces," he says. "Goddamn rain. Goddamn Army." He gets the laces untied and sits up, panting. He stares at the trailer. Goddamn gypsy.

He can't believe those two fools actually went inside there. Yukking it up. Playing around. That shows how stupid they are, because anybody knows that you don't play around with fortune-tellers. There is no predicting what a fortune-teller might say, and once it's said, no way to keep it from happening. Once you hear what's out there it isn't out there anymore, it's here. You might as well open your door to a murderer as to the future.

The future. Didn't everybody know enough about the future already, without digging up the details? There is only one thing you have to know about the future: everything gets

worse. Once you have that, you have it all. The specifics don't
bear thinking about.

Miller certainly has no intention of thinking about the specifics. He peels off his damp socks and massages his white crin-
kled feet. Now and then he glances up toward the trailer,
where the gypsy is pronouncing fate on Kaiser and Lebowitz.
Miller makes humming noises. He will not think about the future.

Because it's true — everything gets worse. One day you are
sitting in front of your house, poking sticks into an anthill,
hearing the chink of silverware and the voices of your mother
and father in the kitchen ; then, at some moment you can't even
remember, one of those voices is gone And you never hear it
again. When you go from today to tomorrow you're walking
into an ambush.

A new boy, Nat Pranger, joins your Little League team. He
lives in a boardinghouse a couple of streets over from you. The
first day you meet Nat you show him the place under the
bleachers where you keep the change you steal from your
mother. The next morning you remember doing this, and you
push your half-eaten breakfast away and run to the ball park,
blindly, your chest hurting. The change is still in its hiding
place. You count it. Not a penny is missing. You kneel there in
the shadows, catching your breath.

All summer you and Nat throw each other grounders and
develop plans to acquire a large sailboat for use in the South
Seas — that is Nat's term, "the South Seas." Then school starts,
your first year of junior high, and Nat makes other friends but
you don't, because something about you turns people cruel.
Even the teachers. You want to have friends, you would
change if you knew what it was that needed changing, but you
don't know. You see Nat struggling to be loyal and you hate
him for it. His kindness is worse than cruelty. By December
you know exactly how things will be in June. All you can do is
watch it happen.

What lies ahead doesn't bear thinking about. Already Miller has an ulcer, and his teeth are full of holes. His body is giving out on him. What will it be like when he's sixty? Or even five years from now? Miller was in a restaurant the other day and saw a fellow about his own age in a wheelchair, getting fed soup by a woman who was talking to some other people at the table. This boy's hands lay twisted in his lap like gloves dropped there; his pants had crawled halfway to his knees, showing pale, wasted legs no thicker than bones. He could barely move his head. The woman feeding him did a lousy job because she was too busy blabbing to her friends. Half the soup went over the boy's shirt. Yet his eyes were bright and watchful.

Miller thought, *That could happen to me.*

You could be going along just fine and then one day, through no fault of your own, something could get loose in your bloodstream and knock out part of your brain. Leave you like that. And if it didn't happen now, all at once, it was sure to happen slowly later on. That was the end you were bound for.

Someday Miller is going to die. He knows that, and he prides himself on knowing it when other people only pretend to know it, secretly believing that they will live forever. This is not the reason that the future is unthinkable to Miller. There is something worse than that, something not to be considered, and he will not consider it.

He will not consider it. Miller leans back against the seat and closes his eyes, but his effort to trick himself into somnolence fails. Behind his eyelids he is wide awake and fidgety with gloom, probing against his will for what he is afraid to find, until, with no surprise at all, he finds it. A simple truth. His mother is also going to die. Just like him. And there is no telling when. Miller cannot count on her to be there to come home to, and receive his pardon, when he finally decides that she has suffered enough.

Miller opens his eyes and looks at the raw shapes of the buildings across the road, their outlines lost in the grime on the windshield. He closes his eyes again. He listens to himself breathe and feels the familiar, almost muscular ache of knowing that he is beyond his mother's reach. He has put himself where she cannot see him or speak to him or touch him in that thoughtless way of hers, resting her hand on his shoulder as she stops behind his chair to ask him a question or just stand for a moment, her mind somewhere else. This was supposed to be her punishment, but somehow it has become his own. He understands that it has to stop. It is killing him.

It has to stop now, and as if he has been planning for this day all along Miller knows exactly what he will do. Instead of reporting to the Red Cross when he gets back to base, he will pack his bag and catch the first bus home. No one will blame him for this. Even when they discover the mistake they've made they still won't blame him, because it would be the natural thing for a grieving son to do. Instead of punishing him they will probably apologize for giving him a scare.

He will take the first bus home, express or not. It will be full of Mexicans and soldiers. Miller will sit by a window and drowse. Now and then he will come up from his dreams to stare out at the passing green hills and loamy plowland and the stations where the bus puts in, stations cloudy with exhaust and loud with engine roar, where the people he sees through his window will look groggily back at him as if they too have just come up from sleep. Salinas. Vacaville. Red Bluff. When he gets to Redding, Miller will hire a cab. He will ask the driver to stop at Schwartz's for a few minutes while he buys some flowers, and then he will ride on home, down Sutter and over to Serra, past the ball park, past the grade school, past the Mormon church. Right on Belmont. Left on Park. Leaning over the seat, saying farther, farther, a little farther, that's it, that one, there.

The sound of voices behind the door as he rings the bell. Door swings open, voices hush. Who are these people? Men in suits, women wearing white gloves. Someone stammers his name, strange to him now, almost forgotten. "W-W-Wesley." A man's voice. He stands just inside the door, breathing perfume. Then the flowers are taken from his hand and laid with other flowers on the coffee table. He hears his name again. It is Phil Dove, moving toward him from across the room. He walks slowly, with his arms raised, like a blind man.

Wesley, he says. Thank God you're home.

FREDERICK BUSCH

✤

Dog Song

I

He always thought of the dogs as the worst. The vet's belly heaved above his jeans, and he cursed in words of one syllable every time a deputy tugged a dog to the hypodermic, or trotted to keep up as a different one strained on its chain for its fate, or when a dog stopped moving and went stiff, splayed, and then became a loose furry bag with bones inside. The deputies and the vet and the judge, who also did his part — he watched without moving — did it twenty-six times, in the yard behind the sheriff's offices. The air stank of dirty fur and feces as though they were all locked in. The yelping and whining went on. When they were through, one deputy was weeping, and the vet's red flannel shirt was wet with sweat from his breastbone to his belt. The deputies threw the dogs into the back of a van.

They might be dangerous, Snuyder had decided. They might have been somehow perverted, trained to break some basic rules of how to live with men. So they had died. And Snuyder, doing his part, had watched them until the last lean mutt, shivering and funny-eyed, was dead. He thought, when he thought of the dogs, that their lips and tails and even their postures had signaled their devotion to the vet or to one of the deputies; they'd been waiting for a chance to give their love. And as the deputies flung them, the dogs' tongues protruded

and sometimes flopped. When their bodies flew, they looked
ardent.

The dogs in the yellow trailer had drawn the attention of the
people in the white trailer across the unpaved rural road : their
howling, their yapping, the whining that sometimes went on
and on and on. Lloyd and Pris, the man and wife in the trailer
with the dogs, came and went at curious hours, and that too at-
tracted the attention of the neighbors, who had their own
problems, but somehow found time — being good country
Christians, they *made* time — to study the erratic behavior and
possible social pathology of the couple in the bright yellow
trailer edged in white, propped on cinderblocks, bolstered
against upstate winters by haybales pushed between the plastic
floor and the icy mud. The neighbors, one working as a janitress, the other as a part-time van driver for the county's geri-
atric ferrying service, finally called the sheriff when there was a
February thaw, and the mud all of a sudden looked awfully like
manure, and an odor came up from the yellow trailer that, according to the janitress (a woman named Ivy), was too much
like things long dead to be ignored by a citizen of conscience.

But only one of the dogs was dead, and it died after the deputies had kicked the door in, and after it had attacked and had
been shot. It died defending a mobile home that was alive with
excrement and garbage. Turds lay on the beds and on the
higher surfaces, counter and sink. Madness crawled the walls.
Lloyd, the husband, had written with dung his imprecations of
a county and state and nation that established laws involving
human intercourse with beasts. Twenty-six dogs were impounded, and the couple was heavily fined by the judge.

The awful part, of course, had been the dogs' dull eyes and
duller coats, their stink, their eagerness to please, and then
their fear, and then the way they had died. Later he decided
that the nurse with her hair that was thinning and her arms
puffed out around the short, tight sleeves of her hissing uniform was the worst part so far. The first sight Richard Snuyder
had seen, when he fell awake like a baby rolling from its crib,

had been a man on crutches at his door, peering. The man had sucked on an unlit filter cigarette, adjusted his armpits on the crutches, and had said, "I heard you did one *jam*-jar of a job. Just thought I'd say so. I was raised to express my appreciation of the passing joys."

Snuyder, hours later, had thought that the man on crutches, apparently a connoisseur of catastrophe, was the worst. He wasn't. The worst became the orderly who brought in a plate of mashed potatoes and open hot roast-beef sandwich in glutinous gravy, who was chased by the nurse who brought the doctor, whose odor of dark, aged sweat and stale clothing did little to dispel that of the roast beef, which lingered in the room as if the pale orderly had hurled it on the walls to punish Snuyder for being on a liquid diet.

The doctor, who had mumbled and left, Snuyder thought for a while, was really the worst part of it: his dandruff, his caustic smell, his dirty knuckles that gave the lie to the large scraped moons of fingernail above the tortured cuticles. This is the worst, Snuyder had thought, though not for long.

Because then the candy striper with her twitchy walk and bored pout had stood at his door, a clipboard in her hand and an idle finger at her ear, though carefully never in it, and had looked at him as though he weren't open-eyed, blinking, panting with pain, clearly stunned and afraid and as lost while being still as dogs are that stand at the side of the road, about to be killed because they don't know what else they should do.

After the candy striper had left, the balding nurse with great arms, and no need for such forms of address as language spoken or mimed, came in to adjust something at his head and something at his leg. His neck didn't roll, so he couldn't follow her movements except with his eyes, which began to ache and then stream. Looking at his legs, she wiped his eyes and took the tissue away. He was about to ask her questions but couldn't think of anything that didn't embarrassingly begin with *Where* or *How*.

He tried to move his legs. That was next, as soon as the nurse left. He worked at wiggling his toes and each foot and each leg. They moved, though they were restrained by something, and he called aloud — it was a relief, during the cry, to hear his own voice and to know that he knew it — because the right leg was pure pain, undifferentiated, and the left, though more flexible, hurt only a little less. His legs, and the stiffness at the neck, his aching eyes and head, a burning on the skin of his face, the waking to no memory of how he had come there, or why, or when, or in what state: *he* was the worst so far. He suspected that little would happen to challenge this triumph. He'd been born someplace, of an unknown event, and every aspect of his arrival on this naked day could be measured against the uncomforting hypothesis that, among the local discomforts he knew, he himself was the worst.

His legs could not be moved, he could not be persuaded to move them again, and he lay with all his attention on his torso, thinking *I will be just chest and balls, I will not be legs or ankles or toes.* He panicked and felt for his legs, then moved an ankle — he yelped — in response to his fear: he did have his legs, and they would move at his command, he wasn't only a chest. *And balls?* He groaned his fear, and groaned for the pain in his legs, and then he groaned with deep contentment: he had found them under his hospital gown, both of them, and everything else, including the dreadful catheter. So all he needed to know now was when he would stop hurting over most of his body, and why and how he was here. *All right. First things first. You have legs, your balls are where you left them, and a little panic is worth a handful of testes during times of trial.*

I have not gone berserk with worry for my wife, he thought.

Do I have a wife?

How do I know my name, if I don't know whether I'm married? How did I know about balls? Are you born with a full knowledge of the scrotum? So that even during amnesia, you still —

I don't want *amnesia.*

I don't want *to be a pendulum in a ward, swinging on crutches and sucking on cold cigarettes and laughing at people forever and never* remembering.

What about my kids, if I do have kids?

The same nurse, with thin dark hair and wide white arms, was at the head of his bed, looking into his eyes this time as she wiped them. She had the voice of a twelve-year-old girl, and the teeth of someone long dead. She said, "Mister Snuyder? Do you remember you're Mister Snuyder?"

He tried to nod. The pain made him hiss.

"We'll give you something for pain after we X-ray your head again. But could you tell me if you know your name?"

"Thank you," he said.

"Yes. And your name?"

"Woke up knowing it was Snuyder"

"Good *boy*!"

"Woke up. Found out I had my scrotum, and I never knew if I had any children or a *wife*." He was crying. He hated it.

"You'll remember," she said. "You'll probably remember. You did take out a telephone pole and a good I say at least half of a Great American Markets rig. Worcestershire sauce and mustard and beerwurst smeared over two lancs for a quarter of a mile. If you don't mind glass, you could make a hell of a sandwich out there, they said."

"Kill anybody? Did I kill anybody?"

"Not unless *you* die on us. The truck was parked. Trucker was — how do you want to put it? — banging the lady of the house? You must of pulled a stupendous skid. The troopers'll be by to talk about it."

"Did you look in my wallet?"

"Doctor'll be by too. I'm off-duty now."

"You don't want to tell me about my family? There wasn't anybody with me, was there?"

"You're supposed to remember on your own. There wasn't anybody killed. You take care now."

"Won't dance with anyone else."

"Good boy."

"Wait," he said. "Wait a minute." He winced. He lay back. He heard himself breathe.

She said, "That's right. You lie down and be good. Good boy."

HE WOKE AGAIN, with a thump, waiting for the nurse to speak. He saw that she was gone, the room dark, the door closed. He couldn't remember waking, ever before in his life, so abruptly, and with so much pain. And that wasn't all he couldn't remember. He thought *baby, baby, baby* to himself, as if in a rapture, and he tried to think of a lover or wife. Was he divorced? What about kids? He thought a gentler *baby* and looked within his closed eyes for children. He thought of maps — blank. He thought of cars and couldn't see the one he'd driven. He remembered that the nurse had evaded the question of who had been with him. But at least she wasn't dead.

And how had he known that his passenger was a woman? And how could he know he was right?

He was tired of questions and tired of hurting. He remembered, then, how they had rolled him through the halls for a CAT-scan and how, when he'd been rolled back, they had looked at him like magic people who could make him fall a-sleep, and he had fallen. He wanted more magic. He wanted to sleep some more and wake again and know one thing more. A woman in the car with him. Should she have been with him in the car? Should she have come with him to this room?

And he woke again, one more question not answered, to see a light that sliced at his eyeballs and to hear a general commotion that suggested daytime and what he had doubtless once referred to as everyday life. The door opened in, and Hilary was inside with him, and through dry lips he said, "I *remember* you!"

She said, "Can you see how little I'm cheered by that?"

No: she started to; he finished her statement in his mind, fed by memory, and he smiled so triumphantly, his face hurt. In fact, Hilary said, "Can you see — "

And he said, "Hilary. Hil."

She shook her head as if winged insects were at her, and then she wept into her wide, strong hands, walking slowly toward him, a child at a hiding game. But she was not a child and there were no children — not here, anyway, because the boys were at school, of course, and he and Hilary, Richard and Hilary Snyder, were alone, they were each forty-seven years old, and they were working at being alone together while Warren and Hank went to school in other states. The states were *other* because this one was New York. Hilary was tall, and she wore her pea jacket, so it must be autumn, and her upper lip came down on the lower one as if she wanted to make love. Richard did, then, and his hand went down to grip himself in celebration where it had earlier prodded for loss. "Hilary," he said. The catheter guarded his loins, and his hand retreated.

She wiped at her eyes and sat on the chair beside the bed.

"Come sit on the bed," he said.

She sat back. She crossed her legs, and he looked with a sideways glance to see her jeans and Wallabees. His eyes stung, so he looked up. He sniffed, expecting to smell perfume or soap. He smelled only gravy and the finger-chewing doctor. And Hilary said, "How could you decide on — going away like that?" She said, "How could you *do* that? No matter what?"

"Hil, I'm having a hell of a time remembering things. I didn't remember *you* until you came in, the boys and you and — would you tell me stuff? You know, to kind of wake me up some more? I don't remember going anyplace. They said I smacked the car up."

Hilary stood, and something on her sweet, pale face made him move. The motion made him whimper, and she smiled with genuine pleasure. Her long hand, suspended above him, was trembling. He felt her anger. His penis burned. He closed his eyes but opened them at once. He was afraid of her hand descending to seize him as if in love or recollected lust, but then to squeeze, to crush the catheter and leave him coughing up his pain and bleeding up into the blanket. He saw her playing the piano with strong bloody hands, leaving a trail of blood on the keys.

She said, "I have to go outside until I calm down. I'll go outside and then I'll be back. Because unlike you I do *not* run out on the people I love. Loved. But I'll leave you a clue. You want to remember things? You want a little trail of bread crumbs you can follow back into your life? How about this, Richard: you drove our fucking car as hard as you could into a telephone pole so you could die. Is that a little crust of some usefulness? So you could leave me forever on purpose. Have I helped?"

The awful doctor came back again, adding the insult of his breath to the injury of his armpits. He was thick, with a drooping heavy chest and shoulders that came down at a very sharp angle, so that his thick neck looked long. His fingers were large, and the knuckles looked dirtier now — this morning, tonight, whenever it was that the doctor stood at the bed, telling Richard where the orthopedic surgeon was going to insert pins of assorted sizes and alloys into the hip and femur, which the instrument panel had cracked in an interesting way. The neck was all right. The back was all right. The head seemed all right, though you never can tell with the brain. A little rancid laugh, a flicker of motion across the big jowls and their five o'clock shadow. And the ribs, of course, although CAT pictures showed no danger to the lungs. "You'll be bound."

"I'm a judge," Snuyder said.

"Good man."

"I'm a district judge with a house in the suburbs and a wife and two kids and two cars. Three cars. We have an old Volvo my son Hank fixed up. A '67 Volvo. It runs pretty well, but it's rusted out. Bound over — you say that when — "

"Yes, you're a judge. Good man. I was talking about a restraint for the ribs, is all. Two ribs. You're lucky."

"Of course, I'm lucky. And I didn't aim to hit some tele-phone pole."

"You remember what happened?"

"No. But I wouldn't have. People with a — people like me don't *do* that."

The doctor looked bitter and weary. "No," he said. "I can call the rescue squad, if you like, and ask them to take you back and drop you off at your car. I'd have to call the garage and tell them that it isn't telescoped. Totaled. All but small enough to use for a Matchbox toy if the grandchildren come over. Of course, you'll probably benefit by using less gas in it from now on."

Richard blushed. He couldn't shut up, though. He said, "I meant suicide."

"I know."

"I meant people like me don't *do* that."

"You want anything for pain?"

"No."

"Don't be stubborn, Your Honor. A petulant patient is still a patient in pain. Can be. Call the nurse if you hurt. I'll leave or-ders in case you do. I'll see you before they sedate you. It might be soon, but I think they'll wait until tomorrow, or late this af-ternoon. We're crowded. Sick people, you know."

"Unlike me."

The doctor let his face say that he was ignoring Richard's childishness. And Richard felt an overwhelming need to cry.

"So if you're so crowded, how come you put me in a private room. Why don't you keep a suicide watch on me? Who *says* it's suicide?"

"First of all, we didn't. Second of all: Two kids in a car, one pedestrian walking her dogs, the cop who was chasing you for DWI and reckless endangerment and all the other violations you probably pronounce on people at your place of work. I'm going. We aren't having much of a doctor-patient relationship right now."

And when he left, Richard lay back, breathless with rage. He panted with hatred for his wife and his doctor, the nurse, the orderly, the hospital, the cops behind him during the chase, and the fact that he had not slowed down when they came into his mirror, no siren on but a band of white and red light that made him blink before — he suddenly could see himself — he crouched over the wheel and then leaned back, pushing his arms straight, locked at the elbows, jamming the accelerator down until the bellow of the engine and wind and, then, the siren of the following police, were almost as loud as the howl that he howled and that he kept on howling until the impact shut him, and everything else, up.

He heard his breath shudder now, in the salmon-colored room, mostly shadows and walnut veneers. Then he heard a man say, "You wanna nurse?"

"Who?"

"It's me. You can't turn, huh? Listen, Your Honor, it's such a pain in the ass as well as the armpit, the crutches, I'm gonna stay flat for a while. I'll visit you later on, you can look at me and remember. I'm the guy said hello the other time."

"You're in here with me?"

"Yeah. Ain't it an insult? You a judge and everything. Like the doctor said, it's real crowded."

"This is *too* crowded."

"Well, listen, don't go extending any special treatment to me, Your Honor. Just pretend I'm a piece of dog shit. You'll feel better if you don't strain for the little courtesies and all. Your wife's a very attractive woman, if I may say so. Hell of a temper, though."

Richard rang for the nurse.

His roommate said, "All that pain. Dear, dear. Listen, remember this when you wake up. My name's Manwarren. Emanuel Manwarren. Manny Manwarren. It's an honor to be with a Your Honor kind of deal." Then, to the entering nurse: "His Honor is in discomfort."

Richard lay with his eyes closed until the nurse returned with water and a large capsule. He looked at her. She was young and intelligent-looking, and very tired. He said, "How shall I take this medicine without drowning? I can't sit up."

She said, "He ordered it by spansule." Her voice was flat. She was expecting a fight.

"He would," Richard said. "What if I die taking medicine?" He heard himself: he sounded worried about dying.

"Don't fret," she said. "I'll telephone for an order change, and I'll bring you a shot."

"You're a charmer, Your Honor," Manwarren said.

"Are we going to engage in class warfare, or whatever this is, for all the time we're in here? Mister Manwarren?"

"Call me Manny. Nah. I'm a prickly personality. I hate the cops, authority figures like that, judges — you know what I mean?"

"Manny, why don't you think of me as a miscreant and not a judge."

"Can I call you Dick?"

Richard closed his eyes and listened to his breathing and the rustle of Manwarren's sheets. The pain was in Richard's bones and in his breath. He said, "There *was* someone with me, wasn't there?"

"Dick, in cases like this, there usually is."

II

THEY LIVED in a renovated carriage house at the edge of a small country road outside Utica. Simple country living at a condominium price, Hilary liked to say. They couldn't quite afford the mortgage, college tuitions, cars, the Macintosh stereo rig — Snuyder felt like a pilot when he turned the power on — or the carpets from Iran or Iraq or India, he forgot which, that Hilary had lately come to buy as investments. He thought of them as insulation.

Looking at his lighted house at 1:25 in the morning, observing a close, clear disk of moon, a sky bluer than black, and veined with cloud — it was a dark marble mural more than sky — Richard said, "We get by."

Hilary was in the living room, at the piano. She was playing little clear crystal sounds with occasional speeded-up patterns of dissonance. He watched the tall, pale woman at the piano, her body rigid, neck tense, all pleasure residing below her moving wrists.

"Hello," Snuyder said softly, removing his jacket and then his tie, dumping them on the sofa. "I was working with the clerks on a case. It's a terrible case. Then we went out for some drinks."

The repetitions in the music came in miniature parts and were very simple. There was a name for that. He was unbuttoning his shirt and he had it off by the time she sensed him and stopped and turned on the piano bench to see him wiping the sweat on his chest with the wadded shirt.

"Ugh," she said, covering her eyes with her big hands.

"How."

"Richard, stop. It's ugly."

"It's a sweaty night," he said. He went for his welcoming kiss. She hugged his waist and kissed his belly.

"Yummy," he said.

"Salty," she said. "Phoo." But she held him, and he stayed there. "Vhere vas you so late?"

"I told you — clerks? case? Just now?"

Richard carried his guilt and his dirty shirt toward the shower and Hilary followed. She stood in the doorway as he slid the cloudy shower door closed and made a screen of water that sealed him away. He groaned and blubbered and shook his head and shoulders and, loosening at last, dopey with comfort, shed of the sweat and oils and inner fluids of somebody else, he heard only part of what Hilary had said.

He called, "What?"

He turned the water off, and her words came over the stall.

"I said you sounded especially like a whale tonight."

"Thank you. You did not. The Satie was beautiful."

"Thank *you*. It was Villa-Lobos, a Chôros. I don't think it's possible to confuse the two unless you've got me at the piano, the Snuyder Variations, eh?"

"Hilary."

"Sorry. Sorry."

"A number of other performers also dislike playing to a live audience. Glen Gould, I remind you, for the one-millionth time, stopped playing concerts altogether. He was not, I think you'll agree, a shabby tickler of the ivories."

"Can you see how *little* I'm cheered by that? I'm sorry Gould is dead. I wish he'd been comfortable at concerts. But he made *recordings*, Richard. He made wonderful recordings."

"And you will too. It'll happen." He made his voice sound matter-of-fact, sincerely casual, casually sincere. But he knew how impatient he must sound to her.

He had intended to leap from the shower, dangle his body before her, and roll her into bed — and pray for performance this third time tonight. But when he came out, tail wagging and his smile between his teeth like a fetched stick, she was gone, his stomach was fluttering with premonitions, and he was very, very tired. He decided to settle for a glass of beer and some sleep. Hilary was in the kitchen when, wearing his towel, he walked in. She was peeling plastic wrap from a sandwich, and she had already poured him a beer. "You always want beer after a day like this. At least I can make the meals."

Richard drank some beer and said, "Thank you. You're very kind, though sullen and self-pitying."

"But I make a fine Genoa salami sandwich. And I look nice in shorts."

She was crying at the sink, turning the instant boiling-water tap on and off, on and off. The mascara ran black down her face. She looked like a clown. He realized that she'd made herself up for him — when? midnight? afterward? — and had worn the face she had made for him to see. He visualized himself, proud as a strapping big boy, stepping from the shower to greet her.

He finished chewing salami and dark bread. He said, "I hate to see you so damned unhappy."

She turned the boiling water on and off, and steam fogged the kitchen window. "So you make me cry to express your dismay with my sorrow?"

"Actually, I wasn't aware that I was making you cry."

"You're such a slob, Richard."

"But well-spoken, and attractive in a towel."

"You aren't unattractive," she said. "But you're so tired, you could never make love. Could you?"

Richard sighed with fear and satisfaction as he drank his beer. "We can do some middle-class perversions if you like. Many were developed for the tired husband after work, I understand. We can — " He had by now stood and moved to her, was moving against her as they leaned at the sink. "We can do a number of exotic tricks they practice in the movies that the D.A. confiscates."

Hilary's eyes were closed. She was unfastening his towel. Her upper lip was clamped over the lower one, and he watched it when it moved. "Movie perversions?" she said. "Where would you pick up movie perversions?"

"You know those evidentiary sessions I sometimes hold? We all sit around and watch dirty flicks."

She said, "Pig."

His skin had been cool and hers hot. His body, had it been a creature with a mouth, no more, would have sung. But it was very tired, and it was crowded with his mind. He thought, now, here, in his hospital room, not about — *damn* it — whoever he had been with in a motel room in Westmoreland, New York, before he wrecked his car. He could remember that — the room, the bedspread's color, the light lavender cotton skirt on the floor, and not her face. He couldn't see her *face*.

Richard, in their house, in his memory now, had taken off

his wife's clothing and had wooed her away from what was sorrowful and true. He'd loved her in their kitchen to the exclusion of everything, for a very little while. And now, in the hospital room, he couldn't see or say the name of the woman he had loved more than Hilary and whom he had washed from his body to preserve her to himself. Naked of clothes and towel and her, they had lain in a nest of Hilary's underwear and blouse and dark Bermuda shorts — skins so easily shed. And Hilary had been watching him. He'd seen her eyes rimmed with black and filling with darkness. She had figured him out, he knew. He had wondered when she would tell him. In his hospital room, he remembered hoping that she would find a way to make it hurt.

III

IT TOOK LLOYD AND PRIS nearly a month to arm themselves and gather their courage and rage. Then they came, through the main doors of the county office building, and past the glass information booth — "Can I help you?" the woman in beige had said to the profiles of their passing shotguns — and down one flight to the basement offices. They thought the dogs would be in the basement, Lloyd later said. "I couldn't figure on anybody keeping animals upstairs where the fancy offices was bound to be." They took eleven people hostage, including a woman who cried so long and loudly that Lloyd — "She sounded like one of the goddamned *dogs*" — hit her with the pump-gun barrel. She breathed quietly and shallowly for the rest of their visit and was hospitalized for a week. The police at first remained outside and were content to bellow over battery-powered hailers. "*I* couldn't understand 'em," Lloyd said. "It sounded like some goddamned cheerleaders on a Friday night over to the high-school game. Except Pris and me wouldn't play ball."

They passed out a note that said, "26 PRIVAT STOCK CRE-

TURS PLUS FREEDOME OF CHOICE PLUS $10,000." The
money was for Pris's sex-change operation, Lloyd said in his
deposition. They wanted to be legally married and live as man
and wife. Pris was tired of costumes and wanted *outfits*. The
police got bored and flushed them out with tear gas, then beat
them badly before the arraignment. Lloyd later said, "I don't
think the operation would of made that much difference, to
tell you the truth. Pris, he didn't — she — whatever the hell he
is. *It*. I don't think he loved me the way you want somebody to
love you." Lloyd was starving himself in the county jail. Pris was
defended from rape by a captured counterfeiter out of Fair-
fax, Virginia, and their affair was two weeks old and going
strong.

And Hilary had not come back. Manwarren had paid for a
television set while Snuyder had slept the sleep of the sedated,
and Snuyder now lay looking at the dimpled ceiling panels,
clenching his fists against the pain, and listening without wishing to. Game-show hosts with voices as sweet and insistent as
the taste of grape soda cried out with delight and mortification
as army sergeants and homemakers and stockbrokers selected
numbers and boxes and squares marked off on walls and were
awarded either bounty or a consolation prize consisting of a
lifetime supply of scuff-resistant, polymer-bound linoleum
clean-'n-polisher for the busy woman who has more to do than
wax, for sweet goodness' sake, her floors. Manwarren also
watched soap operas that had to do with misplaced babies and
frantic adulterers, always on the verge of discovery as in-
cestuous. There were snippets of old movie, fragments of cartoon, crashingly educational disquisitions on the use of *C* — "C,
you *see*, is also in *ka*-ristmas ta-*ree!*" — and Gilligan, eternally
trapped on his island with Tina Louise and constitutionally incapable of hurling himself upon her, continued to invent ways
of extending his imprisonment.

Manwarren, a real critic, commented with alert smugness
and an eye for the obvious. "You believe she wouldn't remember who invented *noodles*?" he sang. He crowed, "Numbers are

from the friggin' Arabs, dummy! No wonder he's a garbage-
man." Snuyder kept waiting to hear the suck-and-pour of passing traffic on the arterial highway leading into downtown
Utica, but all he heard was Manwarren and the objects of his
derision. "Hey," he said, "hey, Judge. You handle yourself like
this *Family Court* guy? He takes *no* crap offa nobody, you know?
He's got a courtroom fulla morons, by the way. No wonder
they ended up in court. They wouldn't know how to cross the
street." A *M*A*S*H* rerun drove Manwarren into silent sniffles,
but he covered well by saying, in a gravelly voice, "I don't think
that's a very realistic way to talk about the Korean conflict." Of
Robin Hood, he said, for the first time approving in tone, "I
never knew Glynis Johns had knockers like that, Judge."

Snuyder listened. The pain made him blink in disbelief. He
looked at the ceiling panels and waited for Hilary to return.
She didn't. The balding nurse, this time in a long-sleeved
dress, came in with a sedative shot. He was so grateful, he felt
embarrassed. His orthopedic surgeon, a tall and slender man
who not only didn't smile, but who made clear both his dis-
approval of the patient and of having to explain to him, explained to him what he would do inside of Snuyder's hip and
leg. Pins. Something about pins that would staple him together
again, he remembered, after the surgeon was gone and the
ceiling had dropped a few feet, and then the orderlies came to
roll him away to be pinned into shape.

There was something about dogs, and their terrible odor,
and somebody riding one around a muddy country lot. He said
No! And, knowing that he dreamed while he dreamed, he
awaited the dream that would tell him who had sat in the front
with him while the police car chased him and he drove — by accident, he insisted to the unseen audience his dream included
— into the slow breaking up of his bones. The dogs whined and
whined, as if steadily, increasingly, wounded by someone patient and cruel.

The intensive care unit was dark and silent and Snuyder was
in very deep pain. His hip burned, and his stomach, and the

groin he ached too much to reach for. He kept seeing the skin
slide open as the angry surgeon sliced. He yelped for assistance
and then shuddered to show the nurse that it was he who needed her promptest sympathies. He was hooked to a drip and a
monitor, she explained. Soon he would be taken back to his
room. He was fine. The procedure had seemed to be effective,
and now his job was to sleep. He slept, but the burning followed him, and he dreamed again of dogs whose fur was stiff
with filth, whose eyes dripped mucous, and whose droppings
were alive with long white worms. He heard the dogs' howling
and he hated Lloyd and Pris. The television set was low, and a
curtain divided him from Manwarren, but he knew, waking
later, that he was back in his room, and still burning, and all
right, alive, not dreaming any more. The world was in color on
the other side of the curtain where a voice electric with triumph told someone named Cecelia that the car she'd won had
bucket seats. She screamed.

The woman in the car with him had screamed.

TONY ARIZONA, his senior clerk, was there in the morning to
discuss adjustments of his trial calendar. He brought a cheap
glass vase filled with blue flowers that Snuyder couldn't name,
and a fifth of Powers' Irish Whiskey. He showed Snuyder how
his cases had been distributed among the other sitting judges
and that certain others — very few of them — had been post-
poned. Snuyder said, "No. You gave the boys with the dogs to
Levinson."

"He wanted it. He hates queers."

"He *is* queer. I want that one, Tony. Hold it over as long as
you can before you give it up. And try not to give it to Levinson.
He'll be cornholing them in chambers by the end of the first
hour. Oh, boy."

"They cut you up some, I understand."

"Not to mention *I* cut me up."

"Judge. Dick. I have to give the dog people to Levinson.

State wants your calendar cleared. You understand? I'm sorry."

"The suicide thing?"

"They think they might want to look into it."

"Tony. *You* think I tried to kill myself?"

"I think you bent your car around a telephone pole. For what it's worth. I don't care — I mean, I *care*, but only about you. You did it, you didn't do it, you'll work it out and the accident's over, that's that. It's not the suicide thing. It's the woman."

Snuyder heard himself sigh. He could see the letters coming out of his mouth and into a comic-strip bubble: Ahhhh. He waited for Arizona to tell him who she was, and whether he was in love as much as he thought he remembered he once had been.

Arizona said, "They have to do it. *I* don't know anything. And nobody else is gonna say word one. I expect a superficial investigation, announced vindication, and a prompt resumption of jurisprudence as usual."

"And then there's the matter of the law," Richard said.

Arizona, handsome and intelligent, with great brown eyes and a fondness for dark striped shirts such as the maroon one he wore, smiled a broad smile. "Absolutely," he said. "There is always the law, and the public trust, Your Honor."

Manwarren called over the curtain, "You guys believe this? They want me to believe this bimbo just won a trip around the world for two, all expenses paid, by telling greaseball over there with the microphone that Columbus didn't discover America?" The muted shrieks of the victor poured around Manwarren's voice.

The woman in the car had screamed. Arizona poured Powers' into Snuyder's glass with its plastic straw, then he held the straw low, near Snuyder's pillow, so the judge could suck it up. He emptied the glass. Arizona might know her, he thought. But he couldn't be asked. Snuyder was ashamed to remember his wife and his children, his work even down to the specifics of the cases he had tried months and years ago, when he could barely remember the presence, much less identity or necessary intimate facts, of a woman he carried with him toward jail for certain, and possibly (if Hilary was right) toward death. But she wasn't dead. The nurse had told him that no one was dead. He thought of someone with no face who sat in a wheelchair, paralyzed. He saw her—she was like a burglar in a stocking mask, terrifying because faceless, unnatural — lying in an iron lung, crushed in a fetal sleep forever, staring through a window and drooling, staggering like a monster with hands like claws at her waist, serving the judge's sentence and locked away from his mind.

Arizona slid the Powers' into the drawer of the bedside table when he left. The pain pills and the Powers' combined, and Snuyder flinched. The doctors would have to cut and cut before they found out what was wrong with such a man as he, he told himself. He closed his eyes against the undeniable blade, as if they were cutting, as if they were at the flaccid organs and slimy bone, searching for what was the matter. For him.

It was Hilary who woke him when she sat in the visitor's chair with some effort, swearing as she fell back into the deep seat. After a silence — she breathed as if she had a cold — she said, "How's your catheter, Judge?"

"Hil. Do you know who she is?"

Manwarren turned the volume down.

Snuyder whispered: "The woman in the car?" He took a breath and then shouted, "Manwarren! Turn the sound up! Mind your own business!" He felt as though he'd been running. "Bastard," he said. He shouted it: "Bastard!"

The sound came up slightly, but Snuyder knew that Manwarren was unchastened.

Hilary said, "Why, who would that be, Your Honor? How *is* your catheter, by the way?"

"I hurt all over. Okay? I'm in a lot of pain. I'm humiliated. I'm under investigation, Hilary. They're looking into my comportment on and off the bench."

"I didn't know you'd done it on the bench. And you can't really blame them. A suicide is not always the most stable interpreter of the law, never mind his other little quirks and foibles."

"It's apparently because of the woman. That was all I could get from Arizona."

Hilary said, "I wish *I* could get more from Tony. He's really a piece."

"Please don't talk like that."

"Do I really need to tell you about the hypocrisy of this discussion?"

"No."

"You know I'm disgusted with you. That's an easy one. Disgust is easy and seeing it's easy. But what *kills* me — "

"Hil, I can't remember a lot. I remember *us*, overall, you know. And a lot of times and things. But I can't remember a lot."

"And that includes the slut in the car? *That's* what kills me. It's so *sad* for you that you can't. I feel *sorry* for you. You son of a bitch."

"Hil, she's literally a slut?"

"Oh. You boy. You infant. You expect me to keep track of your infidelities and log your bedroom transactions, don't you. You'd ask me for help. You know, knowing me, I'd probably give it. You — *boy*." She wept mascara lines down her face.

Snuyder said, "I'm promiscuous? I thought I remembered that I really loved her." Their silence widened, and a woman on the television set said, "I wouldn't dare tell them that!"

Hilary sighed. She said, "I think I'll go home. I understand they'll bring you back for therapy, and you'll use a walker. You'll be able to walk some day. I feel sorry it's so bad. Also, Richard, I'm moving. During the latter part of the week. I'll telephone you."

"Where?" he said. "Did we decide to do this?"

Hilary shook her head. "It started when you told me *you* were moving out."

"Yes," he said. He remembered at once, and as if he looked through transparent overlays: long arguments, slower and longer conversations, Hilary on the phone, Hilary weeping black lines while holding a teacup to her mouth, himself standing before her and wishing aloud that he were dead. He remembered the words about remorse that he had tried to say, and the fear of how they'd tell their sons. Hilary had told him about Warren, calling from college, in tears, because he had sensed that it all had gone wrong. Snuyder said, "I'm sorry. I don't remember women. A woman. *The* woman, I guess you'd call her."

"Yes," Hilary said.

"I apologize. If it's because of her, I apologize. I don't suppose it would make any difference now, seeing that I don't know her anymore. Is she the — "

But Hilary was up and moving. She was at the door. He heard the squelch of her crepe soles on the linoleum floor.

He said, "I suppose not."

She said, "See you, Judge." Then, too brightly, she said, "Actually, I'll see you in court." She laughed too hard, and she left.

Manwarren called over at once. "You know what, Dick? I think you shoulda hit the pole a little harder, you don't mind my saying so. You're in a pickle, to say the least, big fella."

"You think I'm in a pickle, Manwarren?"

"Call me Manny."

"I'm going to make a call, Manny. While you sleep. I'm going to have a man who runs a chain of fish stores in Syracuse — I'm going to ask him to have an employee in the Manlius packing plant come over here while you're sleeping and kill you. He's going to open your chest with his bare hands, and he's going to tear out every vital organ in your body one at a time. And he won't wear gloves. His nails will be dirty. He picks his nose. Do you understand me, Manny?"

The sound increased in volume, and bright voices clung to the ceiling tiles. She had been in the car with him. She had screamed when they'd hit. Hilary was leaving because of her, and he didn't know who the woman was. The set cried out and the voices rose. He was alleged to have attempted suicide. He would never walk normally, and his sons would not come to him. He knew that too. Hilary would take all their money and the ethics committee of the Bar Association might remove him from the bench. He thought they wouldn't, since none of them was terribly honest either, and each was equally impeachable. They would probably reprimand him, and he would suffer a trial-by-headline. But he would return to the bench, he thought. He would live alone in an apartment such as the ones near the Sangertown Mall. Or perhaps he might move into Clinton, where the old large houses east of town were divided into Victorian cells for bachelors and men such as he. He would drive alone to work and sit in his courtroom. He would say who was right in the eyes of the law. He never would know who the woman had been, or what they had been together, or why.

It was an empty mourning, he thought — abstracted, like a statement about how dreadful the starving African babies are. He wondered if the woman he loved and didn't know might have told him she was leaving. Perhaps he had aimed at killing *her*.

He heard himself whimpering, and made himself stop. He heard Manwarren's television set, and then the dogs in the trailer who'd whimpered, he'd been told by the deputies, before they heard the foot on the door; once rescued, they'd begun to bark and wail. He thought of Lloyd and Pris, armed and marching, in their terrible fetor and loss, to recover their starved, sick dogs. They were separated now. Poor Lloyd: he had taken the hostages, and only when his prisoners lay on the floor in the deeds-recording office had he realized that he wanted to insist on one more prize, the operation that would change Pris's sex. It was then, Snuyder remembered realizing, as he'd read Lloyd's deposition, that Lloyd had understood how permanently separate he had always been from Pris and probably always would be. "He don't love me," Lloyd had said. "How could he?"

It was a case he had wanted to try. They were accused of a dozen public-health violations and twenty or more violations of the civil and criminal codes. And they were so innocent, Snuyder thought. No one should be allowed to be so innocent. Shots rang out on a TV show, and wheels screamed. Snuyder jumped, remembering the sound of locked brakes. She had been there with him, in the same small space. And he had leaned back, locked his elbows and knees, and had driven at the pole. He had. And he would not know her. And even that was not the worst part.

SHE *might* return. He would have to decide about trying to heal, or waiting for her next door to death. He forced himself to breathe evenly, as if he slept. The TV set made sounds. The dogs stood on the bed and chairs, they cried their pain and hunger, their fear. Manwarren cackled. The police would come soon with questions. He was held together with pins. He was going to die, but of natural causes, and many years from today. He knew it. He smelled the dark air of the trailer, and he heard the gaunt dogs whine.

ALAN CHEUSE

✛

The Quest

for Ambrose Bierce

THE BUS ROLLED across the bridge to the south bank of the river and Alman breathed at last. He had imagined it to be a broader, swifter stream, but even so he felt newborn. Dark-faced boys in rags played among weeds and stubby cactus along the other shore. They didn't look up as he passed, but he waved anyway.

Oily fumes welled up inside the nearly-deserted bus as the vehicle slowed to a crawl and turned into a parking area at the rear of a group of low stone buildings. *Aduana*. Customs. *Immigración*. Immigration. Alman flexed his college Spanish, a legacy that had finally convinced a doubting editor at *Ohio Magazine* to let him give this assignment a try. Inside one of the buildings a small dark man in an unpressed khaki uniform typed up his tourist card — "What for do you take in this machine?" he asked, pointing to the small portable typewriter Alman had bought at a Columbus discount store just before he departed. "You a journalist?" "To write letters home," Alman said with a straight face. The man nodded. "Not do it by hand?" He held up his hand, palm outward, as though showing Alman a secret sign. Alman shook his head. The man grinned and handed him his card. Alman had been warned about stating that he was entering the country in order to write an article. Nobody warned him about the smells, the noise, the sprightly music that rolled out of the loudspeakers in the small food stands on the edge of the parking lot.

"Señor?"

The smiling, round-faced woman touched his arm just as he stepped into the next building for baggage inspection.

He backed away from her, but only far enough to get a good look at her breasts beneath her light synthetic sweater.

"Do you speak English?"

She smiled, as if approving his glance.

"I wan' hep. You give? I be you' mai'?"

"I don't need a maid."

She shook her head.

"Jes' for now, señor. For his 'spection."

"Oh?" Alman tried to figure out her plan. "You want to say you're my maid when you go through customs?"

"Sí!" She showed him nearly every tooth in her mouth.

They were already walking slowly down the long corridor, their bags in their hands (and a sack slung over the chubby woman's shoulder as well). She didn't look like a drug smuggler or a prostitute. He nodded his agreement. The Mexican woman kept several paces behind him but he could feel her presence. He had a recollection of a news story about Mexican citizens bringing in appliances and new clothes from the U.S. and trying to avoid paying the duty. It was close to Christmas so he figured that this must be the case with the woman who wanted to pose as his maid.

A squat guard patted his typewriter, glanced inside his suitcase, listened to the woman's languid words about her service to this North American. Alman then found himself on the other side of the customs line.

"Graciàs," she muttered as they returned to the bus. She placed her bulky sacks in the overhead rack alongside his typewriter and settled into the set next to him.

He leaned away from her, giving her room to spread her billowy skirt. The woman — she told him her name was Marguerita Aceves after he introduced himself — settled closer to him. Their thighs met, chaperoned by the folds of her skirt. The bus lurched forward through the desert twilight. Blue-black clouds hovered above distant mountains in the west. The last streaks of sunlight turned muddy beyond them. Joshua trees raised their stubby arms toward the darkening sky. Alman used unhappy memories of the past few lonely months as a sleeping pill. He dozed. Upon awakening, he found Marguerita Aceves' hand lying limply on his thigh. A minute passed in which he enjoyed the feel of her palm just above his kneecap. Then he edged toward the dark aisle. Moments later, her body sagged with the leftward movement of the bus, and her hand flopped back onto his leg, her head against his shoulder.

The bus roared like a dragon, approaching mountains on an endless incline of curves and more curves. It climbed and climbed into the high desert. Marguerita Aceves snored lightly in his ear. He imagined himself in bed with her, on top of her, married to her, raising her children. At least she smuggled for family and not just for herself. A faint tinge of heartburn swelled his breast at the thought of his own marriage in Columbus. But he didn't want to carry such excess baggage with him on this trip. And so he tried to imagine Ambrose Bierce's bitter journey across the desert. And imagined leads for his article, his first but not, he hoped, his last.

Brap-ap-ap-ap-ap! The bus expelled bad gas from its exhaust as it slowed down, steadying into a lower speed, then turning the curve that led westward. Alman must have dozed. Lights of a city flickered across his eyelids. Moments later the bus thumped along a roadway with special strips of concrete spaced out every few yards to slow them down. Alman shook off sleep and gazed at the lights of the bus terminal at the end of the long street.

"Permit me," said the awakening Marguerita, her voice fuzzy with sleep. He launched himself to his feet to allow her to pass down the aisle. As he watched her move lithely toward the

door, he felt the heaviness in his bowels, thirst, heavy eyes. A
few dark passengers from the rear brushed past him. Then he
plunged after them into the aisle, into the terminal. In the
brightly lighted but foul-smelling lavatory, he hurriedly unloaded his bladder and bowels, then bought a can of papaya
juice and returned to the bus. Noxious engine fumes made it
difficult for him to enjoy the sweet, thick juice of the tropical
fruit.

Old passengers filed back into the vehicle, new ones arrived.
A thin woman in black appeared at his side. He shook his head,
telling her in signs that the seat was taken. Stoically, she passed
on. Next a swarthy Indian peasant. More hand signals. The
man protested. Alman sat up to full height. The man shuffled
to the rear of the bus. Hurry now, he said to Marguerita Aceves
in his mind. She ought to know better. These buses left on
schedule. The driver revved the engine.

He did not panic when the overweight man sat down. Sliding
to the window, he searched the terminal yard for a glimpse of
Marguerita. The bus bumped over the hump that slowed it
down before the ticket window at the exit. Foreign chatter ex-
ploded around him, then subsided as the passengers settled
down for the rest of the ride. No sight of her on the platform,
he realized as he twisted around for one final look. He had not
asked her her destination. He had not even known what con-
traband she had been smuggling. She had walked so lightly
that it seemed that it must have been small cargo, perhaps even
drugs or diamonds. The bus slowly rolled through the outskirts of the city, then plunged into the dark desert again at an
ever increasing speed. Alman settled back, closed his eyes,
rubbed his nose where the pain still tingled slightly, and tried
to rehearse an outline for the article on Bierce. Not until he
opened his eyes at the first touch of daybreak, as they slowed
down once again amid vast tracts of grey and dun-brown
dunes, did he discover that his typewriter was missing.

2

Armed with pen and notebook, Alman continued his search, a little bit wiser about his surroundings. His hotel room in Chihuahua was a perfect base — it was so dust-laden and depressing that he hated to return there. This encouraged him to spend hour after hour in the hall of records at the State capitol, and to take excursions into the countryside where lay the small villages frequented by the rebel soldiers of Villa during their campaign here in the north.

North? It was as far south as Alman had ever travelled, and the heat of noon on a winter's day convinced him that he didn't want to travel any further south, even in winter, if he could help it. But this was his story, and if it required that he follow tracks southward he would do so. Besides, he told himself, I might somehow meet up with that woman again and get my typewriter back. And he laughed at himself because he knew how naïve a thought that was.

Much to his own surprise, he accepted the rhythm of his new life in Chihuahua, a round of boring research, spicy meals, churning bowels, and lonely nights. Now and then he ate a new dish that pleased him — from time to time he heard himself making noises resembling laughter and others like cries of pain. No friends, no acquaintances cheered or annoyed him. He avoided calling Columbus although a few afternoons found him straying in the direction of the long-distance office. One morning an old man in the newspaper office showed him a yellowed sheet of newspaper with a story referring to the gringo journalist who was accompanying a Villa scouting expedition on an excursion to the coast. Alman was amused at how dislocated he felt when he left the city in the smelly, fuming third-class bus. He had been there only a week and a half but it had felt like home.

Pez de Espada. The name of his destination made him feel all the more uncertain. It was an ocean name — swordfish — and from his window he saw only desert, hour after hour nothing but flat sandy plain with few distant mountains on the horizon. Only after dark did they begin to make their descent, and though he could not see much more than an occasional light in a peasant hut at the side of the highway, he felt the heat of the jungle rising up to meet him even as the bus spiralled its way downward toward the sea. By daybreak they rolled along a track under a canopy of palms and tall bushes, many of them heavy with red and yellow blossoms as large as his fists. The passengers who had boarded with him in Chihuahua trickled away stop by stop in tiny villages nestled along the downward-turning roadway. Few others boarded. By the middle of the night, Alman had the seat to himself. He had suffered, cramped up in the small space, but he had won some deserved sleep as well.

He awoke to discover the sea. The broad curve of the azure Pacific, sparkling in the morning light, punished him with its beauty. As the bus spiralled its way down through the welcoming jungle, he sweated beneath the same blanket that had kept out the chill during the night. Alman stripped it off. The bus rounded a turn in the jungle and a collection of palm-roofed hovels appeared down the road. Beyond them the sea burned with the fire of early morning sunlight. The bus driver spat out an oath.

The bus station was the only modern building in the village, a square stucco structure with posters plastered all over its outside walls and its waiting room laid with dirty tiles on which school children had painted a mural of butterfly-shaped fishing boats putting out to sea. From the ferocious glare of the sun, umbrellas, trees, stucco-roofed and -walled houses offered some surcease. But Alman had little time to worry about the heat.

An infant cried out. He glanced over his shoulder at a short, bulbous-nosed woman bundled up in a serape with an infant bulged against her chest. "Can you help me?"

Her voice was pure New York, so out of keeping with her ap-

pearance that Alman first looked around to see if someone else
was speaking.

"Hello," he said, finally looking into her eyes. These were
brown, as was the fringe of unkempt hair that hung down from
beneath the hood formed by her serape. She had large cheeks,
pocked and red, and her large nose was also cratered. Either
her eyes were her only beautiful feature or they merely looked
beautiful by comparison with her face.

"Can you help?"

"What's wrong?" Alman tried to catch a glimpse of the baby
that the woman bundled so close to her body. Unlike the silent
children he had seen on the streets of Chihuahua, this child
made tiny mouse-like squeaks that penetrated the heavy cloth
in which its mother had swaddled it.

"My name is Marsha." The woman blinked several times.

"Tommy Alman. Sounds like the nut."

"Tommy," she said, as though she had known him since
grade school, "I need your help."

"What's wrong?" He swung his hand around and touched
his wallet, an action that had become a habit since his encounter with Marguerita Aceves. Then he felt silly to imagine that
he might be threatened by this dumpy American girl with her
pathetic bundle of a baby.

"Help me get the bus to the border. I'm afraid to go by myself."

The woman trembled, and the cloth fell away from her
head, revealing a tangled mess of dirty orange hair that was
dark at the roots. She smiled feebly, yet invitingly, motioning
toward the bundle of baby clothes heaped at her feet.

Alman paused a moment, as if thinking it over, but he was
not truly thinking. In Columbus he had returned early from a
trip to New York and had walked into his living room to find
his wife in the arms of a stranger, and he walked out again,
bumping his nose and shoulder against the door frame as he
departed, returning to the office to demand an assignment

and receiving the word about Bierce. Alman now picked up
the bundle and headed to the ticket window.

3

He had made a number of stupid mistakes in his life, but
they seemed nothing compared to the troubles of Marsha
Heinrich, or Em, as she said her friends called her at college.

"I was an English major," she said, "but really I was into
Latin-American stuff. Have you read — ?" She spoke of some
authors whose names Alman didn't recognize. But then he had
never read much; he had in fact never read of Bierce until he
had left the magazine office and stopped at a bookstore, found
a couple of his books and then decided to take the bus south so
that he had time to read them. He wanted to mention his assignment (or what had *been* his assignment, he had to admit to
himself now that the bus took a curve that cut them off at last
from the sight of the sea), but Marsha kept on chattering.

" — Teatro Boriqueño. Ever hear of that?"

"Sorry. What was that?"

"You weren't listening, Tommy. I said I met Enrique at the
Teatro Boriqueño. The Puerto Rican Street Theater where I
was an intern over the summer? He was one of the directors.
He never went past eighth grade, but he read a lot of drama on
his own and wrote some wild plays and also directed them. We
were very simpatico, and I moved in with him on the Lower
East Side. We had a really grungy place over on East 2nd
Street, the part that looks like East Berlin but we loved each
other and it didn't matter. Enrique was getting back to his
roots, so I had to learn Spanish, which was really neat because
even though I was away from him during the spring term, I felt
close to him during the week because of my Spanish class, anyway it turned out I was pregnant and one of his things was his
macho pride so that he didn't want me to get an abortion even
though my parents were going crazy, and so I moved in with

him at the end of the term. His family wanted us to get married, my family wanted an abortion, and I didn't know what I wanted except Enrique, so we got a little money together from friends and selling things and moved down here, not to Pez but to Oaxaca and then over here to Pez, the baby was born in Oaxaca and then Enrique decided he had to make some money and . . ."

They travelled for several hours while she put the story together for him, and he was as interested in the news about herself that she was giving him as in the terrain he had missed in the dark.

" — you know they bust you here for the smallest amount of anything, I mean, like aspirin without a prescription makes them look cross-eyed at you, it's a racket they use to shake down gringos, and I begged and begged him to stop carrying the stuff but he didn't listen and one day he was up in the city and bam, they picked him up and locked him in and except for a visit a couple of months ago, I haven't seen him . . ."

What an idiot that Enrique was! Alman wanted to tell her. But since it had taken her so long to get control of herself in order to tell him her story, he feared upsetting the balance she had regained. She had been through a lot of bad times and didn't need him to chip away at her feelings. If for no other reason than taking care of the baby, he didn't want her to become hysterical. Her plan was to cross back over into the States, call her parents, and then find a lawyer for Enrique. But what was his story? The bus rocked from side to side on the narrow highway through the jungle as he gave her an account of his own. Their hips bumped together and he told his tale in bits and pieces, wondering now and then about the lust he felt rising in his lap since she was such a striking picture of ugliness.

She wanted to stop in Chihuahua to buy some supplies for the baby.

"It's been weeks," she said, her voice returned to what was obviously its full strength, "since this little kitten has had clean diapers."

In the cool shade of the drug store, Alman volunteered to pay for the box of paper diapers.

" 'Kleen-Bebe,' " she read from the label, "far out." Then she thrust the infant into his arms and announced that she was going shopping. "I'll meet you back at the bus station."

"What time?" he called after, the unfamiliar bundle squirming in his arms.

"When's the bus leave?" she asked over her shoulder.

He told her the time.

"I don't know anything about what to do with this!"

"It's good practice!"

She waddled off along the sun-bleached avenue, leaving him the object of curiosity of a number of admiring pedestrians. The infant had calmed down, but now he realized that it was giving off a sweetish but repugnant odor. Wandering back toward the bus station, he spied a small park and lay the baby down on the grass, letting it kick and make fists at the trees. He undid its filthy wrapping, marvelling that a few thin streaks of excrement could emit such a foul smell. He daubed carefully at the boy's genitals with his handkerchief — which he then rolled up into a ball and left lying at the base of a tree — and after ruining the tapes on only two diapers, successfully negotiated the change.

Vendors approached them, asking him to buy slices of fruit or vegetables, roasted seeds and nuts. He didn't feel hungry although he hadn't eaten in half a day. When the infant stopped its silent calisthenics and slept, he dozed off only to be awakened by a pinch on his neck and another on his cheek. A scouting party of red ants had attacked him, and as he brushed them aside, he remembered the baby. But the thing slept peacefully, apparently invulnerable to the marauding insects.

"Hey!"

Alman looked up to see Marsha kicking the grass in front of him with the toe of a cowboy boot. She wore a western shirt, faded jeans, and her hair was pulled back to show off all the more starkly the jutting ugliness of her nose and the craters of cheeks. But now that she had shed her serape, he could see a nicely-shaped body that distracted him from the unpleasantness of her face.

"Where'd you change?" Alman asked, sitting up and then scooping up the baby in his arms.

Marsha smiled. "You look good with the kid, man. I met a friend of Enrique's. He let me clean up in his place."

"You should have taken the baby with you," Alman said. "It smells."

Marsha relieved him of the child.

"Can't face up to the essential odor of the human race, can you, man? I thought we were supposed to meet in the bus station. I was looking all over for you."

"You didn't think I'd run off with him, did you?"

He stood up and they started walking toward the station, Alman slinging her bags over his shoulders, Marsha with the baby in her arms.

"Actually I think you'd be very good with it." She smiled slyly.

Alman thought she was taunting him and ignored her look. They had missed one bus to the border and now had an hour to wait for another. While Marsha sat on a bench with her blouse open and nursed the baby, he went out to buy them some food for the trip.

Darkness settled over the desert by the time they rolled north out of the flat dry city. El Paso, their destination, lay hours away across the dunes. Marsha, in the window seat, asked him to hold the baby while she ate, and then did the same for him. The food was peppery, but the milk nicely cooled his burning tongue.

"He'll sleep all the way," Marsha said, "and I'll change him just before we cross the border so that he doesn't make a mess while we're in customs. Like I once got stuck there for hours one time with Enrique, man, and the baby nearly went berserk."

"Is that where he got caught?"

"Huh? Oh, yeah, but not at the border. He was driving along in Sinaloa and ran into a roadblock. What a bad break, man. They wanted to crucify him and now he's rusting away in prison." There was something in her voice that disturbed him.

"I hope you're going to try and do something for him once you get home."

Marsha had been bumping shoulders with him as they rode. Now she pulled herself toward the window.

"What kind of a chick do you think I am?"

Alman retreated as far as he could toward the aisle.

"I don't know, Marsha, it just sounded like . . . "

"Let me tell you, everything isn't always the way it sounds. And that's not something they teach you real well in college. Tommy Nut, you think it's time to get aggressive with me? Now I know exactly why your wife left you."

The remark hit Alman in the chest like a fist.

"Why was that?"

"Because you pretend you're macho when you're really just a pushover."

Marsha burped loudly, adjusted the sleeping baby in the crook of her arm as though the infant were a limp-limbed rag doll, closed her eyes, and went to sleep.

A large bright moon dominated the desert highway. Alman would have liked to have blamed its piercing light for his own inability to sleep, but he knew that what kept him awake were the facts of his life rolling about in his brain like loose luggage on the upper rack of the bus. Without even feeling very sorry for himself, he understood that up until now his days had simply caved in on him, like sand in a pit in the desert through which the bus now carried him. He had no momentum of his own — having staggered out of his family home and college days he finally had slowed down and fallen over. His marriage, or the end of it, marked the place where he tipped over and stopped running. Though he was rolling north toward the border of his country and knew absolutely nothing about what he would do once he got there, he prayed that he would find something. Something. Something. To the tune of his seat-mate's stertorous breathing, finally he dozed.

More than a moment but less than an hour had gone by when he opened his eyes. The moon had slipped down behind them, and the bus roared forward toward Texas and darkness. Either the baby or the woman had stirred, rousing him from his slumber. When he moved slightly in the seat, he felt the heel of a hand resting on his upper thigh while the fingers worked open the zipper of his corduroy trousers.

He glanced over at Marsha, but she lay back, eyes closed, the baby still asleep on her arm, as though she knew nothing about the stealthy steady progress of her own hand. Suddenly she had the zipper unlatched, and spread open the metal teeth. Like a ferret after a rabbit, her hand swiftly entered the slit in the front of his undershorts and grasped his flaccid penis.

The shock pressed him back against the seat, and he rolled his eyes about, fearing that some full-bladdered passenger might this very moment stumble down the aisle toward the bathroom in the rear of the bus. But no one stirred; only the fuss and roar of the engine, and the thumpedty-thud of the tires on the bumpy desert highway, broke the silence that encircled him like her fingers tightening around his organ. It was a dream, it was a fantasy out of the pages of a magazine, it was a dilemma, it was a pleasure, it was a tricky quickening sense of the improbable taking place right there in his own lap, a daydream at night, a surging, mounting, thickening, a blurring of sight and urging of feeling, a buckling of his hips; he spurted into her hand.

No less quickly than she had found him, she pulled away, sliding her slick fingers across his thighs. She wiped them on the baby's blanket, and withdrew back into the sleep that she had surprised him from, like a sea animal retiring into its shell. Alman, lulled into a stupor, closed his eyes, listened to the bus, remembering only when he noticed the shape of another passenger against the darkness of the aisle that he had to adjust his trousers.

He must have slept because a faint touch of light dappled the horizon just beyond the supine girl's shoulder. He was glad that she hadn't awakened because it gave him a minute to decide how to treat the whole thing when she opened her eyes. As it turned out, he needed no strategy. When in the next few moments the bus swerved to avoid a cow grazing at the roadside, Marsha sat up, bright-eyed, and inquired after the time. When he told her, she beamed.

"We're almost to the border," she said. "Don't you need to take a piss or something? I want to stretch out and change the baby."

He nodded, pleased that nothing of their encounter in the darkness showed in her eyes. He got up, and she immediately set down the sleeping infant on his seat, reaching into her knapsack for a fresh diaper. The stench inside the tiny bathroom nearly made him gag. But he took advantage of the small sink with the pump faucet to wash himself. When he returned to the middle of the bus, Marsha was nursing the baby whose tiny birdlike noises spoke of hunger unlike any he had known in a long while.

The moon had departed, the sun lolled up over the dunes. Within minutes he could make out the towers and rooftops of Juarez with El Paso on the northern bank of the winking river. In a few more minutes, they were rolling past shacks made of corrugated tin, and then small brick houses with dry front yards full of cactus trees and bluebonnets. They had to switch buses at the Juarez station for their trip across the border. With its odor of insecticide, whiskey, cigarettes, and body odor, the ancient vehicle that carried them onto the bridge might have been the same one that had transported him southward only a few weeks ago. Except that this time no dumpy Mexican women looked nervously about as they approached the customs checkpoint. Only a few laborers who had boarded in Juarez accompanied him and Marsha into the U.S. customs building at the side of the broad cement bridgeway.

A dour Mexican official collected their tourist cards — and then motioned for them to move on to American territory. There a uniformed Texan, narrow as a reed, looked him in the eye, asking if they had anything to declare.

"No, sir," Alman said.

"Open these, please," the official said stiffly, rummaging through Alman's small suitcase and Marsha's knapsack.

"How old's the baby?" he asked.

Alman said, "Uh . . . "

"New fathers!" Marsha broke in with a snort, telling the man the infant's age in months.

The man kept on feeling about in the knapsack, but his voice took on a more gentle quality than the movement of his hand suggested.

"That all you have with you, son?"

Alman nodded.

"I had a typewriter but it was stolen."

"That's the way it is down there," the official said, as though he were talking about a pit or the ocean bottom. "Okay, you can get back on the bus now."

"Thank you, sir," Alman said. Marsha remained silent as they left the customs booth and reboarded the reeking bus. When they were turning down a short street that led to the El Paso Greyhound Station, she said, quietly, "You're terrific."

Alman had no idea what she meant, and was still too embarrassed about the incident in the night to ask about it. At least one thing had become clear: he wasn't going to go back to work for the magazine, and that was fine with him.

"Baby needs a change," Marsha declared when the bus came to a stop.

"I'll do it," Alman volunteered, pulling their luggage down from the rack and following her out of the bus and into the depot. They had a number of benches to choose among in the nearly deserted station. Marsha selected one in the corner by the baggage room which at this hour had not yet opened. She spread a blanket on the bench and gently lay the infant on top of it.

"Listen, you check the time of the New York bus, okay, honey? I'll change the baby."

"Honey?" Alman saw that she was about to pull open the child's diaper. "Okay." He ambled over toward the ticket counter where the schedule was mounted on a board in white plastic letters and numbers. New York? Why New York? Her husband was in jail in Mexico. Why did she want to go all the way up to New York? Maybe he could convince her to go somewhere else. She seemed quite footloose for all of the needs of the baby. He checked the time of the next bus to New York but also of the next one to Los Angeles. He'd only been there a few times selling space, but it was a new town and maybe a better town for him, or them, than New York.

"I'm just going to get rid of this poo-poo," Marsha said when he returned to the bench. She held up at arm's length a neatly-folded diaper.

Alman nodded, sitting down alongside the infant who seemed to be asleep again and watching Marsha walk slowly off in search of a place to dispose of the loaded diaper.

She folds a diaper nice, he thought. You'd think even the kid's shit was precious. He decided that he would try to talk her out of going to New York and into trying another town, maybe L.A. or Houston, he had sold space in Houston, too, and it was a growing town. You don't want to go all that far away from your husband, do you? he'd say. Think of the baby, he'll want to see the baby. I'll convince her. She probably only wants to go to see her own family a while and then come back down. He remembered what she did for him in the dark of the bus. We'll stop, we'll take a hotel room. He pictured all kinds of pleasure for them in the dark room. When you came right down to it, her face wasn't all that bad, and besides she was a good mother. Honey, she had called him. Tommy the Nut. He listened to her voice in his mind.

A bus full of workers from the other side of the river unloaded noisily, filling the depot with Spanish and cigarette smoke. Alman stood up and looked around. She's in the ladies, he decided. He sat down.

A second bus load of workers arrived. The ticket seller opened the booth, illuminating his sign with a flick of a switch. Alman poked around in the knapsack, found that it was full of paper diapers and small bottles, cans of powdered milk, clothing. A policeman appeared in the center of the depot, and when he strolled near the bench, Alman, for some reason he could not explain, turned to look after the baby.

The ticket seller called out the times of departing buses. When Alman heard the New York bus announced he picked up the sleeping infant, amazed as before at its near weightlessness, and hurried outside into the light of full dawn. She wasn't anywhere in sight. He rushed back to check the gate where a small group of dark-skinned travellers shuffled in toward the bus.

"New York?" asked the driver at the gate.

Alman shook his head, retreating to the bench.

"Jesus," he muttered. He waited on the bench a while longer, then scooped up child, knapsack, and his own suitcase, and walked to the ticket counter. "Did you see?" The baby stirred, and he rocked it gently in his arms, hoping that it would remain asleep.

"Is a boy?" The brown-skinned ticket seller looked at him blankly.

Alman nodded.

"What's it call?"

Alman shook his head.

Later, as they departed for Las Cruces, with the morning sun behind them, Alman, hands trembling, heart beating wildly despite the calm and certitude of the humming American bus, patted the wailing infant on its bottom until its noisy fears subsided.

In Tucson, amidst the ammoniac fumes of the men's room, he changed the infant yet one more time. In Phoenix, after picking a cigarette butt from the drain, he sat the naked creature in the sink, bathed it with a paper towel and rubbed it with ointment he found in the knapsack. Dabbing water on its brow, he took a deep breath and gave the child an old-fashioned masculine name.

CHRISTOPHER ZENOWICH

✤

On the Roof

THE YELLOW FIAT CHASE drove was towed back to the farm and put behind the barn. The winter snow kept it hidden for a while, but after that melted, it stayed there. Bob couldn't understand why they wanted to be reminded of the accident. At least the sight of it reminded him. Once in a while, he would try to imagine how she managed to survive. The snowplow that side-swiped the car ripped off the left side of the windshield and the roof above it, cracked the steering wheel in half, shredded the top of the driver's seat and tore out the door frame. The metal there had popped out the way a party noisemaker looks after it's been yanked. It was beginning to rust.

What impressed Bob about Apley was how well he kept himself under wraps. His joking had turned a little flat, but overall he appeared to be in the same easy-going mood, quick to cut up on Bob whenever he did anything wrong. The only other change was in the quantity of beer he consumed. Before the accident, Bob took the 50-gallon drum filled with cans to the dump about once-a-month. Now it was close to every two weeks.

Ted wasn't as easy to read. But Bob didn't see that much of him. He almost always worked out in the fields or was off doing chores when Bob worked. When he was in high school, he had been a legendary drinker. Everyone in the family had him pegged to follow in Apley's shoes and to take over the farm. But when Ted grew his hair out and started hanging around with the set of rich kids in town, he changed. Bob had heard people say he grew pot on the farm. But it was hard to imagine Apley not knowing that. When he started going out with Chase, it seemed like he became a whole other person. And when they took a summer off to hitchhike the country, the family started talking about him as a problem. He got married somewhere out West without even telling anyone beforehand. When he announced that he was joining a stock car team as a mechanic, it was a big ho-hum. The family had given up on him.

That had been four years ago. When he returned to the farm with Chase the fall before, everyone just forgot his past. His pony tail was gone. He had gotten a little soft around the middle, and his arms were pillowy like a fat man's. But he was still strong. He could carry two cinderblocks pinched together in each hand like they were lunch boxes. The accident had to be bothering him, but you'd never know it from his face. It was like Trudy's — puffy and round — but without animation, an effect that Bob took for either controlled grief or some sort of numbing high.

Trudy was more visibly upset. With Ted home, Bob wasn't invited in for lunch. There was too much family business to discuss. But he'd catch a glimpse of her once in a while when she came out to fetch Ted or Apley. Her face was whiter, her forehead tight and wrinkled.

Bob guessed that babysitting an adult could do it to anyone. What made it worse was the feeling everyone shared that Chase somehow knew, or at least felt much of what she used to be. That she had some hazy recollection of former abilities. Once when Bob helped him pile bags of citrus in the barn loft, Apley said he couldn't help feeling that she had just enough of a mind left to know some of it was missing. The thought had never occurred to Bob. He stood there, the tang of citrus dust on his tongue, trying to imagine how awful that would be.

Whenever Bob drank orange juice, he remembered what Apley said.

As far as Bob was concerned, Ted had scored a big coup in marrying Chase. She was rich and looked it. Her face was small and angular, with a thin perfectly defined nose — the result of two centuries worth of the eugenics known as good marriages. She smiled easily and often, and used her smile to communicate a range of feelings — from surprise to cool dismissal. That too was a product of breeding. But her face had lost its tone. The jaw had been broken, and either the doctors hadn't put it together right, or somehow her whole face drooped. There was a flap of puffy flesh where her chin used to be. And her hair had gone from pure blonde to a dull brown streaked with silver. The medication, Apley said. But Bob's mother thought she might have been a bleached blonde after all. "A rich girl?" Bob asked. "Sure," his mother said. "Today, everyone bleaches."

THE SECOND WEEK in August the roof over Chase's room sprung a leak during an all-night thunderstorm. She didn't say a word about it. She beat a path between her bed and the bathroom, bringing towels to sop up the water. When she used up all the towels, she emptied her dresser of sweaters and jeans, and then her closet of dresses, skirts and blouses. Everything got stained. The water seeped down through the floor and ruined the ceiling in the family room. Trudy was still crying when Bob got to the farm the next morning.

Apley asked Bob to come with him to check the corn. They took the pickup and Apley asked Bob to drive. When they got out on the dirt road, he started rambling.

There was no logic to it, Apley said. The accident, the problems, they just couldn't be understood. Trudy was on thin ice herself. He'd never seen her so upset and nothing seemed to help. She had her heart set on Ted staying, but after this? Who could blame him for leaving? She spent half the day resenting Chase and the other half feeling guilty about it. One thing for sure, she couldn't take looking after Chase for much longer. It was a situation where every other option you thought of just stunk.

When Bob swung the truck into the cornfield, Apley stopped talking. Bob could feel his stare, and didn't return it. Why was Apley telling him this? What could he do? He started thinking it was high time for Apley and his family to have a little bad luck in life. It isn't all hard work and brains, he found himself thinking. People get screwed for no good reason. Maybe Apley could understand what Bob's father felt like now. Then he felt bad. How could he wish all this on anyone? Especially on someone who'd been so fair with him.

"Do you want me to park here at the edge of the field?" Bob asked finally.

"Oh, well," he said. "Got to keep our chin up."

Apley stared straight ahead into the corn. Bob put the pickup in park, and opened the door to get out. But Apley shook his head. "Turn back," he said, "The corn's okay."

As they drove back to the farm, Apley said he'd be needing as much help as Bob could give over the last three weeks before school. From five in the morning to seven at night, if Bob was up to it. There'd be time-and-a-half for every hour over forty. It was perfect. Bob had counted on earning a couple of grand over the summer. Besides saving for college, maybe enough for a junker of a car. For the first time, it looked like he had a chance.

"We'll start by fixing the roof," Apley said. "You and Ted can tackle that. We'll be doing the whole thing, not just where it leaked. Right down to the beams — so Trudy can relax."

TED KNEW about roofs. He also knew better than to get involved stripping the old shingles and ripping out the rotted slats. It was dirty, hot work. "I'll help you set up the tarpaulin and lay down the plywood when you get to it," he said. "We'll work together putting down flashing and shingles, too."

The roof was a bitch. You had to watch what you were doing all the time. Each day, for the first few minutes, Bob felt like he was going to fall. That was okay, because he knew he'd be careful. It was later on that things got really scary. When he was sure he wasn't going to fall, when he was nonchalantly tossing old shingles over the edge — that was when he found himself almost going over. He'd get cocky and forget to stay on the board supported by angle irons. Next thing he knew, he was sliding down the worn surface of the old shingles, following the force of his toss and propelled by his own bulk. There was always a moment — how long it seemed — a split second in which he believed he was going over. After it happened a third time, Bob began to appreciate that moment — that instant of panic. It was more intense than winning a race. More than feeling like a total fool at a junior high dance. A split second when he truly believed, right down in his gut, that it was all over — he was going down. That all he could do now was to concentrate on falling feet first so only his legs would break. Of course he always managed to gouge and claw to a stop.

THE JOB stretched on for two weeks. Several of the beams below the slats had to be reinforced. And since the house was 200 years old, Apley fussed over how that was to be done. Everything had to be authentic.

Once a day, Ted showed up at the top of the ladder to monitor Bob's progress. Sometimes he'd head back down without saying a word. When Chase caught sight of him, she would come out from the house and stand on the lawn below watching. If Ted didn't pay some attention to her, she'd start to act up. "I'm running away," she said once. And she turned and started walking toward the fields in the exaggerated way kids do. Ted let her go until she was out of sight. After a few minutes, Bob could hear her screaming from somewhere near the cornfield. Ted didn't say a word. He climbed down and went after her.

Bob's mother had heard that she had the mental age of a fourth grader. "Sad," she said. "Such a talented girl." The entire family had a chorus of comments to the same effect. Chase was a topic for all of the aunts and uncles and cousins. She was different. Who ever heard of a dairy farmer's wife named "Chase"? Not in Connecticut, anyway. But it wasn't just the name. And it wasn't the fact that she had been to Miss Porter's School, which she had been enrolled in since the day she was born, or that she spent two years at Vassar. It wasn't even the fact that she played guitar and sang folk songs and had a tape looking for a record company. It was the way she walked that told you she was no farmer's wife. She was too light on her feet — not like a young girl is — but as if she wasn't subject to the force of gravity. A real farmer's wife walked more flatfooted than that. Jackie, Carol and Becky had it down. So did Trudy. They walked as if they were prepared to withstand a sudden gust or the blindside whack of a barn door. Chase didn't have to. No barn door would ever have hit her.

She had had it all, now she had nothing. It was the same angle network news shows found for all disasters. Bob could almost imagine the drone of Walter Cronkite or of one of his correspondents. "People said she was a girl that had it all . . . and then, the impossible happened." While you're safe in your living room, Mr. Jones, recovering from your rotten little day, the world for someone else is going up in smoke and fire, collapsing in an earthquake, being buried in mud and water, or baked to a barren cinder. There were countless catastrophes, coups and assassinations, serial killers, cult murders, mysterious illnesses, carcinogenic wells. But if you've got your health and a weekly lottery ticket, by God, you've got just about everything a man could ask of this life. Sure, an occasional headache or a bout of constipation or acid indigestion, but our sponsors take care of that. And that's the way it is, this night, tomorrow night, night after night.

First hand, though, you could see that a catastrophe doesn't make you any more thankful for your life. Instead, it becomes a logistical problem. Its shock wears off quickly and in the wake practical considerations take over. Those things which must be encountered and dealt with every day on the same level as a bodily function. They weren't even worth discussing.

TED CLIMBED the ladder carrying two 60-lb. packages of standard black shingles, one over each shoulder. He'd already brought up four packages, and was trying to flip the fifth off his shoulder. But it had slipped too far back during his climb. He held it like a knapsack over his shoulder, his face turning bright red as he strained to pull it up. Bob slid along the board to offer a hand when he saw the ladder wobbling. Quietly, as in a dream, it swayed back from the roof. Ted made a sound with his mouth — not a shout — sort of a gasp, something that might come from a person turning over in his sleep. He let go of the shingles. The ladder hovered in the air like a giant pair of stilts and Bob bellied to the edge and held out a hammer. Ted snatched it by the handle, and Bob, holding the claw, pulled. He closed his eyes and shut off his hearing and could feel only the hot stretching of his muscles trying to move the ladder and Ted back to the roof. Then Ted flipped the other package to the roof in one great slap, the aluminum ladder clanking back to the edge.

There was a quiet. A deafness. Slowly, other sounds returned. The hiss of leaves across the street. A car on the road a few hundred feet away. A radio inside the house. Bob looked at Ted, who grinned and said, "Shit."

That was when Bob first noticed Ted had grown a moustache — wispy and long, the whiskers hanging down over his lower lip. "When did you grow that?" Bob asked after Ted pulled himself onto the roof. His hands were shaking.

"Two weeks ago," he said. "I can tell you're pretty observant." He grinned. "I'm going down to get those shingles. Be back in a few minutes."

Ted had been gone for a few minutes before Bob looked over the edge and saw the shingles still spread across the lawn like a fallen deck of cards. Ted was nowhere in sight. Bob thought about getting back to work but decided he needed a break. He lay back on the roof and waited, trying not to think about how close the farm had come to another accident. Then he peered over at the ground again. It looked even farther down than usual.

Bob lay back down on the roof, its warmth rising into his back, his feet propped against the board. The sky was filled with dark little clouds, the color of bread mold. He couldn't decide whether a storm was coming, or had broken up. Someone banged on the ladder to test its position. "Coming up," Ted said. Bob listened to the tap of his shoes against the metal rungs.

"Sorry I took so long," he said, bellying onto the roof. "Had to change my underwear." He grinned and held out a joint. "Thought we could make things up here real safe. What do you say?"

"Why not. Heck, we can't come any closer to falling. You gave me a scare."

"You? What do you think I felt like?"

Bob exhaled. "That would have been a heck of a fall." He handed the joint to Ted.

"Yeah," he said. "That would have been a great fall."

"Have you ever come that close before?"

"Here? No, not here. But when I worked on the stock car crew, I took our car out for a spin after some engine work. I was heading into a corner at about a hundred when the stabilizer bar snapped and I spun out. Bounced off the wall and skidded back into the infield. I think if I'd come off the wall rolling it would have been all over."

The pot was mild. Just right for a roof. Bob watched the smoke cloud he exhaled tumble off toward the horse farm up the road.

"I don't think I'd take either way if it was up to me." Bob said.

"Either way for what?"

"To die. Falling or a car crash." He regretted saying that as soon as the words left his mouth. The pot made him thoughtless.

"You mean if we could choose?" Ted asked, and toked. Exhaling: "Sure, no one would take an auto accident. That's not even in the scope of this discussion. In an accident, you're out of control. We're talking about choosing. You could drive your car over a cliff or something."

Bob found it odd to talk about death so casually. He enjoyed it. "Nothing in a car," he said. "Nothing off a ladder."

Ted took the stub of the joint and pulled a roach clip from his pocket. "I can't say I'm opposed to the idea of falling. If it was that or cancer, I'd take a fall. Not off a ladder though. Off a plane. And at least a mile up. Time enough so you could take in the view on the way down. Imagine how free you'd be those last few seconds. You'd have no future to consider, just the moment you were in."

Bob nodded. He hadn't thought about falling in that way. He wasn't sure "free" was the word he'd use to describe it, but the general idea was there. "I'm beginning to think there ought to be more options for us when it comes to death. Nice options. Like a fantasy park. You choose the fantasy, say a rock and roll star or G.I. Joe — you name it — and you do it along with the drug that puts you out. An arcade for death. Think how much Medicare this nation would save."

Ted blew smoke in his face.

"I'm serious," Bob said. "The problem with our prospects is they're all horrible, and death shouldn't be that way. You get cancer or some other disease. You forget who you are and cause pain to everyone you care about. You go in the nuclear flash, or die of the runs from radiation poisoning. Or you kill someone and get the chair. It all stinks."

"In California, it's gas," Ted replied. "They drop a pellet in water, and presto, you're gone. That can't be so bad."

"Bull. You can probably hear the hiss of the gas leaving the water. And when it hits, it probably scorches your nose and fills your lungs with blood and water. I'll bet you feel your tongue foaming and your body twitching before you check out."

"There are other ways. In Texas, it's a needle. What about that? I've got friends in Florida who keep a lethal dose of heroin on hand just in case of a war. They're going to put the Grateful Dead on, and check out on one big numbing wave."

Bob whacked the roof with his hand. "There you go. No pain, just pleasure — that's more what interests me." Bob looked over at the barn. He could hear Apley steam the milking equipment. It would be time to do the herd pretty soon. "Pleasure has the most appeal," he said. "Get a pellet planted in your brain that explodes during orgasm. You come, and boom — you're out."

Ted laughed. "Some women will tell you that's already the case.

Bob was careful when it came to talking about sex. He could talk about death because no one listening could contradict him. But sex was different. Lots of guys had been laid by his age. "Right now, I'd take it any way I could get it," Bob said. "One shot or more."

"No luck with the women this summer?" Ted asked.

Bob could have lied. He could have said he just hadn't had it in a while. But he decided to be truthful. "Not just this summer," he said.

"You're kidding."

"I don't want to sound like I'm making excuses," Bob said, "But, shit, I can't keep up with these guys who spend all summer on the beach or at some house in Maine. Christ, those guys got it made. But by the time I get back to school from a summer of dirty work, my face is pocked with zits."

"You've got a girlfriend, though — right?"

"Yeah, but she's off at her parents' summer house on the Sound. I've already told you what that means."

"So go down and see her some weekend. My father will let you off. For that, he understands."

"I've been down. It wasn't any fun. Too short of a time. She had two twelve-year-old cousins — twins — to look after. And a house full of relatives at night. It's hard to get my parents' car, too. They work on the weekends. Just having a car would help."

"Go out with someone else."

"You got to be careful. Some of the girls around here, they're out for the long haul. They're too serious about it. Their pants come down only for marriage. They're procreators. I'm looking for recreators."

Ted lay back on the roof and exhaled, long and slow. "Man, if you knew what I know now. Don't let it bother you. Forget it. I wish I could see women only as procreators or recreators. My problem is . . . what is it, anyway? Every one needs a good time here and there. But eventually, you expect more in a relationship."

"That's where your procreator comes in."

"No way. Not like you have it figured. Not with the Sears living room and the new pickup. There's a whole lot more."

"Like what?"

"Like a whole lot more," Ted said shutting his eyes and leaning back on the roof.

Bob wasn't sure whether Ted expected a response. He couldn't imagine what to say. So he sat there. It seemed like for minutes. But that might have been the pot.

Finally Ted opened his eyes. He sat up and stretched. "Is it milking time?"

"I don't have a watch. But I hear your Dad."

"So do I," he said, lying back down. "I hear him all the time. No matter where I am."

Bob shut his eyes and drifted. He was a lizard in the sun, somewhere in another land without trees or ponds or snow. Without seasons. A land of baked dirt and hot boulders.

"What would you think about taking that old Fiat if I fixed it up for you?" Ted asked.

Bob opened his eyes and the light stung. He looked over at Ted. His eyes were shut. "Are you serious?"

"Were you thinking of something else? Another car? This won't race a Camaro, you know."

"Do you want to do that?"

"I want to get rid of that car."

"How much?"

"Just what I put into it. Is it a deal?"

"Yeah, it's a great deal."

"It's a good deal. Not a great one."

Bob was quiet. He heard the slap of the screen door to the dairy. The sound of Apley moving across the dry grass of the lawn.

"How you doing up there?" Apley said from below. "You still awake?"

Those words. Apley said the same nearly a year before when Bob was in the silo. He wore a pith helmet and two sweat shirts to protect him from the silage blowing in from above. He was raking it level. Or trying to, trying in a great warm storm of falling vegetation. It had sat in wagons overnight, fermenting in the heat of an Indian summer. Sour smoldering greens and the sweet decay of corn kernels, the air thick the way he imagined the tropics. He was in the tropics. On a Caribbean island. So high, so high. Raking the sugar cane and so high when he couldn't move. It was up to his thighs and he was so high. Stop, he was saying. Stop. And he could hear Apley say, cut the auger, shut it down. Bob swayed in the silage, thinking it was time to free his legs. He was being buried. Then Apley showed up. He put a pill under Bob's nose. Bob jerked his head back and smiled. His eyes cried. "You're too high to be in here," Apley said, burrowing around Bob's legs and pulling him out. Apley went down first. Bob's hands were wet and slipped off the cold rungs. But Apley held him up. When Ted drove in and surprised everyone, Bob was sitting at the picnic table. He had never met Chase and here he couldn't stand up to say hello. She had beautiful sisters, they said. Now he knew it was true. Ted was pouring a dixie cup of wine for him to drink. And Chase was leaning toward him, smiling the way Bob had always hoped a woman would smile at him.

PAUL GRINER

✤

Worboys' Transaction

F. T. WORBOYS, parked twenty yards from the highway on a dusty access road, sat in the cab of his wrecker, listening for the hum of approaching cars and watching the reflected glow of his cigarette brighten and fade on the windshield as he breathed. It was two o'clock in the morning. Crickets chirped in the underbrush around him and he heard the wind pushing through the leaves of the overhanging maples and oaks like rain. He was waiting for someone to come down the road and hit the small bits of sharpened metal he'd spread over one lane of the highway. He'd placed them carefully, about fifty yards after a turn, so that whoever hit them wouldn't be going too fast when they did. From a distance, with the moonlight glinting off them, they looked like a small puddle on the macadam.

He figured he'd get at least two tires out of the deal and maybe three; with the towing charge thrown in the bill wouldn't come to less than two hundred and fifty dollars. Business had been slow for a while. F. T. was twenty-nine and single. He knew that if he was going to make something of himself he'd have to do it soon; a man, he figured, was only given so much time to work with. The metal bits were part of his continuing plan, which had begun two years before when he'd bought the Texaco station. It was on Route 88, once the main road across northern New York, but nearly forgotten since the opening of the Thruway twenty miles to the south. F. T. had come across the station after working in a series of others. It was failing, and selling cheap, and he'd bought it with money he'd put aside for just that purpose. The first thing he'd done was to order new denim workshirts so that everyone who worked for him advertised the place. Written in yellow thread above the red and white Texaco logo, the letters raised like a fresh scar, were the words, "F. T. Worboys' Texaco." Below the logo were the words, "Trust the man with the Star."

He hadn't had many workers; a couple he'd fired, a few had been drifters, going from town to town and job to job on some invisible schedule. He knew when he hired someone just what type he'd be. The drifters usually stood with their hands in their back pockets and their eyes focused beyond his shoulder when he talked to them, as if they were already thinking about their next job. He didn't mind; he paid them less. Some lasted longer than others. One, a wiry little runt named Bolen, had stayed only a week. When he left though, he'd nearly cleaned out the garage, taking among other things two sets of socket wrenches, a compressor, three drills, a set of metric wrenches for foreign cars, and boxes of spare engine parts. As far as F. T. was concerned that was about as low as you could get. Stealing was one thing, taking the means of a man's livelihood another.

After that Worboys never hired another drifter and he always stood the night shift himself. He moved into a shed behind the station and set up a cot and a dresser in there, with a big standing fan he bought from a junk dealer for five dollars and fixed up himself. It stirred up the hot air a little on summer nights when otherwise it wouldn't move. He'd lie awake on his bed, waiting for cars to come, crunching over the gravel towards the pumps. He had a telephone on his dresser so that if anyone called for a tow — he'd posted signs all up and down Route 88 — he wouldn't have to run to the station to answer it; almost no one ever did. One night when he was lying on his cot, listening to the mosquitoes buzz around below the ceiling, he'd gotten the idea for the metal.

So now he sat, one big-knuckled hand on the wheel, the other nervously tapping time on the stem of the sideview mirror, wondering if his plan would work. He heard a car coming, not too fast, and guessed by the pitch of its engine that it was a big American model, something with a V-8 that could unwind pretty good but that hadn't been aired out in a while. It passed the road where he waited and Worboys saw in the moonlight that it was a '72 Buick Electra, light colored, and in pretty good shape. Ten seconds later he heard the concussive pop of its tires blowing out followed by the squeal of its brakes, then gravel kicking up against the car's sides.

"Must have left the road," he said, throwing his cigarette out the window. The sound of his voice echoing in the cab startled him. He hadn't talked to anyone in a while. He wondered who was in the car and hoped it might be a pretty girl. He got out of the truck and walked a few steps into the woods, unzipping his pants as he went; he didn't want to appear too soon after the accident and raise any suspicions. As soon as he started pissing the crickets stopped their singing. He thought again of who was in the car. A girl, sure, and lonely and scared, out in the middle of nowhere with two flat tires. It'd be natural for her to take a liking to him. He laughed at himself, but in his hurry to get back to the truck caught himself in his zipper.

He turned the truck around and headed off the access road to a smaller one. This one led back to the highway further up, so he could come up to the car from the other direction and not have to drive over the metal himself, or avoid it and then have to explain how he knew it was there. He drove with his shoulders bunched up and a cold sweat beginning under his arms; he'd hit thirty-five by the time he'd reached the car. When he saw the old man bent over one of its wheels he felt like driving on by, but the man turned and saw him and he pulled off the side of the road. When the dust had settled he stuck his head out the window.

"What seems to be the problem?"

Worboys guessed the man was near eighty. He was still

strong, with a big round head as bald as a pumpkin. He stood next to his car, looking at Worboys, his hands in his back pockets, his jaw thrust forward. Two teeth, all he had left, stuck up into space, as if to challenge Worboys. He reminded Worboys of a cracked anvil — It couldn't take too many shots, but you wouldn't want it to drop on you.

"What are you asking me for?" the man said, and his teeth bobbed up and down a few times. "You know damn well what the problem is."

"I know?" Worboys said, looking down for a moment in spite of himself. "How the hell should I know what the problem is?"

He reminded himself to wait longer the next time.

"All my tires are blown."

"*All* of them?" Worboys was genuinely surprised.

"That's right," the man said, less belligerently. He seemed somewhat mollified by the tone of Worboys' voice. "All of them."

"Christ. It's lucky you weren't hurt."

"Yeah, and I suppose it's luck that brought you here."

"Not really. I cruise this highway two or three times a night, seeing if anyone's disabled. This was my last run before getting some shut-eye."

He walked around the car once, keeping an eye on the old man, who looked like he wanted to fight, then squatted down and began rubbing his hands lightly around one of the tires. When he found pieces of the metal embedded in the rubber he pulled a few free by working them from side to side. The old man stood silently behind him, watching. He had on blue Bermuda shorts, a pressed, button-down shirt, and sneakers; he looked like he'd planned on going to the beach. But a bar of dirt stretched across the shirt's front and one of its buttons was missing. One of his shins was scraped and bloody.

"See these?" Worboys said, standing and showing him the metal. "They're in all your tires." He looked out onto the road. "Someone must have spread them on the highway."

"Must have been your twin brother," the man said, his teeth sticking up even higher.

"I don't have a brother," Worboys said, dropping the metal and dusting his hands on his overalls.

"Then it must have been you."

Worboys lowered his head and shook it sadly, giving the guy a chance to swing. He made a neat pile of the metal with the side of his boot, tensed his jaw for the blow, then looked up.

"Mister, I don't know where you're from, but around here we just don't do that kind of thing."

"Somebody did. Who was it, Peter Pan?"

"Probably kids." He squinted towards the woods. "Did you see anything after it happened?"

"I heard your truck."

"Once you get a notion you just won't let it go, will you?"

"I've got a notion to punch you right in the nose."

"Why's that?"

"Because this didn't happen five minutes ago and you're already here, ready to tow me. You might as well have parked where you are and saved the gas." He snorted. "I'll bet you've got a warehouse full of these tires just waiting for me."

"These?" Worboys said, kicking one. "Sure. I got plenty. They're standard size."

"And you expect me to believe you didn't plan this?"

"If I'd'a planned this, you'd be sixty years younger and female."

He took out a cigarette and lighted it, cupping the match from the wind. If the guy was going to swing, he figured, he'd have done it by now.

"I expect you'll believe whatever you want to. Now, how far back did you hit?"

" 'Bout a hundred feet, near that puddle," he said, nodding up the road.

"Puddle?" Worboys said, starting for it. "We haven't had rain in a week."

He gathered the metal, some of which had been scattered into the other lane, and piled it beneath a roadside bush. When he came back he said, "That way no one else'll hit it, and it's there if you want to make a police report."

"Police?" the old man said, his teeth dropping back into his mouth for the first time all night. "What do I want with them?"

"A report might get you back the money from your insurance agent."

"What money?"

"The money you're going to spend on the four tires from my warehouse, plus the tow to get you there." He smiled at the old man. "Unless you carry four spares."

"No," he said, looking around, as if hoping to see someone else whom he might bargain with. He stuck his chin out again, hesitating, and for a moment Worboys thought he was going to tell him to go to hell. Finally he sighed, the air whistling as it pushed between his teeth, his chin receded and his hands dropped to his sides.

"All right. How much will it be?"

Worboys rolled his head upwards. His lips moved as if he were counting to himself, but he already knew the total.

"Four hundred dollars. Fifty for the tow and three-fifty for the four tires."

"I only need three. I got a spare."

"Three-fifty then. They're a buck a piece, but seeing as how you're in trouble, I was going to give you a deal." He wondered how far he could push it. "You might want to take it. Getting caught out here without a spare isn't exactly a good idea."

"Some deal." He shook his head, but Worboys knew he'd take it. Getting him to agree to the tow had been the difficult part.

"Okay. Four hundred. You take Triple-A?"

"Nope. They're too hard to collect from."

"How about American Express?"

"Cash or personal check."

"Who the hell's got that kind of cash?" the old man said, sud-

denly flaring. "And what would you do if I didn't have a check?
Leave me here?"

His teeth showed, and abruptly he raised his trembling
hands in front of his chest, then dropped them.

"Ah, the hell with you," he said and turned away. "I don't
have a check, and I don't have the money." He began inspect-
ing one of the tires.

Worboys bounced lightly against the car, arms folded across
his chest. The old guy was turning out to be tougher than he
had expected.

"All right," he said, bluffing. He climbed back up to his cab.

"I'll call the cops, tell 'em you're out here." His was the only
station open for miles around. They'd just call him back and
ask him to come for the tow.

"No, don't call the cops," he said, his head snapping up so
fast that moonlight glinted off his glasses like a spark. "I'll be all
right out here on my own."

That was the second time he'd gotten nervous about the
cops: Worboys wondered what he was afraid of. He figured
the barked shin had something to do with it. The car's tags
were out of state, and he knew nobody went too far from home
without money. Besides, he found himself liking the old man's
feistiness.

"All right," he said reluctantly, swinging the door back and
forth as he leaned on it. It squeaked beneath his weight.

"Just get in the truck."

"I told you I can't pay."

Jesus! Worboys thought. This guy really wants to come out
on top. "Look, just get in the damn truck!"

He did as he was told. Worboys reached inside the car and
the smell of wine nearly knocked him over. Three full bottles
clinked together on the floor. A fourth, on the seat, had
dripped a purple stain. That explained some of the nervous-
ness. Worboys whistled silently, impressed. If the guy had been
drinking, he showed no signs of it. The ignition key was by itself, no trunk key, no key ring. He put the car in gear so it

wouldn't roll on him when he went underneath it, jockeyed the truck into position and attached the sling. Getting into the truck he slammed the door behind him.

"Name's F.T. Worboys," he said, starting the truck and shoving it into gear. It bucked once as the slack went out of the cable, rattling the tools in the toolbox, then pulled smoothly onto the highway.

"Fred, Fred Mostone," the old man said, smiling into the darkness.

Soon they saw the station. Its lights were ablaze, and the sound of people talking floated towards them over the fields and empty gravel lot surrounding it.

"Say," Fred said. "Who's that talking?"

"The radio. Keeps thieves away." He looked over at Fred, then back at the white line along the edge of the road.

"Makes the place seem less dead when I come back to it," he almost added, but kept it to himself.

Fred leaned forward to look it over. He turned to Worboys and chuckled.

"Not too many cars you're working on," he said.

F.T., who hadn't liked giving in to Fred back on the road, liked this even less.

"Nope," he said, popping the emergency brake and kicking open his door. "But I got yours, and right now that's all I need."

WORBOYS TURNED the dial to get a late night baseball talk show, cranked the volume to full blast, then ignited the compressor and plugged in the pneumatic wrench's air hose. The compressor roared to life, belching a cloud of diesel smoke, and echoing loudly in the nearly empty garage. He dragged the wrench over to the back of the car and pried off the hubcaps with a pinch bar. He took off all the nuts, moving counterclockwise from the top one, each time letting the nut come off in the socket, then flicking it loose into the hubcap where it rattled around until coming to rest with the others. The wrench made a noise like a muffled jackhammer but Worboys, used to it, didn't notice. Fred snapped off the radio.

"Hey!" Worboys said. "What are you doing?"

"I can't talk with that thing on."

"Then talk."

Worboys went back to his work.

"There's easier ways of doing that."

"Like what?"

"Put it chest high and hold the wheel steady with one hand, then you won't have to bend so much."

"You a mechanic?"

"No."

"Used to be?"

"No."

"I'll do it my way then." He took off another nut. "I'd rather listen to the radio than to that kind of advice."

Fred walked around the garage, poking into open drawers and looking at the white spaces on the walls where tools and parts had hung.

"Kind of low on tools, aren't you?"

"Somebody stole 'em."

"Your radio didn't do you much good."

F. T. ignored him. Fred peered outside the garage, then came and stood next to Worboys.

"I stole something once."

"Yeah? What was that, bubble-gum?"

"This car."

"Sure. And this ain't my station; I'm only using it while the owner's out of town."

"Don't believe me?"

"Nope."

Worboys eyed him, then moved to the next wheel. He squatted, pulling the hubcap close to him; it rasped across the cement. He worked a bag of chewing tobacco from a side pocket, took a plug, and offered the bag to Fred.

"No thanks, I can't chew anymore on account of my gums."
He drew back his lips, showing F. T. his pitted gums. "Besides,
I never liked that brand. I used to grow my own."

"Grew it? Where?"

"On a farm, not thirty miles down the road."

"You're shitting me," F. T. said, lowering the wrench. "You
can grow tobacco in New York?"

"And just about anything else. Anyway I could once; I don't
know about now. I haven't seen the farm in a while."

Worboys, getting interested, didn't want to speak too soon.
He raised the car shoulder high and removed the wheels, then
rolled them against the far wall where he pulled off the rubber
with the pinch bar. He stacked it neatly; later he would sell it to
the junk dealer. He pulled four new tires from an overhead
rack and let them bounce on the floor. They sounded like un-
der-inflated basketballs.

While working them onto the rims and inflating them he
said, "So why'd you steal the car?"

"Change your mind?"

"Nope. I'll listen to your story, then decide."

"It's my birthday."

Worboys laughed. "You always steal a car on your birthday?"

"No, just this one."

Worboys started putting on the wheels.

"I done everything in my life, everything," Fred said, and
when he spoke he thrust his jaw forward and showed his teeth,
as if he were ready to fight anyone who contradicted him.
"Carpenter, painter, electrician. You name it. But I'm getting
old." He looked up at Worboys as if that fact had come to him
as a great and sudden surprise. He lifted his hands and looked
at them. "My goddamn hands shake so much that I can't even
hold a screwdriver steady, and without my glasses I'm blind."
He dropped his hands back onto his thighs. "But hell, I'm not
helpless."

He worked his jaw for a minute. Worboys went on to the
next tire.

"All my relatives came over this afternoon. Kids, grand-children, nieces, nephews." His voice was sing-songy. "They talked about me like I was already dead. 'Give Gramps some pasta.' 'Don't let Gramps get tired.' 'Make sure Gramps doesn't drink too much wine.'

"Hell, I gave up drinking wine before most of them were born."

He kicked at a piece of scrap metal.

"Listening to them gave me a headache, so I told them I was going to lay down for a minute. I could see the car from my bed. It used to be mine, a long time ago, but I gave it to my nephew, Tommy. He's a good kid, kind'a strange. Drinks by himself, doesn't have any friends, won't drive the car except on nice days in the summer. He says he's saving it."

Fred patted the car.

"For what? I remembered I had an extra key, so I climbed out and took it."

"Just like that? No problems getting out the window?"

"Nah," Fred said, dismissing the suggestion with a wave of his hand. "Popped a button on my shirt, scraped a shin, but that's about it." He smiled. "They probably think I'm still sleeping. Didn't want to disturb me about Tommy's car."

"Freddie," Worboys said, laughing again. "You're all right. It'll be a while before you see the boneyard."

He finished putting on the last wheel, then lowered the car.

"How come you ended up here?"

"Didn't have anything in mind when I took it, but Tommy had four bottles of homemade wine on the seat, and I remembered we used to make wine up here on the farm. My wife's buried there and I wanted to see it again."

"Where exactly is this place?"

"Between here and Canajoharie."

"Another twenty miles and you'd have made it."

"I'd probably have made it if it hadn't been for you," Fred said, straightening.

"If it hadn't been for me, you'd have been out there all night."

Worboys coiled the hose beside the compressor and cut the switch. He started the car and slowly depressed the accelerator to the floor; finally he let the motor idle and came around and opened the hood.

"What are you up to now?" Fred asked.

"Trying to get you to your farm all right. I don't want to go to bed and then have to get up and tow you again. This thing's idling way too slow."

He took a long screwdriver and turned a screw just beneath the carburetor, first almost bringing the engine to a stop, then raising its idle until he was satisfied with the pitch. He bent over the engine and opened the carburetor. He clucked and shook his head.

"It's all gummed up. Engines like this weren't made to turn-over this slowly."

"That's all right. I'll live with it. It got me this far."

Worboys got back in the car as if he hadn't heard him and held the accelerator to the floor a full two minutes. A cloud of blue smoke filled the garage and the engine's vibration bounced the screwdriver across the workbench and onto the floor. When he let up, the engine ran more smoothly.

"So how long are you going to be on this farm?"

"About a week, I guess. I'll let them worry some about me first, and I might fix up the house before heading back to Boston."

"You going back this way?"

"I been by here once."

"Well, a week'll be plenty of time to get this running clean. Take it out every day on the highway, just for an hour or so. That'll unclog the lines and keep it out of the shop."

He picked up the carburetor cap and bent to replace it, then hesitated, holding it over the engine as if weighing it, and said, "I'll tell you what. You've run up a pretty big bill here. I'll throw in an oil change for free. Go on into the office there and get me a case of thirty-weight."

After Fred left, Worboys reached into the back of his toolbox for a plastic film container. Inside, rattling a little as he picked it up, were twenty or so BB's. He poured a couple onto his palm and picked the shiniest of the bunch; the rest he put back in the case. He held the BB above the open carburetor and as he did an image of Freddie clambering out his window rose to his mind: the old man grunting as he turtled his fat stomach over the sill, his feet searching for the ground, finally popping a button and dropping onto his unsteady legs. He was lucky he hadn't killed himself. Worboys smiled, glad he'd get the chance to see Fred again, then dropped the BB. He was just closing the hood as Fred struggled back into the garage with the case of oil.

When he had finished, he backed the car out and pocketed the key. He was going to be gone a minute or two and didn't want Fred to clear out without paying.

"All set?" Fred asked.

"Just a minute." He went back into his shed and rummaged around. When he came back he had an extra shirt and jacket.

"Here," he said, giving them to Fred, who put the shirt over his own. "You'll need a change of clothes there. These are all I've got."

The shirt had the Texaco logo, and F. T.'s name.

"Thanks," Fred said, looking at it. "You won't see these again."

"That's all right. You can advertise me down in Boston. And who knows? It's an old car. If you run into problems, my card is in the pocket."

"What, did you give me leaky tires?"

Worboys chuckled as they walked outside. A faint pink glow was spreading across the eastern sky and all but a few crickets had stopped their singing. The air was sharply clean after the exhaust fumes in the garage.

"I'll come right back here if you did."

"I'm sure you will."

"What do I owe you?"

"Four even. No tax if I keep it off the books."

"Fine." Fred took out a checkbook.

"I thought you didn't have any checks."

"I remembered them when you threw in the oil change."

"You sure it's good?"

"Yeah, but I can always cancel it."

"That's all right," F. T. said, looking at the address. "I'll know where to come looking for you, too."

They shook hands and said their good-byes; Worboys gave him the key and Fred backed out of the lot.

Worboys waved, and the last thing he saw clearly, before the Buick pulled out of the station's circle of light, was his own logo shining at him from Freddie's left breast.

He tried to figure out how long the BB would take to work its way through the carburetor to the manifold — a day, two at most. From there it would roll into the cylinders. At 1500 RPM's that would blow a cylinder-head. There'd be plenty of money in that. He went inside to check his engine parts. As he'd thought, Bolen had stolen the ones he needed. He called a twenty-four hour auto parts supply place, ordered, and then, yawning and swatting at a few early morning flies, Worboys went off to bed.

TIM O'BRIEN

✛

The Things They Carried

FIRST LIEUTENANT JIMMY CROSS carried letters from a girl named Martha, a junior at Mount Sebastian College in New Jersey. They were not love letters, but Lieutenant Cross was hoping, so he kept them folded in plastic at the bottom of his rucksack. In the late afternoon, after a day's march, he would dig his foxhole, wash his hands under a canteen, unwrap the letters, hold them with the tips of his fingers, and spend the last hour of light pretending. He would imagine romantic camping trips into the White Mountains in New Hampshire. He would sometimes taste the envelope flaps, knowing her tongue had been there. More than anything, he wanted Martha to love him as he loved her, but the letters were mostly chatty, elusive on the matter of love. She was a virgin, he was almost sure. She was an English major at Mount Sebastian, and she wrote beautifully about her professors and roommates and midterm exams, about her respect for Chaucer and her great affection for Virginia Woolf. She often quoted lines of poetry; she never mentioned the war, except to say, Jimmy, take care of yourself. The letters weighed ten ounces. They were signed "Love, Martha," but Lieutenant Cross understood that Love was only a way of signing and did not mean what he sometimes pretended it meant. At dusk, he would carefully return the letters to his rucksack. Slowly, a bit distracted, he would get up and move among his men, checking the perimeter, then at full dark he would return to his hole and watch the night and wonder if Martha was a virgin.

THE THINGS THEY CARRIED were largely determined by necessity. Among the necessities or near-necessities were P-38 can openers, pocket knives, heat tabs, wrist watches, dog tags, mosquito repellent, chewing gum, candy, cigarettes, salt tablets, packets of Kool-Aid, lighters, matches, sewing kits, Military Payment Certificates, C rations, and two or three canteens of water. Together, these items weighed between fifteen and twenty pounds, depending upon a man's habits or rate of metabolism. Henry Dobbins, who was a big man, carried extra rations; he was especially fond of canned peaches in heavy syrup over pound cake. Dave Jensen, who practiced field hygiene, carried a toothbrush, dental floss, and several hotel-size bars of soap he'd stolen on R&R in Sydney, Australia. Ted Lavender, who was scared, carried tranquilizers until he was shot in the head outside the village of Than Khe in mid-April. By necessity, and because it was SOP, they all carried steel helmets that weighed five pounds including the liner and camouflage cover. They carried the standard fatigue jackets and trousers. Very few carried underwear. On their feet they carried jungle boots — 2.1 pounds — and Dave Jensen carried three pairs of socks and a can of Dr. Scholl's foot powder as a precaution against trench foot. Until he was shot, Ted Lavender carried six or seven ounces of premium dope, which for him was a necessity. Mitchell Sanders, the RTO, carried condoms. Norman Bowker carried a diary. Rat Kiley carried comic books. Kiowa, a devout Baptist, carried an illustrated New Testament that had been presented to him by his father, who taught Sunday school in Oklahoma City, Oklahoma. As a hedge against bad times, however, Kiowa also carried his grandmother's distrust of the white man, his grandfather's old hunting hatchet. Necessity dictated. Because the land was mined and booby-trapped, it was SOP for each man to carry a steel-centered, nylon-covered flak jacket, which weighed 6.7 pounds, but which on hot days seemed much heavier. Because you could die so quickly, each man carried at least one large compress bandage, usually in the helmet band for easy access. Because the nights were cold, and because the monsoons were wet, each carried a green plastic poncho that could be used as a raincoat or groundsheet or makeshift tent. With its quilted liner, the poncho weighed almost two pounds, but it was worth every ounce. In April, for instance, when Ted Lavender was shot, they used his poncho to wrap him up, then to carry him across the paddy, then to lift him into the chopper that took him away.

THEY WERE CALLED legs or grunts.

To carry something was to "hump" it, as when Lieutenant Jimmy Cross humped his love for Martha up the hills and through the swamps. In its intransitive form, "to hump" meant "to walk," or "to march," but it implied burdens far beyond the intransitive.

Almost everyone humped photographs. In his wallet, Lieutenant Cross carried two photographs of Martha. The first was a Kodachrome snapshot signed "Love," though he knew better. She stood against a brick wall. Her eyes were gray and neutral, her lips slightly open as she stared straight-on at the camera. At night, sometimes, Lieutenant Cross wondered who had taken the picture, because he knew she had boyfriends, because he loved her so much, and because he could see the shadow of the picture taker spreading out against the brick wall. The second photograph had been clipped from the 1968 Mount Sebastian yearbook. It was an action shot — women's volleyball — and Martha was bent horizontal to the floor, reaching, the palms of her hands in sharp focus, the tongue taut, the expression frank and competitive. There was no visible sweat. She wore white gym shorts. Her legs, he thought,

were almost certainly the legs of a virgin, dry and without hair,
the left knee cocked and carrying her entire weight, which was
just over one hundred pounds. Lieutenant Cross remembered
touching that left knee. A dark theater, he remembered, and
the movie was *Bonnie and Clyde,* and Martha wore a tweed skirt,
and during the final scene, when he touched her knee, she
turned and looked at him in a sad, sober way that made him
pull his hand back, but he would always remember the feel of
the tweed skirt and the knee beneath it and the sound of the
gunfire that killed Bonnie and Clyde, how embarrassing it was,
how slow and oppressive. He remembered kissing her goodnight at the dorm door. Right then, he thought, he should've
done something brave. He should've carried her up the stairs
to her room and tied her to the bed and touched that left knee
all night long. He should've risked it. Whenever he looked at
the photographs, he thought of new things he should've done.

WHAT THEY CARRIED was partly a function of rank, partly of
field specialty.

As a first lieutenant and platoon leader, Jimmy Cross carried
a compass, maps, code books, binoculars, and a .45-caliber
pistol that weighed 2.9 pounds fully loaded. He carried a
strobe light and the responsibility for the lives of his men.

As an RTO, Mitchell Sanders carried the PRC-25 radio, a
killer, twenty-six pounds with its battery.

As a medic, Rat Kiley carried a canvas satchel filled with
morphine and plasma and malaria tablets and surgical tape
and comic books and all the things a medic must carry, including M&M's for especially bad wounds, for a total weight of
nearly twenty pounds.

As a big man, therefore a machine gunner, Henry Dobbins
carried the M-60, which weighed twenty-three pounds unloaded, but which was almost always loaded. In addition, Dobbins carried between ten and fifteen pounds of ammunition
draped in belts across his chest and shoulders.

As PFCs or Spec 4s, most of them were common grunts and carried the standard M-16 gas-operated assault rifle. The weapon weighed 7.5 pounds unloaded, 8.2 pounds with its full twenty-round magazine. Depending on numerous factors, such as topography and psychology, the riflemen carried anywhere from twelve to twenty magazines, usually in cloth bandoliers, adding on another 8.4 pounds at minimum, fourteen pounds at maximum. When it was available, they also carried M-16 maintenance gear — rods and steel brushes and swabs and tubes of LSA oil — all of which weighed about a pound. Among the grunts, some carried the M-79 grenade launcher, 5.9 pounds unloaded, a reasonably light weapon except for the ammunition, which was heavy. A single round weighed ten ounces. The typical load was twenty-five rounds. But Ted Lavender, who was scared, carried thirty-four rounds when he was shot and killed outside Than Khe, and he went down under an exceptional burden, more than twenty pounds of ammunition, plus the flak jacket and helmet and rations and water and toilet paper and tranquilizers and all the rest, plus the unweighed fear. He was dead weight. There was no twitching or flopping. Kiowa, who saw it happen, said it was like watching a rock fall, or a big sandbag or something — just boom, then down — not like the movies where the dead guy rolls around and does fancy spins and goes ass over teakettle — not like that, Kiowa said, the poor bastard just flat-fuck fell. Boom. Down. Nothing else. It was a bright morning in mid-April. Lieutenant Cross felt the pain. He blamed himself. They stripped off Lavender's canteens and ammo, all the heavy things, and Rat Kiley said the obvious, the guy's dead, and Mitchell Sanders used his radio to report one U.S. KIA and to request a chopper. Then they wrapped Lavender in his poncho. They carried him out to a dry paddy, established security, and sat smoking the dead man's dope until the chopper came. Lieutenant Cross kept to himself. He pictured Martha's smooth young face, thinking he loved her more than anything, more than his men, and now Ted Lavender was dead because he loved her so much and could not stop thinking about her. When the dust-off arrived, they carried Lavender aboard. Afterward they burned Than Khe. They marched until dusk, then dug their holes, and that night Kiowa kept explaining how you had to be there, how fast it was, how the poor guy just dropped like so much concrete. Boom-down, he said. Like cement.

IN ADDITION to the three standard weapons — the M-60, M-16, and M-79 — they carried whatever presented itself, or whatever seemed appropriate as a means of killing or staying alive. They carried catch-as-catch-can. At various times, in various situations, they carried M-14s and CAR-15s and Swedish Ks and grease guns and captured AK-47s and Chi-Coms and RPGs and Simonov carbines and black-market Uzis and .38-caliber Smith & Wesson handguns and 66 mm LAWs and shotguns and silencers and blackjacks and bayonets and C-4 plastic explosives. Lee Strunk carried a slingshot; a weapon of last resort, he called it. Mitchell Sanders carried brass knuckles. Kiowa carried his grandfather's feathered hatchet. Every third or fourth man carried a Claymore antipersonnel mine — 3.5 pounds with its firing device. They all carried fragmentation grenades — fourteen ounces each. They all carried at least one M-18 colored smoke grenade — twenty-four ounces. Some carried CS or tear-gas grenades. Some carried white-phosphorus grenades. They carried all they could bear, and then some, including a silent awe for the terrible power of the things they carried.

IN THE FIRST WEEK of April, before Lavender died, Lieutenant Jimmy Cross received a good-luck charm from Martha. It was a simple pebble, an ounce at most. Smooth to the touch, it was a milky-white color with flecks of orange and violet, oval-shaped, like a miniature egg. In the accompanying letter, Martha wrote that she had found the pebble on the Jersey shoreline, precisely where the land touched water at high tide, where things came together but also separated. It was this separate-but-together quality, she wrote, that had inspired her to pick up the pebble and to carry it in her breast pocket for several days, where it seemed weightless, and then to send it through the mail, by air, as a token of her truest feelings for him. Lieutenant Cross found this romantic. But he wondered what her truest feelings were, exactly, and what she meant by separate-but-together. He wondered how the tides and waves had come into play on that afternoon along the Jersey shoreline when Martha saw the pebble and bent down to rescue it from geology. He imagined bare feet. Martha was a poet, with the poet's sensibilities, and her feet would be brown and bare, the toenails unpainted, the eyes chilly and somber like the ocean in March, and though it was painful, he wondered who had been with her that afternoon. He imagined a pair of shadows moving along the strip of sand where things came together but also separated. It was phantom jealousy, he knew, but he couldn't help himself. He loved her so much. On the march, through the hot days of early April, he carried the pebble in his mouth, turning it with his tongue, tasting sea salts and moisture. His mind wandered. He had difficulty keeping his attention on the war. On occasion he would yell at his men to spread out the column, to keep their eyes open, but then he would slip away into daydreams, just pretending, walking barefoot along the Jersey shore, with Martha, carrying nothing. He would feel himself rising. Sun and waves and gentle winds, all love and lightness.

WHAT THEY CARRIED varied by mission.

When a mission took them to the mountains, they carried mosquito netting, machetes, canvas tarps, and extra bug juice.

If a mission seemed especially hazardous, or if it involved a place they knew to be bad, they carried everything they could.

In certain heavily mined AOs, where the land was dense with Toe Poppers and Bouncing Betties, they took turns humping a twenty-eight-pound mine detector. With its headphones and big sensing plate, the equipment was a stress on the lower back and shoulders, awkward to handle, often useless because of the shrapnel in the earth, but they carried it anyway, partly for safety, partly for the illusion of safety.

On ambush, or other night missions, they carried peculiar little odds and ends. Kiowa always took along his New Testament and a pair of moccasins for silence. Dave Jensen carried night-sight vitamins high in carotin. Lee Strunk carried his slingshot; ammo, he claimed, would never be a problem. Rat Kiley carried brandy and M&M's. Until he was shot, Ted Lavender carried the starlight scope, which weighed 6.3 pounds with its aluminum carrying case. Henry Dobbins carried his girlfriend's panty hose wrapped around his neck as a comforter. They all carried ghosts. When dark came, they would move out single file across the meadows and paddies to their ambush coordinates, where they would quietly set up the Claymores and lie down and spend the night waiting.

Other missions were more complicated and required special equipment. In mid-April, it was their mission to search out and destroy the elaborate tunnel complexes in the Than Khe area south of Chu Lai. To blow the tunnels, they carried one-pound blocks of pentrite high explosives, four blocks to a man, sixty-eight pounds in all. They carried wiring, detonators, and battery-powered clackers. Dave Jensen carried earplugs. Most often, before blowing the tunnels, they were ordered by higher command to search them, which was considered bad news, but by and large they just shrugged and carried out orders. Because he was a big man, Henry Dobbins was excused from tunnel duty. The others would draw numbers. Before Lavender died there were seventeen men in the platoon, and whoever drew the number seventeen would strip off his gear and crawl in headfirst with a flashlight and Lieutenant Cross's .45-caliber pistol. The rest of them would fan out as security. They would sit down or kneel, not facing the hole, listening to the ground beneath them, imagining cobwebs and ghosts, whatever was down there — the tunnel walls squeezing in — how the flashlight seemed impossibly heavy in the hand and how it was tunnel vision in the very strictest sense, compression in all ways, even time, and how you had to wiggle in — ass and elbows — a swallowed-up feeling — and how you found yourself worrying about odd things — will your flashlight go dead? Do rats carry rabies? If you screamed, how far would the sound carry? Would your buddies hear it? Would they have the courage to drag you out? In some respects, though not many, the waiting was worse than the tunnel itself. Imagination was a killer.

On April 16, when Lee Strunk drew the number seventeen, he laughed and muttered something and went down quickly. The morning was hot and very still. Not good, Kiowa said. He looked at the tunnel opening, then out across a dry paddy toward the village of Than Khe. Nothing moved. No clouds or birds or people. As they waited, the men smoked and drank Kool-Aid, not talking much, feeling sympathy for Lee Strunk but also feeling the luck of the draw. You win some, you lose some, said Mitchell Sanders, and sometimes you settle for a rain check. It was a tired line and no one laughed.

Henry Dobbins ate a tropical chocolate bar. Ted Lavender popped a tranquilizer and went off to pee.

After five minutes, Lieutenant Jimmy Cross moved to the tunnel, leaned down, and examined the darkness. Trouble, he thought — a cave-in maybe. And then suddenly, without willing it, he was thinking about Martha. The stresses and fractures, the quick collapse, the two of them buried alive under all that weight. Dense, crushing love. Kneeling, watching the hole, he tried to concentrate on Lee Strunk and the war, all the dangers, but his love was too much for him, he felt paralyzed, he wanted to sleep inside her lungs and breathe her blood and be smothered. He wanted her to be a virgin and not a virgin, all at once. He wanted to know her. Intimate secrets — why poetry? Why so sad? Why that grayness in her eyes? Why so alone?

Not lonely, just alone — riding her bike across campus or sitting off by herself in the cafeteria. Even dancing, she danced
alone — and it was the aloneness that filled him with love. He
remembered telling her that one evening. How she nodded
and looked away. And how, later, when he kissed her, she received the kiss without returning it, her eyes wide open, not
afraid, not a virgin's eyes, just flat and uninvolved.

Lieutenant Cross gazed at the tunnel. But he was not there.
He was buried with Martha under the white sand at the Jersey
shore. They were pressed together, and the pebble in his
mouth was her tongue. He was smiling. Vaguely, he was aware
of how quiet the day was, the sullen paddies, yet he could not
bring himself to worry about matters of security. He was beyond that. He was just a kid at war, in love. He was twenty-two
years old. He couldn't help it.

A few moments later Lee Strunk crawled out of the tunnel.
He came up grinning, filthy but alive. Lieutenant Cross nodded and closed his eyes while the others clapped Strunk on the
back and made jokes about rising from the dead.

Worms, Rat Kiley said. Right out of the grave. Fuckin' zom-
bie.

The men laughed. They all felt great relief.

Spook City, said Mitchell Sanders.

Lee Strunk made a funny ghost sound, a kind of moaning,
yet very happy, and right then, when Strunk made that high
happy moaning sound, when he went *Ahhooooo,* right then Ted
Lavender was shot in the head on his way back from peeing.
He lay with his mouth open. The teeth were broken. There was
a swollen black bruise under his left eye. The cheekbone was
gone. Oh shit, Rat Kiley said, the guy's dead. The guy's dead,
he kept saying, which seemed profound — the guy's dead. I
mean really.

THE THINGS THEY CARRIED were determined to some ex-
tent by superstition. Lieutenant Cross carried his good-luck

pebble. Dave Jensen carried a rabbit's foot. Norman Bowker, otherwise a very gentle person, carried a thumb that had been presented to him as a gift by Mitchell Sanders. The thumb was dark brown, rubbery to the touch, and weighed four ounces at most. It had been cut from a VC corpse, a boy of fifteen or sixteen. They'd found him at the bottom of an irrigation ditch, badly burned, flies in his mouth and eyes. The boy wore black shorts and sandals. At the time of his death he had been carrying a pouch of rice, a rifle, and three magazines of ammunition.

You want my opinion, Mitchell Sanders said, there's a definite moral here.

He put his hand on the dead boy's wrist. He was quiet for a time, as if counting a pulse, then he patted the stomach, almost affectionately, and used Kiowa's hunting hatchet to remove the thumb.

Henry Dobbins asked what the moral was.

Moral?

You know. *Moral.*

Sanders wrapped the thumb in toilet paper and handed it across to Norman Bowker. There was no blood. Smiling, he kicked the boy's head, watched the flies scatter, and said, It's like with that old TV show — Paladin. Have gun, will travel.

Henry Dobbins thought about it.

Yeah, well, he finally said. I don't see no moral.

There it *is,* man.

Fuck off.

THEY CARRIED USO stationery and pencils and pens. They carried Sterno, safety pins, trip flares, signal flares, spools of wire, razor blades, chewing tobacco, liberated joss sticks and statuettes of the smiling Buddha, candles, grease pencils, *The Stars and Stripes,* fingernail clippers, Psy Ops leaflets, bush hats, bolos, and much more. Twice a week, when the resupply choppers came in, they carried hot chow in green Mermite cans and large canvas bags filled with iced beer and soda pop. They carried plastic water containers, each with a two gallon capacity. Mitchell Sanders carried a set of starched tiger fatigues for special occasions. Henry Dobbins carried Black Flag insecticide. Dave Jensen carried empty sandbags that could be filled at night for added protection. Lee Strunk carried tanning lotion. Some things they carried in common. Taking turns, they carried the big PRC-77 scrambler radio, which weighed thirty pounds with its battery. They shared the weight of memory. They took up what others could no longer bear. Often, they carried each other, the wounded or weak. They carried infections. They carried chess sets, basketballs, Vietnamese-English dictionaries, insignia of rank, Bronze Stars and Purple Hearts, plastic cards imprinted with the Code of Conduct. They carried diseases, among them malaria and dysentery. They carried lice and ringworm and leeches and paddy algae and various rots and molds. They carried the land itself — Vietnam, the place, the soil — a powdery orange-red dust that covered their boots and fatigues and faces. They carried the sky. The whole atmosphere, they carried it, the humidity, the monsoons, the stink of fungus and decay, all of it, they carried gravity. They moved like mules. By daylight they took sniper fire, at night they were mortared, but it was not battle, it was just the endless march, village to village, without purpose, nothing won or lost. They marched for the sake of the march. They plodded along slowly, dumbly, leaning forward against the heat, unthinking, all blood and bone, simple grunts, soldiering with their legs, toiling up the hills and down into the paddies and across the rivers and up again and down, just humping, one step and then the next and then another, but no volition, no will, because it was automatic, it was anatomy, and the war was entirely a matter of posture and carriage, the hump was everything, a kind of inertia, a kind of emptiness, a dullness of desire and intellect and conscience and hope and human sensibility. Their principles were in their feet. Their calculations were biological. They had no sense of strategy or mission. They searched the villages without knowing what to look for, not caring, kicking over jars of rice, frisking children and old men, blowing tunnels, sometimes setting fires and sometimes not, then forming up and moving on to the next village, then other villages, where it would always be the same. They carried their own lives. The pressures were enormous. In the heat of early afternoon, they would remove their helmets and flak jackets, walking bare, which was dangerous but which helped ease the strain. They would often discard things along the route of march. Purely for comfort, they would throw away rations, blow their Claymores and grenades, no matter, because by nightfall the resupply choppers would arrive with more of the same, then a day or two later still more, fresh watermelons and crates of ammunition and sunglasses and woolen sweaters — the resources were stunning — sparklers for the Fourth of July, colored eggs for Easter. It was the great American war chest — the fruits of sciences, the smokestacks, the canneries, the arsenals at Hartford, the Minnesota forests, the machine shops, the vast fields of corn and wheat — they carried like freight trains; they carried it on their backs and shoulders — and for all the ambiguities of Vietnam, all the mysteries and unknowns, there was at least the single abiding certainty that they would never be at a loss for things to carry.

A FTER THE CHOPPER took Lavender away, Lieutenant Jimmy Cross led his men into the village of Than Khe. They burned everything. They shot chickens and dogs, they trashed the village well, they called in artillery and watched the wreckage, then they marched for several hours through the hot afternoon, and then at dusk, while Kiowa explained how Lavender died, Lieutenant Cross found himself trembling.

He tried not to cry. With his entrenching tool, which weighed five pounds, he began digging a hole in the earth.

He felt shame. He hated himself. He had loved Martha more than his men, and as a consequence Lavender was now dead, and this was something he would have to carry like a stone in his stomach for the rest of the war.

All he could do was dig. He used his entrenching tool like an ax, slashing, feeling both love and hate, and then later, when it was full dark, he sat at the bottom of his foxhole and wept. It went on for a long while. In part, he was grieving for Ted Lavender, but mostly it was for Martha, and for himself, because she belonged to another world, which was not quite real, and because she was a junior at Mount Sebastian College in New Jersey, a poet and a virgin and uninvolved, and because he realized she did not love him and never would.

Like cement, Kiowa whispered in the dark. I swear to God — boom-down. Not a word.

I've heard this, said Norman Bowker.

A pisser, you know? Still zipping himself up. Zapped while zipping.

All right, fine. That's enough.

Yeah, but you had to see it, the guy just —

I *heard,* man. Cement. So why not shut the fuck *up?*

Kiowa shook his head sadly and glanced over at the hole where Lieutenant Jimmy Cross sat watching the night. The air was thick and wet. A warm, dense fog had settled over the paddies and there was the stillness that precedes rain.

After a time Kiowa sighed.

One thing for sure, he said. The lieutenant's in some deep hurt. I mean that crying jag — the way he was carrying on — it wasn't fake or anything, it was real heavy-duty hurt. The man cares.

Sure, Norman Bowker said.

Say what you want, the man does care.

We all got problems.

Not Lavender.

No, I guess not, Bowker said. Do me a favor, though.

Shut up?

That's a smart Indian. Shut up.

Shrugging, Kiowa pulled off his boots. He wanted to say more, just to lighten up his sleep, but instead he opened his New Testament and arranged it beneath his head as a pillow. The fog made things seem hollow and unattached. He tried not to think about Ted Lavender, but then he was thinking how fast it was, no drama, down and dead, and how it was hard to feel anything except surprise. It seemed unchristian. He wished he could find some great sadness, or even anger, but the emotion wasn't there and he couldn't make it happen. Mostly he felt pleased to be alive. He liked the smell of the New Testament under his cheek, the leather and ink and paper and glue, whatever the chemicals were. He liked hearing the sounds of night. Even his fatigue, it felt fine, the stiff muscles and the prickly awareness of his own body, a floating feeling. He enjoyed not being dead. Lying there, Kiowa admired Lieutenant Jimmy Cross's capacity for grief. He wanted to share the man's pain, he wanted to care as Jimmy Cross cared. And yet when he closed his eyes, all he could think was Boom-down, and all he could feel was the pleasure of having his boots off and the fog curling in around him and the damp soil and the Bible smells and the plush comfort of night.

After a moment Norman Bowker sat up in the dark.

What the hell, he said. You want to talk, *talk*. Tell it to me.

Forget it.

No, man, go on. One thing I hate, it's a silent Indian.

FOR THE MOST PART they carried themselves with poise, a kind of dignity. Now and then, however, there were times of panic, when they squealed or wanted to squeal but couldn't, when they twitched and made moaning sounds and covered their heads and said Dear Jesus and flopped around on the earth and fired their weapons blindly and cringed and sobbed and begged for the noise to stop and went wild and made stupid promises to themselves and to God and to their mothers and fathers, hoping not to die. In different ways, it happened to all of them. Afterward, when the firing ended, they would blink and peek up. They would touch their bodies, feeling shame, then quickly hiding it. They would force themselves to stand. As if in slow motion, frame by frame, the world would take on the old logic — absolute silence, then the wind, then sunlight, then voices. It was the burden of being alive. Awkwardly, the men would reassemble themselves, first in private, then in groups, becoming soldiers again. They would repair the leaks in their eyes. They would check for casualties, call in dust-offs, light cigarettes, try to smile, clear their throats and spit and begin cleaning their weapons. After a time someone would shake his head and say, No lie, I almost shit my pants, and someone else would laugh, which meant it was bad, yes, but the guy had obviously not shit his pants, it wasn't that bad, and in any case nobody would ever do such a thing and then go ahead and talk about it. They would squint into the dense, oppressive sunlight. For a few moments, perhaps, they would fall silent, lighting a joint and tracking its passage from man to man, inhaling, holding in the humiliation. Scary stuff, one of them might say. But then someone else would grin or flick his eyebrows and say, Roger-dodger, almost cut me a new asshole, *almost.*

There were numerous such poses. Some carried themselves with a sort of wistful resignation, others with pride or stiff soldierly discipline or good humor or macho zeal. They were afraid of dying but they were even more afraid to show it.

They found jokes to tell.

They used a hard vocabulary to contain the terrible softness. *Greased,* they'd say. *Offed, lit up, zapped while zipping.* It wasn't cruelty, just stage presence. They were actors and the war came at them in 3-D. When someone died, it wasn't quite dying, because in a curious way it seemed scripted, and because they had their lines mostly memorized, irony mixed with tragedy, and because they called it by other names, as if to encyst and destroy the reality of death itself. They kicked corpses.

They cut off thumbs. They talked grunt lingo. They told stories about Ted Lavender's supply of tranquilizers, how the poor guy didn't feel a thing, how incredibly tranquil he was.

There's a moral here, said Mitchell Sanders.

They were waiting for Lavender's chopper, smoking the dead man's dope.

The moral's pretty obvious, Sanders said, and winked. Stay away from drugs. No joke, they'll ruin your day every time.

Cute, said Henry Dobbins.

Mind-blower, get it? Talk about wiggy — nothing left, just blood and brains.

They made themselves laugh.

There it is, they'd say, over and over, as if the repetition itself were an act of poise, a balance between crazy and almost crazy, knowing without going. There it is, which meant be cool, let it ride, because oh yeah, man, you can't change what can't be changed, there it is, there it absolutely and positively and fucking well *is*.

They were tough.

They carried all the emotional baggage of men who might die. Grief, terror, love, longing — these were intangibles, but the intangibles had their own mass and specific gravity, they had tangible weight. They carried shameful memories. They carried the common secret of cowardice barely restrained, the instinct to run or freeze or hide, and in many respects this was the heaviest burden of all, for it could never be put down, it required perfect balance and perfect posture. They carried their reputations. They carried the soldier's greatest fear, which was the fear of blushing. Men killed, and died, because they were embarrassed not to. It was what had brought them to the war in the first place, nothing positive, no dreams of glory or honor, just to avoid the blush of dishonor. They died so as not to die of embarrassment. They crawled into tunnels and walked point and advanced under fire. Each morning, despite the unknowns, they made their legs move. They endured. They kept humping. They did not submit to the obvious alternative, which was simply to close the eyes and fall. So easy, really. Go limp and tumble to the ground and let the muscles unwind and not speak and not budge until your buddies picked you up and lifted you into the chopper that would roar and dip its nose and carry you off to the world. A mere matter of falling, yet no one ever fell. It was not courage, exactly; the object was not valor. Rather, they were too frightened to be cowards.

By and large they carried these things inside, maintaining the masks of composure. They sneered at sick call. They spoke bitterly about guys who had found release by shooting off their own toes or fingers. Pussies, they'd say. Candyasses. It was fierce, mocking talk, with only a trace of envy or awe, but even so, the image played itself out behind their eyes.

They imagined the muzzle against flesh. They imagined the quick, sweet pain, then the evacuation to Japan, then a hospital with warm beds and cute geisha nurses.

They dreamed of freedom birds.

At night, on guard, staring into the dark, they were carried away by jumbo jets. They felt the rush of takeoff. *Gone!* they yelled. And then velocity, wings and engines, a smiling stewardess — but it was more than a plane, it was a real bird, a big sleek silver bird with feathers and talons and high screeching. They were flying. The weights fell off, there was nothing to bear. They laughed and held on tight, feeling the cold slap of wind and altitude, soaring, thinking *It's over, I'm gone!* — they were naked, they were light and free — it was all lightness, bright and fast and buoyant, light as light, a helium buzz in the brain, a giddy bubbling in the lungs as they were taken up over the clouds and the war, beyond duty, beyond gravity and mortification and global entanglements — *Sin loi!* they yelled, *I'm sorry, motherfuckers, but I'm out of it, I'm goofed, I'm on a space cruise, I'm gone!* — and it was a restful, disencumbered sensation, just riding the light waves, sailing that big silver freedom bird over the mountains and oceans, over America, over the farms and great sleeping cities and cemeteries and highways and the Golden Arches of McDonald's. It was flight, a kind of fleeing, a kind of falling, falling higher and higher, spinning off the edge of the earth and beyond the sun and through the vast, silent vacuum where there were no burdens and where everything weighed exactly nothing. *Gone!* they screamed, *I'm sorry but I'm gone!* And so at night, not quite dreaming, they gave themselves over to lightness, they were carried, they were purely borne.

On the morning after Ted Lavender died, First Lieutenant Jimmy Cross crouched at the bottom of his foxhole and burned Martha's letters. Then he burned the two photographs. There was a steady rain falling, which made it difficult, but he used heat tabs and Sterno to build a small fire, screening it with his body, holding the photographs over the tight blue flame with the tips of his fingers.

He realized it was only a gesture. Stupid, he thought. Sentimental, too, but mostly just stupid.

Lavender was dead. You couldn't burn the blame.

Besides, the letters were in his head. And even now, without photographs, Lieutenant Cross could see Martha playing volleyball in her white gym shorts and yellow T-shirt. He could see her moving in the rain.

When the fire died out, Lieutenant Cross pulled his poncho over his shoulders and ate breakfast from a can.

There was no great mystery, he decided.

In those burned letters Martha had never mentioned the war, except to say, Jimmy, take care of yourself. She wasn't involved. She signed the letters "Love," but it wasn't love, and all the fine lines and technicalities did not matter.

The morning came up wet and blurry. Everything seemed part of everything else, the fog and Martha and the deepening rain.

It was a war, after all.

Half smiling, Lieutenant Jimmy Cross took out his maps. He shook his head hard, as if to clear it, then bent forward and began planning the day's march. In ten minutes, or maybe twenty, he would rouse the men and they would pack up and head west, where the maps showed the country to be green and inviting. They would do what they had always done. The rain might add some weight, but otherwise it would be one more day layered upon all the other days.

He was realistic about it. There was that new hardness in his stomach.

No more fantasies, he told himself.

Henceforth, when he thought about Martha, it would be only to think that she belonged elsewhere. He would shut down the daydreams. This was not Mount Sebastian, it was another world, where there were no pretty poems or midterm exams, a place where men died because of carelessness and gross stupidity. Kiowa was right. Boom-down, and you were dead, never partly dead.

Briefly, in the rain, Lieutenant Cross saw Martha's gray eyes gazing back at him.

He understood.

It was very sad, he thought. The things men carried inside. The things men did or felt they had to do.

He almost nodded at her, but didn't.

Instead he went back to his maps. He was now determined to perform his duties firmly and without negligence. It wouldn't help Lavender, he knew that, but from this point on he would comport himself as a soldier. He would dispose of his good-luck pebble. Swallow it, maybe, or use Lee Strunk's slingshot, or just drop it along the trail. On the march he would impose strict field discipline. He would be careful to send out flank security, to prevent straggling or bunching up, to keep his troops moving at the proper pace and at the proper interval. He would insist on clean weapons. He would confiscate the remainder of Lavender's dope. Later in the day, perhaps, he would call the men together and speak to them plainly. He would accept the blame for what had happened to Ted Lavender. He would be a man about it. He would look them in the eyes, keeping his chin level, and he would issue the new SOPs in a calm, impersonal tone of voice, an officer's voice, leaving no room for argument or discussion. Commencing immediately, he'd tell them, they would no longer abandon equipment along the route of march. They would police up their acts. They would get their shit together, and keep it together, and maintain it neatly and in good working order.

He would not tolerate laxity. He would show strength, distancing himself.

Among the men there would be grumbling, of course, and maybe worse, because their days would seem longer and their loads heavier, but Lieutenant Cross reminded himself that his obligation was not to be loved but to lead. He would dispense with love; it was not now a factor. And if anyone quarreled or complained, he would simply tighten his lips and arrange his shoulders in the correct command posture. He might give a curt little nod. Or he might not. He might just shrug and say Carry on, then they would saddle up and form into a column and move out toward the villages west of Than Khe.

AUTHOR BIOGRAPHICAL NOTES

✜

CHARLES BAXTER is the author of *First Light, Through the Safety Net*, and *Harmony of the World*. He teaches at Wayne State University.

FREDERICK BUSCH's books include *Rounds, Hardwater Country, The Mutual Friend, Invisible Mending, Sometimes I Live in the Country,* and *Too Late American Boyhood Blues.* He lives in Sherburne, New York.

RAYMOND CARVER is the author of three collections of short stories: *Will You Please Be Quiet, Please?, What We Talk About When We Talk About Love, Cathedral,* and several collections of poetry. *Where I'm Calling From: New and Selected Stories,* will be published in April by The Atlantic Monthly Press. He lives in Port Angeles, Washington and in Syracuse, New York.

ALAN CHEUSE is the author of *The Grandmothers' Club, The Bohemians, Candace & Other Stories* and *Fall Out of Heaven.* His fiction has appeared in *The New Yorker* and other magazines. He is a regular commentator for National Public Radio.

STUART DYBEK is the author of *Brass Knuckles,* a collection of poetry, and *Childhood and Other Neighborhoods,* a collection of short stories. "Chopin in Winter" is part of a short story collection to be published by Knopf. Stuart Dybek teaches at Western Michigan University in Kalamazoo.

RICHARD FORD is the author of *Rock Springs,* a collection of short stories, and the novels, *The Ultimate Good Luck, A Piece of My Heart* and *The Sportswriter.* He lives in western Montana and in Mississippi.

PAUL GRINER lives with his wife in Syracuse where he is the Cornelia Ward Fellow in the Creative Writing Program at Syracuse University. This is his first published story.

226

WILLIAM KITTREDGE is the author of a short story collection, *We Are Not In This Together,* and *Owning It All,* an essay collection, both published by Graywolf Press. He teaches Creative Writing at the University of Montana.

DAVID LONG is the author of two collections of short fiction, *The Flood of '64* and *Home Fires.* He is also the author of *Early Returns,* a book of poems. He lives in Kalispell, Montana.

TIM O'BRIEN is the author of *The Nuclear Age, If I Die in a Combat Zone,* and *Northern Lights.* His novel *Going After Cacciato* was the winner of the National Book Award in 1979.

ROBERT OLMSTEAD is the author of *River Dogs,* and a forthcoming novel, *Soft Water.* He is currently the writer-in-residence at Dickinson College in Carlisle, Pennsylvania.

TOBIAS WOLFF's fiction appears frequently in *The Atlantic, Esquire, Vanity Fair, Antaeus,* and other magazines. He is the author of two story collections, *In the Garden of the North American Martyrs* and *Back in the World,* and a short novel, *The Barracks Thief.*

CHRISTOPHER ZENOWICH has just received his M.A. in Creative Writing from Syracuse University where he was a Cornelia Ward Fellow. His novel, *In Search of Excellence,* and short story collection, *Economies of the Heart* are forthcoming from Harper & Row.

Other Books in

THE GRAYWOLF SHORT FICTION SERIES

Text and cover design by Tree Swenson

The text type is Baskerville,
and was set by The Typeworks

Manufactured by Edwards Brothers

✛